cross over water

WITHDRAWN

WEST WORD FICTION

cross
over
water

Richard Yañez

University of Nevada Press
RENO AND LAS VEGAS

WEST WORD FICTION

University of Nevada Press, Reno, Nevada 89557 USA
Copyright © 2011 by Richard Yañez
All rights reserved
Manufactured in the United States of America
Design by Kathleen Szawiola

Library of Congress Cataloging-in-Publication Data

Yañez, Richard, 1967–
Cross over water / Richard Yañez.
p. cm. — (West word fiction)
ISBN 978-0-87417-838-8 (pbk. : alk. paper)
1. Mexican Americans—Fiction.
2. Mexican-American Border Region—Fiction.
3. Domestic fiction. I. Title.
PS3625.A677C76   2011
813'.6—dc22   2010035063

The paper used in this book is a recycled stock made from 30 percent
post-consumer waste materials, certified by FSC, and meets the
requirements of American National Standard for Information
Sciences—Permanence of Paper for Printed Library Materials,
ANSI/NISO Z39.48-1992 (R2002). Binding materials were selected
for strength and durability.

FIRST PRINTING
20   19   18   17   16   15   14   13   12   11
5   4   3   2   1

for my family

for fronterizos

—BOTH SIDES—

"The desert exhaled as he sank into the water."

—ARTURO ISLAS,
The Rain God

1   Ruly learned how to drown the summer his family left Lomaland for good.

The moment he struck the plane of water the world he knew bridged with one that awaited him.

Rather than climb the rope of bubbles escaping his mouth, he hugged himself and closed his eyes. With faith that he'd rise to the top, he didn't panic.

Many lessons later, he remembers how his arms betrayed him when he needed them most. How water almost replaced the air in his lungs. How his legs became anchors. His weight under water.

Between the excitement of turning twelve and the nervousness of entering junior high, the house he'd been born into was left behind like a lizard tail in the desert. As his family drove away for the last time, he imagined a boy like himself walking along and crushing the dried skin of his house into dust.

In the first weeks of the new house, he developed a routine. As morning sunlight trespassed his bedroom curtains and he heard his parents and older brother empty the house, he stumbled out of his room with a pillow in each hand. Waking up naked (Fruit of the Looms always came off in his sleep), he fit himself in the master bedroom closet and draped his mother's rabbit-skin coat over his legs. Alone with the drool on his cheek, he fell back asleep till midmorning, and after going to the bathroom, toasting white bread, and moping around, he'd return to discover more of the closet.

His skin excited him. Firmer than rubber but softer than leather. The inside of his elbow. The creases where his thighs met his crotch. The love handles of his waist. Naked, he navigated his body like an explorer would leagues of oceans or acres of wilderness.

Dressed, he felt lost, as if someone had buried his birth-map. The closet in his parents' bedroom was where he journeyed into the world of his body. The space smelled like his pillowcase after he'd drooled on it for several nights. The drool stains, like the rings on his dresser, were a collection of shapes—pear and eggplant, the state of Texas, inflated lungs, a flat football. He turned his pillows frequently so his mother wouldn't change the pillowcases. Saliva on cotton with a touch of fabric softener was one smell he craved.

A world of more odors rested in the body of the biggest closet. Dad's muddy cowboy boots. Stinky sneakers. His mother's curled-up slippers. Brightly colored high heels. A hamper pregnant with underwear, slips, socks, pantyhose.

Ruly rubbed his butt on the carpeted closet floor like the dogs did outside on the grass. Much of his parents' things—mechanic manuals, bags of photographs, paperback romances, a movie projector—were still packed in boxes shoved under hung clothes. His mother's dresses, skirts, blouses on the right; Dad's slacks and cowboy button shirts on the left. He crawled around the closet like Columbus had through jungles. Lewis and Clark followed rivers, he also remembered from *Big Blue Marble,* a favorite morning TV show.

While he'd decided from day one that he wouldn't give this new house a chance, he guessed that he did like one more thing about his parents' bedroom closet. It was only four big steps from the larger of the two bathrooms. Every morning that summer, not fully awake, he sat on the toilet and held down his palito. He'd heard Pancho, his brother, use other names ("dick," "chorizo," "boner," "verga"), but his penis was stubby and the moist brown of mud. A *palito.* A branch from one of the large cottonwoods all over Lomaland.

Waiting to pee, he reached from the toilet and turned on the bathtub faucet. The running water helped him go. Of the two bathrooms in the new house, his parents' was the only one with a tub. It was the second space he confessed to no one that he liked. The tub was the color of eggshells and as smooth. After flushing, he plugged up the tub and turned the hot water faucet on all the way. Steam filled the bathroom and sweat dripped down the walls. Puddles slept on the tile floor. More shapes: a whale on its back and a pyramid that bowed into an igloo.

He liked that the bathroom was clean. No hairs and scum in the cracks and corners like in the only bathroom at their old house. That bathroom was not as big or fancy. Maybe it was the new mats and towels, the print of flowers and shells, and the gold dish filled with star-shaped soaps, all things from Kmart.

The bathwater was too hot to get his body in all at once. He put one foot in first, then the other, stepped in to one knee, then the other leg, and finally, he squatted like a dog. The heat crawled up his legs and arms. Goose bumps sprouted on his hairless flesh.

The best part of taking a bath was the sound inside his head. He heard it by tilting his head back far enough into the water so that his ears were submerged. After a few seconds, the water plugged up the space behind his eyes. He thought of walking into a cave, like his family had done on past trips to Carlsbad Caverns. And if he closed his eyes and concentrated, he heard the muffled beating of what he took to be his heart. He kept his eyes closed as long as he could, way longer than he could ever hold his breath.

In this moment of stillness, he struggled to keep his head from slipping fully underwater. If the water came up to his nose, he'd panic and pull himself up by the soap dish. He never risked sinking completely below the water level. No way. Not having at least his nose ready to breathe was too hard to imagine.

Lime green tiles covered the area around the tub. Squiggly lines on each tile crawled up to the bumpy ceiling. They reminded him of Lomaland's maze of canals, where he and his brother and their Lomaland friends had fished out guppies and crawdads. He missed putting his hands in the caliche and having mud wars. Water somehow reminded him more of getting dirty than of getting clean.

Sitting in the tub, distracted by his senses, he usually forgot to wash and only remembered when he noticed his fingers had aged into ten tiny viejitos, pruned and pale. Time to pull the plug and drain the water. He'd remain in the tub until it emptied, enjoying the sucking sounds. More and more, he allowed himself to imagine being pulled down under the new house, draining into the canals, and somehow floating all the way back home to Lomaland.

The move from the heart of the Lower Valley to a suburban neighborhood off North Loop Drive was supposed to be the best thing to happen to his family since his mother graduated from El Paso Community College and got promoted to management. During the weeks of packing, she'd done everything she could to sell him and his brother on the idea. Not only would they each get their own room, which made his brother the happiest, but there would also be a bigger neighborhood, with sidewalks and fences, his mother bragged. No more dirt roads. No more tumbleweeds. A bigger school where he could make new friends. And a swimming pool only blocks away.

"I don't know how to swim," he had to remind his mother.

"You'll take lessons," she said.

"What if I'm no good?"

"Everyone can learn how to swim, Raul Luis. It's like breathing, except sometimes you have to do it underwater."

He knew she was serious when she used both his first names. He'd inherited them from uncles on both sides of the family tree. They were reminders that he'd come from people who'd migrated all the way from interior Mexico to the country's northern edge. Imagining them traveling that long distance, settling in El Paso, Texas, their first stop in the United States, a whole other country, always made him tired and wheezy.

It didn't help that he also had a history of real bad allergies. Back when they lived in Lomaland, acres and acres of sand dunes, creosote bushes, mesquite trees, there'd been many nights of sneezing and coughing. Absences from school increased with the changes in weather. And the morning he woke up with eyes as red as hot coals and his throat swollen like a bullfrog's, his mother had had enough and dragged him to an allergist.

Pollution. Avocados. Weeds. Dirt. Dog hair. Lint. Grass. Melons. Flowers. Plants. Leaves. Bees. Feathers.

After a test of needle pricks on his back (he lost count at thirteen), Dr. Goldfarb's diagnosis was that he was allergic to everything. At least everything in the Chihuahuan Desert: grains of sand, cactus needles, scorpion bites, you name it. It didn't matter if this landscape was home to three generations of the Cruz family.

After four weeks in the new house, the second big change of that summer occurred when Laura moved in. His cousin was almost two years older than he was, and although no one talked about it, he knew that she'd lived with each of his four aunts for different periods of her life. Tío Manuel, his mother's only brother, was Laura's father, but he was somewhere en el otro lado. Laura called no one "Mother," much less "Mamá."

One past Christmas Eve, on the drive home from the annual family get-together at Tía Linda's, Ruly asked his parents who was Laura's mother. He'd heard an older cousin mention something about the family that he didn't understand. After pretending to not hear him, his mother said, "It's not important." He would've asked more questions if she hadn't turned up the radio. "Silent Night" filled the space of their Datsun.

As with most hard questions he had as a boy, his brother was the one he went to for answers. Pancho dug through a Revco Pharmacy bag of photos and showed Ruly a photo of a woman holding a baby. "That's Aunt Lilly, Laura's mom. She left." Nobody knows why or where, his brother added. And he shouldn't ask more questions, if he knew what was good for him.

He'd misplaced the photo of the fair-skinned woman and over the years thought of his cousin as an orphan. A word he looked up in their new encyclopedia set to make sure it meant what he thought it did. The encyclopedia's illustration of a boy and a girl, barefoot and in torn clothes, left him sad for his cousin.

At first, Laura started coming over on Saturdays to help his mother with settling into the new house. "My three boys," as his mother called Ruly, Pancho, and their dad, "aren't much help," she said. After a day of cleaning the pantries, hanging new curtains, arranging furniture, it got late and Laura spent the night. His mother said it was too much trouble to drive her back to whichever aunt she was staying with at the time. Eventually, that summer, she spent weeknights with them too.

One morning around the Fourth of July, his mother came into his bedroom and asked what he thought of Laura living with them for the rest of the summer. Her asking him surprised him even more than the actual question. *Maybe she knows that I'm still sad about leaving Lomaland,* he thought. In a sleepy daze, he shifted his head to try and hide a fresh drool spot. His mother took this as "okay."

"Treat her like your sister, Ruly," she said as she left for work. Her rose-scented perfume hung in the air as he went back to sleep, and he remembered the conversation only later when he soaked in the bathtub.

He'd always thought about having another sibling, maybe a little brother he could make flinch and punch in the arm and outrun if he had to. But he'd never known anything else but being the younger of two brothers. Although he and his brother weren't that close anymore, especially after Pancho got his driver's license, he'd always been an "hermanito."

Laura got the bedroom between his and Pancho's. One day the room was full of unpacked boxes, Dad's collection of *Hot Rod* magazines, and abandoned exercise equipment, and the next day it was a girl's room: yellow-flowered curtains, a new dresser and chest of drawers, and a canopy bed covered in stuffed animals. Tía Antonia even bought Laura a parakeet as a good-bye gift. "I had four others," she said on the first day she officially moved in, "but they all died." He stroked the bird's wings until the roof of his mouth started itching.

Birthday parties. Midnight Masses. Memorial Park picnics.

These were the only occasions when he spent much time with his seventeen cousins, ten boys and seven girls. He thought of them as good friends although he didn't like everything about them. At least it's not Cousin Sammy moving in, his brother told him: "He stinks and always gives enchiladas." Ruly shuddered thinking of his cousin's painful kneading of your forearms that left your skin chile red.

As it turned out, he didn't have to worry about the changes the youngest of his girl cousins was bringing. While he still felt lost in the new house, he discovered that Laura made the summer days go by quicker. They hung out in the new house from the moment they woke up to the time his parents and brother came home from work.

They stayed busy playing old maid, tic-tac-toe, or Chinese checkers or trying to pick the lock to Pancho's room. They did have chores, but they finished making the beds, washing the dishes, and dusting furniture in the half hour before his mother came home.

One afternoon, after they'd made grilled cheese sandwiches for lunch and turned through all the TV channels ("nothing . . . nothing . . . nothing"), he decided to show his cousin his favorite space in the new house. Since she'd moved in, he hadn't spent much time in his parents' bedroom closet.

"Come in. Close the door," he said to Laura.

"C'mon, Ruly, what's the big deal?"

He reached into Dad's extra toolbox. In each direction he pointed the flashlight, there were objects for which he had stories. Some true, some almost true, most made up.

"This stuff is from when my dad was in the Army." A tote bag contained a scrapbook with pictures and postcards, a box with medals and pins, a stack of airmail letters addressed to "My Bucko." His cousin agreed that it wasn't a very cute pet name for his mother.

"These are from Sweden." He handed her a pair of decorated wooden shoes that fell out of the bag. "I bet they dance in them. Or maybe mash grapes."

His cousin shook her head but said nothing. He clipped some of the tarnished medals on his striped shirt. He threw out his chest. His cousin still wasn't impressed. She looked bored and bothered.

"Hey, check this out." He grabbed a thing he'd named "Sit-on Slinky." It was his mother's and made of hand-sized pieces of plastic held together by a thick spring.

His cousin laughed as he sat and hopped on the Sit-on Slinky. "That's not a toy, menso. Use it like this." She took it away from him and with both hands squeezed it in front of her chest. Her muscles fluttered like small wings.

"Really?" He tried it and felt silly.

She laughed louder. "It stinks in here. Let's go look around in the garage."

"No, wait. You'll like this."

He switched off the flashlight and negotiated the dark closet. Extra instincts born from exploring in the days before his cousin moved in. A couple of times, his legs did rub up against her skin, much softer than his.

As her breathing turned to sighs, she told him to hurry up. He did and soon switched on the featured attraction.

In the glow of a home movie projector, 16 mm black-and-white images came alive on the closet wall. His mother's dresses parted like movie house curtains.

The home movie is of a family party. All their aunts, uncles, and cousins are at their Lomaland home to celebrate his fifth birthday. Spider-Man is the special guest, a piñata taller than the birthday boy. After his mother blindfolds him and spins him around, he is the first to take swings at the papier-mâché superhero. Following many misses, he finally makes contact with Spider-Man's foot.

In coveralls and pigtails, Laura takes her turn at Spider-Man after Cousin Bonnie. Laura knocks one of Spider-Man's arms loose. Then Javi, their oldest cousin, finishes the job. The clay pot inside the piñata explodes and drops a treasure of candies and small toys.

In the closet, the cousins laughed at their younger selves scrambling on hands and knees.

"Your piñata parties were the best," Laura said. "Tía Angie always put good candy. Not that cheap Mexican kind Tía Toni put in Bonnie's Minnie Mouse."

In the home movie, everyone eats cake and ice cream in the backyard. The yard in Lomaland is bigger than the space of the two-bedroom house. Beyond the grass area where they have parties and cookouts, there is a section where Dad grows green chiles, squash, even corn. The ears of corn are never good enough to eat, but the stalks are a good hiding place for when Ruly gets into trouble. In the rear of the yard is a makeshift corral. Pancho won the burro in a Cristo Rey Church raffle and named it Cholo.

"Did Cholo die?" Laura, enjoying the movie, asked.

"I don't think so." Ruly couldn't remember what happened to the animal. "I think Dad sold it. Or los del City made him get rid of it."

"Cholo was fun." The light from the projector lit up her teeth when she smiled.

Now that Ruly saw his old backyard again, he missed his former home even more.

He wondered if he would ever return to Lomaland, which might as well have been in a faraway desert on the other side of the world. He'd learned from *Big Blue Marble* that they rode camels, not burros, in the Sahara Desert.

The home movie of the party ends with him and his cousins playing with his birthday presents: Battleship, Mr. Mouth, Worm Wrestle, Rock 'Em Sock 'Em Robots.

"Do you still have any of those games?" Laura asked.

He shrugged. "They may be in the garage somewhere. We threw a bunch of stuff out when we were packing."

On the same film after the birthday party is a rare snow day in El Paso, Ruly and Pancho with sock-gloves building a snowman in the front yard. After some more blank film, there appears a family gathering after a funeral. Sad faces of relatives: each of their tías, some uncles, godparents, older cousins.

The movie camera jolts around the living room, down the hall, into the kitchen and to the bedrooms. A portrait of objects: wall heater that hums, a ball-shaped gold lamp hanging in the den, and pine trees outside the brothers' bedroom window.

He found it strange that his mother would have filmed this solemn occasion. Maybe it was what he'd heard her say, "Funerals and Christmases are the only times the Santos and Cruz sides of the family get together."

He was about to turn off the movie when Laura sat up on her knees. She put her arms out and leaned closer to the wall, as if one of the voiceless images had grabbed her.

"What is it?" he asked.

"Go back," she urged. "Can you do that?"

"Yeah, why?"

"Just do it, menso."

He pushed a few buttons and rewound the film. It screeched. When he played the film again, his cousin got right up to the wall and touched the grayish figures sitting on the plastic-covered couch.

"There. There. You see her?"

He didn't know who she was talking about. He rewound it again and again and managed to slow the movie enough to prove her right. Although they could see only the woman's profile and shoulder, they agreed it must be his cousin's mother. He barely remembered Aunt Lilly from the photo his brother had shown him, but he saw in his cousin's face that it was her mom.

They stared at the ghost on the wall.

When the film tore and cracked like a whip, they both jumped back. The projector's light cast his cousin's shadow where her mother's image once was.

He fumbled around with the projector's buttons as the spinning film slapped him in the face. Although it stung a little, he couldn't help laughing. When he finally turned the motor switch off, he heard his cousin over his laughter. She was lost in the black space of the closet. With Dad's flashlight, he spotted her crouched in a corner under his mother's skirts. Cheeks wet with tears.

He didn't know what to do or say. The flashlight dropped out of his hands. When her soft sighs turned to loud sobs, he said, "I'll fix it. I can. Wait."

He turned his attention back to the projector, got his fingers tangled, and hurried to rethread the film. The closet closed in around him. His heartbeat echoed, as if his head was being held underwater. Before he got the projector ready, his cousin was gone.

He stepped out of the closet into the afternoon light and heard a door open and shut. Rather than go check if it was to her bedroom or the front yard, he went back into the closet and stored away any evidence of their family matinee.

In the last weeks of that summer, Laura kept to herself. Either in her room, from which the sounds of KPSO, El Paso's oldies station, could be heard, or out back, running through the sprinklers with the dogs. With his ear to her bedroom door or his chubby face pressed on the rear sliding-glass door, he wished she would let him into her world.

Didn't I let her into mine? he asked himself.

He would've risked an attack of sneezing and coughing and gone outside to the backyard, but his cousin's body language told him to keep away. He knew because he'd embodied the distant stare and heavy slouch of a person wanting to be left alone from the day they'd left Lomaland up until the day Laura moved in.

2   Ruly went back to spending his summer days like when he was alone in the new house. Napping in the closet, eating fish sticks in front of the TV, looking through Dad's *Hot Rod* magazines on the toilet. Since he'd experienced the warmth of another body next to his, none of these satisfied him as much anymore. Having shared a close space with Laura was like growing a new skin—a more sensitive one.

On one of the hottest days of that summer, he woke up excited. The tepee his palito made of his bedsheet was the tallest he remembered. The drool spot on his pillowcase smelled like the glass of strawberry milk he had drunk before going to sleep. After he spun the globe by his bed nearly a hundred times, something he'd started doing when he couldn't fall asleep, his palito softened. He slipped on his underwear and shorts, as he'd reminded himself to do since his cousin had moved in.

His parents and brother were at work, and it appeared his cousin wasn't around. He pressed his ear to her bedroom door. Nothing. No crying. No radio. Juanito, her parakeet, had flown out of its cage a few weeks after she moved in. One of their mutts chased it down and ate everything but the legs and beak.

He checked the whole house, even the garage, and peeked out the windows to the back and front yards. All empty.

He went to the kitchen. On the refrigerator door was a note: "L's dentist appt. @ 9:30." The date on the note was today. He figured his mother had taken his cousin to get braces in Juárez. Everything was cheaper across the border, he'd heard them say at the dinner table. The oven clock let him know that he had hours before anyone came home. The rapid rhythm of his heart signaled his body's cravings.

With a clean towel from the hall closet, he stripped as he walked to his parents' bathroom. After plugging up the tub, he turned on the water, cold to warm to hot. Steam rose from the tub.

As a special treat, he went out and searched through his mother's vanity. He poured a palm of purple pellets in the tub. A rose-smelling cloud filled the bathroom.

Inhale. Exhale. Inhale. Exhale.

As he took his usual time and steps to get in the tub, tiny brown hills lined his arms and legs. Palito an exclamation point to his excitement. Bubbles blew out of his butt and got lost in the sudsy water. Head tilted back, he spotted something new hanging from the showerhead. He'd seen his mother unpack it after a trip to Kmart. "Loaf," was what he thought she'd called it.

In one quick move, he stood, balancing himself on the shower door, and grabbed the loaf. It felt like sandpaper before he soaked it in the water. He wiped the bar soap on the loaf and rubbed his heels, knees, thighs. When he brought the loaf up to his crotch and scratched his sack of huevitos, it hurt and soothed at the same time. Sparklers behind eyelids. As he continued to rub the soaked loaf on his crotch, up and down his palito, an urge jolted him out of the tub. Not picking up the toilet seat, he peed in short squirts.

Forgetting to flush, he wrapped a towel around himself. Steam fogged up the vanity mirror when he stepped out of the bathroom into his parents' bedroom. Soggy footprints plastered the carpet.

On any other day, he would've taken the four large steps into the closet, curled up in his nakedness, and inhaled a familiar combination of smells: moist skin, smelly slippers, unwashed clothes. But on this morning, a new desire was born. To not only touch himself but to watch himself, too.

He stood on his mother's vanity stool and wiped his hand across the steamed mirror, wearing the towel like a cape. In the moisture of the mirror appeared his reflection. Distorted. Shadowy. A phantom image belonging to ones projected onto closet walls.

Poised on the stool, he struck different poses. Chest out like Superman. Biceps flexed like Tarzan. Lips puckered like Bugs Bunny.

Although he'd touched and smelled more of his body this summer than ever before, the figure in the mirror was almost a stranger. Especially when he didn't look up from his body to his face.

Seeing his belly sag above his palito, soft and shrunken, made him wonder how his body would continue to change as he got older.

Will I get muscles? More hair? Will my palito grow? My huevitos?

He turned around and was about to look over his shoulder at his backside when he saw someone else in the room. In person in front of him and her twin in the mirror.

"What are you doing, menso?" His cousin plopped down on his parents' bed and rubbed the sleep from her eyes.

"Huh?" He half fell, half jumped off the vanity stool.

"What were you doing? Acting like Brooke Shields or somebody?"

"Nothing." He grabbed the towel and shrank inside of it. He wanted to retreat—bathroom on his left and closet on his right.

"Pancho's right. You're weird." She looked at the clock on the night table next to the bed and then at the light coming through the curtains. She appeared to be figuring something out.

He managed to catch his breath while his heart drummed against his chest. "I thought you went to the dentist's."

"Naw, I told Tía Angie that I felt sick."

"Are you?"

"Am I what?" She'd gotten off the bed and walked past him to the bathroom door.

"Sick?"

"No, menso, I just didn't feel like having a stranger's fingers in my mouth." She playfully poked at his face.

Although he resented her sneaking up on him, he found some comfort in their shared allergy for doctors.

"Did you leave any hot water?" She peeked into the bathroom, where the tub was still full.

"I think so."

She walked into the bathroom. "Good. I'm taking a bath."

A towel on his lap, he sat on the vanity stool and wondered if she was going to get in the same bathwater that he'd used. As if she was reading his mind, she stuck her hand in the murky water and pulled out the plug.

Before he could think of what he should do, in one movement she took off her pajama bottoms and panties and kicked them toward him. Her pointed toes rested for a second in the air like a ballerina. He gazed at her polka-dot panties bunched at his feet and resisted the urge to hold the soft fabric.

The bathroom door was slightly open, and he heard her flush the toilet, pee, flush again, and turn on the tub's faucet. He sat outside the bathroom for a moment longer, his only thoughts having to do with the closet, polka-dot panties, and his stiffening palito.

About to take his mixed excitement to his room, he heard Laura call out for him: "Get me a towel, weirdo."

Holding the towel around his waist, he walked out of the bedroom, down the hall, and reached into the linen closet's top shelf. That's where his mother kept the towels "too nice to get dirty." The purple towels with small bows had been a housewarming gift.

Like approaching the confessional at Sacred Heart for the first time, he hesitated returning to his parents' bedroom.

"Here's the towel." After a few moments without an answer, he said, "I'll leave it here, okay?" He laid the towel outside the bathroom door.

As he started to walk away, "Hey, where's my towel?" came shouting out of the bathroom.

He turned back, picked up the towel, and followed the voice into the bathroom.

Inhale. Exhale. Inhale. Exhale.

Laura pushed the shower door to one end. He turned his head away but not before being able to film a mental image. Her lower body soaked underwater; her torso, from her belly button up, exposed. Long legs stretched to the other side. She rubbed the loaf on her neck. Taking one more look, he clicked his eyes like camera shutters right before he hung the towel and walked out.

His towel slipped off as he rushed to his bedroom. Naked under the covers, he gripped his hard palito. Working the flesh around, like his Atari's joystick, he wished it would soften. But the more he tried not to think of Laura—the two fleshy buttons on her breasts, the shade of hair between her legs, her pink toenails bobbing in the water—the stiffer his penis got. While it hurt to twist and pull, it also felt good.

Like what he'd first felt on a deep dip of the Bandido roller coaster, a sensation sparked from his belly button straight to his butt. It tickled but he didn't laugh. With his right hand on his penis, he pinched his love handle with his left hand. The tighter he gripped, the more his body stiffened. Finally, it was too much—he turned his head and buried his face in his pillow. Deep breaths. A groan escaped his mouth, followed by a stream of moans.

The hotter the summer got, the more he wanted to be around Laura. While his favorite place in the new house was the skin of the closet, he figured she would always associate that space with bad memories. He learned to avoid everything that reminded her of her absent mother. She never talked about it, so he left it alone.

After weeks of doing all their chores that summer, they were finally rewarded. His mother said they could get cable TV, like most of their cousins already enjoyed. Cable gave him and Laura something new to do together. They were no longer left with only soap operas and game shows to watch during the day. The world of reruns and channels from as far away as Los Angeles was now available from a brown box with thirty-six white buttons.

To prevent them from arguing, his mother made the two of them write up a list of what shows they'd watch during the week. Laura had better handwriting, so she did the list. Even with so much to choose from, they found that they liked some of the same programs.

9:00, channel 5—*Hong Kong Phooey* (R's choice)

9:30, channel 5—*Scooby Doo* (my choice)

10:00, channels 12/24/5—*Gilligan's Island/I Love Lucy/Good Times*
      (whichever ones we haven't seen)

11:00, channel 17—*The Addams Family* (R's choice)

11:30, channel 17—*The Munsters* (black-and-white)

12:00, channel 24—*The Beverly Hillbillies* (nothing else on)

1:00, channel 5—*The Brady Bunch* (our most favorite)

1:30, channel 12—*Love American Style* (my favorite)

2:00, channel 20—*I Dream of Jeannie* (R's favorite)

2:30, channel 20—*The Brady Bunch* (older years)

3:00, channel 12—*Sanford and Son* (R's choice)

3:30, channel 24—*Bewitched* (2 episodes, my choice)

Although the TV in the den was bigger, the only one hooked up to cable was in his parents' bedroom. He enjoyed lying next to Laura on the king-sized bed. On his stomach, his head propped up by pillows, he tried not to drool whenever Shaggy or Gilligan, who he suspected were the same guy, made them laugh. Laura's laughter reminded him of the tub's gurgling when it drained.

"You hungry?" she asked him one morning during *The Addams Family.*

"Not really." He turned on his side and saw her, in shorts and a SIT ON IT! tank top, rubbing her stomach for added effect.

"Get me some cereal."

"You get it."

"C'mon, Ruly, don't be like that." She playfully pushed him on the shoulder.

"Like what?" He tried to hit her back but missed

"A big baby." This time her shove nearly knocked him off the bed.

"Shut up." He put one foot on the floor to balance himself.

"Please. Pretttyyy pleeeaaase." She clasped her hands like the statue of La Virgen on his parents' dresser.

He didn't want to miss the start of the next show, so he hopped off the bed during the car commercial with the man and chimp riding a buffalo. He ran through the hallway, through the den, and into the kitchen. His dirty tube socks wagged like long tongues ahead of him.

He grabbed the milk from the fridge, the box of Froot Loops on the counter, and two bowls, which he guessed were clean, from the sink. *The Munsters* was just starting when he slid back into the bedroom. He fantasized himself Pete Rose completing an in-the-park home run.

Sitting on the edge of the bed, his cousin took a bowl, wiped off something green with her tank top, and poured in cereal and milk.

"Spoons?"

"Dang, I forgot."

"Go get 'em."

"It's your turn." Sitting at the foot of the TV, he poured himself some cereal and milk. "Just eat it like this." With both hands, he rested the bowl on his bottom lip and slurped. Rainbow-colored milk spilled down Captain America's shield on his T-shirt.

"That's sick."

"Try it."

She imitated him. Rivers of milk ran from the sides of her mouth down her chin. When she put the bowl to her mouth again, he tickled her bare foot.

The bowl slipped out of her hands and cereal poured all over her chest. Soggy circles dribbled down through her legs onto the bedspread. He cracked up along with the program's laugh track as Herman Munster walked through a wall.

"You dork. Look what you did." She jumped off the bed and tackled him on the floor. His bowl of cereal spilled on the carpet, which soaked the milk up like a sponge.

They wrestled and bumped into the TV stand, its flimsy legs wiggling a dance. He was surprised at how strong she was. No matter how much he tried to get the advantage, she fought him off. When his face pressed against her stomach, he smelled milk and baby powder. She was saying something, but he couldn't make it out since she had him in a headlock.

He struggled and squirmed out of his T-shirt. When he got tangled in her slippery legs, an electric charge traveled from the middle of his stomach to his penis. The excitement doubled when he flipped over and came face-to-face with her chest. With her tank top stretched to one side, his cheek pressed against her breasts. This moment happened quickly, like when he tilted his head back in the tub. The rush of blood left him feeling light-headed. When she finally pinned him to the floor, her nipples were as hard as his palito.

"Give up, nerd?" She sat on his stomach, held down his arms with her knees, and tickled him. His back stuck to the soggy carpet. He couldn't stop laughing.

"Okay . . . okay." Saliva bubbles came out of his mouth. "You win. . . . I give . . . I give up."

She got off and raised her arms. "The Champ!"

As she turned and walked away, he reached up and picked a Froot Loop off the back of her thigh. He put it on his tongue and swallowed the cherry-flavored circle, like if he was taking communion.

With the end of summer vacation a few weeks away, he received the worst news since his mother had announced that they were leaving Lomaland. She came home one afternoon and told him and Laura that she'd signed them up at the neighborhood pool.

The lifeguard had invited the family to try the pool for a week at no charge. If they liked it, they could get a membership. To not go would be rude, his mother warned. "It's time the two of you made friends," she added. "You can't stay inside all your life. TV eats your brain cells. And aren't you bored of each other yet?" Laura turned to him and nodded. He pushed her and told her he was bored of her. That was as far from the truth as anything he'd ever said to her. Even more than when he lied that he'd never seen a picture of her mother.

When his "I-can't-swim" excuse didn't hold up, he turned to the allergies born from Lomaland's desert. The night before his first swimming lesson, he acted out his surefire plan. He went to the backyard and crawled into the dog-house. The cramped wooden box, which the dogs used only when it rained, felt as familiar as the crawl space of the closet. When he didn't get any allergic reactions, he chased down Oso, the slowest mutt, and stuffed his nose right in its neck. The dog squirmed away as his allergies kicked in.

Eyes watered. Mouth itched. Good start.

When the dogs started barking, he went back inside the house. Intent on waking up feeling as awful as possible, he hid a handful of weeds from the back-yard under his pillow. He slept through a few bouts of sneezing and coughing and awoke to the sounds of his parents and brother getting ready for work. He used this time to guarantee his plan.

Nose deep in the tuft of weeds, he inhaled. He was surprised that the smell was a little like the cilantro in his mother's arroz. He took long breaths and still nothing. Had he grown immune to the things that Dr. Goldfarb had planted in his back?

He smiled when his throat began to itch. Pressure built around his nose. He took one last whiff and fired snot onto his pillowcase. Rather than get out of bed to blow his nose, he suffered through the itchiness and congestion.

His cousin came into his room excited about going to the pool. When she saw his eyes swollen red and his nose running, she reported it to his mother. He thought she suspected something, but if she did, she didn't act on it. She told him to stay in bed and to take a steaming-hot bath later. A half smile. Before she left for work, she brought him some pills, a glass of water, and his inhaler, which he hadn't used since they'd left Lomaland for good. It tasted like metal and expanded his mouth like a blowfish.

Before his cousin went to the pool, she returned to his room. She had a Betty Boop beach towel wrapped around her body. He imagined the polka-dot bathing suit his mother had bought her at Kmart underneath the towel. They'd all gone to buy what they needed for the pool the day before. His trunks and goggles sat on his dresser. As his cousin bounced out of his room, she said she'd be back to make him his favorites for lunch: grilled cheese sandwiches and instant mashed potatoes. His plan had worked better than he'd predicted. Being allergic had advantages, it seemed for the first time.

In the final days of that summer, he continued waking up looking like he'd slept facedown in the open desert, and his mother gave up trying to convince him that he needed to learn how to swim. She did make him go to Dr. Goldfarb's. The doctor even helped when he said that he was most likely allergic to chlorine: "A pool is home to all kinds of bacteria."

"You see," he said to his mother, surprised that he and the doctor were on the same side.

What his No Swimming Plan hadn't included was losing his cousin Laura. After the first few days of going to the pool, when she came home to eat lunch and watch TV with him, she now spent the entire day outside the house. Her skin was getting so dark that she looked like the Apaches in *High Chaparral*. When he tried to lure her back inside the house with promises of hot dogs and red gelatin, her favorites, she told him that Debbie, the lifeguard, took an extra sandwich for her. They even had the radio on KPAS all day long.

In the evenings, he ate by himself in the den, a TV dinner warming his lap. He pretended not to listen to his cousin talk about the pool. How she was learning to swim underwater. How Debbie was showing her how to jump off the diving board. How there was a boy who chased her in the pool. She smiled after she said the boy's name: "Arturo Romero." The way she rolled the *r*'s in his name gave Ruly a lump in his throat. He sneezed and coughed his way to his room. When no one noticed, he figured that they'd all become immune to his allergic symptoms—real or fake, it didn't matter.

Although the neighborhood pool was only two blocks away, it was as foreign to him as any of the oceans or lakes on his globe. And now that his cousin was part of it, he found it harder not to feel its presence, especially since she brought it home with her. The smell of chlorine and suntan lotion covered her towel and bathing suit, which hung on the shower door.

Like eating avocados or watermelons, which were on Dr. Goldfarb's list of foods that he should avoid, he knew he'd also have to risk swimming. *Bad reaction or no bad reaction, I have to,* he thought.

On one of the last days of summer vacation, he awoke early, and after taking a quick shower, he went to tell his cousin that he'd decided to go to the pool. But she'd already left. He wondered if she was mad at him. Since she'd been spending all her time at the pool, she'd become the stranger he had worried she would be when she had first moved in.

The thought of losing her for good made him hurry. He went to his room, put on his trunks, and placed his goggles on his head. Flip-flops slapped his feet as he half walked, half ran to the pool. The price tag of his trunks dangled on his butt like a pig's tail.

The chain-link fence surrounding the pool made it a scarier place than he'd imagined from his cousin's descriptions. When he stepped into the pool area, he thought it was loud for a space without a roof. Laughing and yelling. Kids everywhere. A few adults talking. Water splashing. Diving board thumping and vibrating. Radio playing.

Not seeing Laura either in or out of the pool, he sat on a bundle of towels. The number of boys and girls with naked arms and stomachs, bare legs, and bare feet comforted him. He took off his DYN-O-MITE! T-shirt and tossed his flip-flops with the family of other plastic and leather sandals. He adjusted his trunks, slipping the waistband over his belly.

In the short time that he sat poolside, his armpits and crotch moistened with sweat. The sun pricked his shoulders and back like Dr. Goldfarb's instruments. The last time he'd looked in the mirror only a tiny circle of needle pricks remained on his lower back.

A group of girls around Laura's age strolled by. Their wet hair pointed down to their nalgitas, small rolls of their behinds slipping out of their bathing suits. The shiny material stuck to their bodies like an extra layer of skin. His eyes ran from a girl's long toes up to her shaped thighs to her flat stomach to her curved chest. His palito stiffened and pushed on the sheer underwear of his trunks. He put his towel over his boner.

Laura came out of an office on the other side of the pool. She was with a skinny blond woman he figured was Debbie the lifeguard, and a boy. He knew he was Arrrturrro Rrromerrro by how happy Laura looked at his side. He was almost twice as tall as Ruly, certainly older.

Ruly wished for his palito to soften so he could walk over to his cousin. "Surprise, I made it," he would announce.

The more he spied on Laura and Arturo, the more fun they appeared to be having. The dizzy feeling of being out in the sun traveled to his stomach. He felt bloated, like after eating too many pork rinds. He burped and worried that he'd fart in the pool if he ever made it into the water.

He forced his attention to the opposite side of the pool. When he saw the diving board, he was reminded of a pirate movie he and his cousin had seen one Saturday afternoon. They both found it a cool way to punish one's enemies. Or their least favorite cousin. Cousin Sammy first came to mind for both of them.

After putting down his towel, palito now half-soft, he got up and walked toward a group of boys and girls. They huddled together, laughing and joking around. Their excitement made him feel like if he was at a birthday party back in Lomaland. He pictured a piñata hanging over the pool and remembered the taste of chile con queso and brisket. Great times.

One by one, the kids climbed a ladder, jogged a few steps, and jumped off the diving board. Heads up, backs arched, they hung in the air for a split second before making a great splash.

Next to shooting webs out of his palms (Spidey's coolest power), he'd always wanted to fly through clouds, like the black-and-white Superman.

And that's what the boys and girls were doing from the diving board. *Flying.*

He followed a redheaded girl's nalgitas. They wiggled. Excitement carried him up the ladder.

His skin tingled with each step he took to the edge of the diving board.

He slipped the goggles down over his eyes and stared into the pool. His distorted reflection was greeted by voices.

"Jump. . . . Come on."

" . . . Jump. Jump. Go on."

"Hurry up."

Silence

    Blue slipping through fingers

River of

       tiny

           bubblesbubblesbubbles

    Feet, toes swaying

    half-bodies waving

Mouth open

       Water

  No air

       More bubblesbubblesbub

Bottom

       Weight

  Wait

His body surfaced.

Light.

Blue.

Air?

Face stuck to a woman's breasts.

FEGUA

At first the two consonants and three vowels didn't spell any word he knew in either English or Spanish.

Lying on his back, head tilted, he was struck by how bright they were—the sky and the lifeguard's eyes, both blue like his favorite shooties. Teeth like white Chiclets and a confetti of freckles around a flat nose.

His thoughts were still underwater when Debbie asked him a question. Before an answer could swim out of his throat, her mouth swallowed his.

Water jumped out of him with each thrust to his stomach. Debbie's hands pushed all the way to his back. He coughed and turned his head. Couples of bare feet circled him.

Debbie told someone, "He's gonna be all right."

He spotted his cousin behind Debbie. Her pale face stood out against her tanned body. "I think he's had enough swimming for one day," Debbie said. His cousin had her arms across her chest. Her eyes were as wet as her bathing suit, and her bottom lip quivered. He'd seen this spooked look before in the closet. Right now, however, she was the one who looked like a ghost.

His cousin said nothing. He wanted to tell her that he was fine, but before his lungs completely filled with air, she walked off.

Debbie asked him if he was okay. He blinked several times.

With his back sticking to the pool deck's wet tile, he peered at the late-summer sky.

No clouds. Far-off sun.

His eyes roamed the sky for anything to hold on to. He spotted a chalk mark and traced it to a distant plane. The higher it soared, the more it disappeared into the blue canvas. Reverse drowning.

Goose bumps crawled up his arms and legs. He turned his head and shoulder and shifted his weight. Debbie took him in her arms and stood him up before he was drawn back into the deep end.

3. The curtain was drawn and covered the stage where Principal Boone had stood during the Welcome Assembly a few weeks ago. Ruly didn't hear everything the scrawny, practically bald man had said. The boys next to him kept making fun of the "Puto Pelón." Ruly didn't laugh until later when he asked his brother what the insult meant. Understanding two languages was better than knowing just one, even if just for insulting someone. This was one of the many lessons he'd learned while attending Valle Vista Junior High.

No matter how dark the cafetorium was for the GIANTS FALL DANCE, the name painted in green on white butcher paper, he knew the lunch tables and chairs were folded and pushed against the back wall. Today's lunch: sloppy joes, Tater Tots, and banana pudding. He loved sloppy joes, although Chris and Santi said they looked and tasted like a run-over dog. "How do you know?" Ruly always challenged his Junior High Best Friends.

After a long summer in the new house and almost drowning, seventh grade overwhelmed him. Music coming from a discotheque filled his ears with booming bass. At midcourt, his senses drowning in sound, he enjoyed the disorientation. The vibrations of the huge speakers crawled into his stomach and spun it around like a pinwheel. The queasiness from the loud rock music made him think that Pancho wasn't so dumb after all for enrolling in a record club. Every two weeks a new album came in the mail. Ruly didn't dare open the cardboard box for fear of getting smacked. DON'T TOUCH MY STUFF, GORDO-BOY might as well have been one of the bumper stickers his brother had plastered all over his bedroom door.

None of the songs the discotheque was playing seemed familiar, but he guessed they might be by the groups that Pancho had posters of in his room. STYX. RUSH. JOURNEY. These band names were printed in ornate letters under photos of the bands. Ruly didn't like their long hair as much as their loose-fitting clothes, especially the elaborate ones sparkling like glitter.

As the music of the junior high dance flooded his head, the strobe lights seduced his eyes. They flashed faster than he could blink and trapped the bodies of the seventh- and eighth-grade boys and girls in action. He knew they were dancing, but it looked more like some sort of awkward posing. Jerking of arms and legs. Thrusting of hips and butts.

It was hard to tell the boys from the girls—everyone in jeans and T-shirts, with hair lengths almost the same. Not many girls wore skirts. He noticed that a few of the least popular girls wore the kinds of dresses you saw at church.

One of these girls was Amy Applegate. She was holding hands with Randy, one of the other ten or so gringos at Valle Vista Junior High. The strobe lights made their white faces even paler. They were both in Ruly's English class, but he pretended not to know them.

Smoke covered the gym. Rising from behind the DJ playing records, the white clouds hovered over the dancers. A cool sensation filled his lungs. He breathed deep and pretended he could blow smoke rings à la Kojak, one of Dad's heroes.

Ruly walked along the far wall, near the cafeteria's kitchen, out of the way of the strobe lights, trying to locate the exit. *Where did Chris and Santi go?* he wondered. He hadn't seen them since the music started and practically everyone paired off. He was almost to the exit when a large group rushed the dance floor. Even if he'd tried, he wouldn't have been able to get past the wave of girls and boys. Pushed and shoved, he was in trouble. It was useless to fight the momentum going opposite the open doorway.

He knew immediately that he was doing everything wrong. His arms flapped like a squawking chicken. His legs kicked like he was trying not to drown. He tried to imitate what others were doing, but it was hard to see. Too much smoke, too many strobe lights, too loud. He hoped nobody witnessed what his limbs were trying to do.

In the middle of the song, he realized he must be dancing. No one seemed to notice this was his first time. At least in public. He and his cousin Laura had danced plenty of times watching *Schoolhouse Rock!* Saturday-morning TV, one of many things he missed doing with Laura, who had moved in with another aunt and now attended Ysleta High School.

After a second song, faster than the previous one, he started to have fun. Being on the dance floor, close to other moving bodies, began to calm him. The drowning-out-of-water feeling numbed his thoughts. Relaxed for the first time this school year, he kept dancing, still not totally in control of his limbs.

Arms waving like a broken windmill, he felt his right hand meet flesh. He winced. Immediately, he knew it wasn't his body. He didn't react fast enough and struck again with his other hand. In that moment, he thought about running, afraid he might have started something he didn't want to be a part of. But on the free throw line of the crowded dance floor, he was boxed in. No quick exit.

More bad luck: The song ended and all the lights came on. Sweat ran down his forehead and stung his eyes. When he wiped them clean, he saw his victim. She had her arms wrapped around her chest. He thought about hurrying past her, all the doors now open and accessible, but he didn't. His heart danced to its own beat. The rhythm of the music and strobe lights echoed inside him (more cavelike than underwater). As the sensations dulled, his legs went stiff.

"What happened?" The question came out of his mouth like a burp.

"Huh?"

"Are you all right?"

She continued to hug herself without smiling. When she turned her back to him, she brushed her long hair over her shoulders. He took this to mean that she knew he was the one who'd hit her. The soft flesh he'd touched was her boob. He wanted to apologize but thought he'd better not risk anything else. *Haven't I already dared too much?* he thought. Simply coming to the dance had been scary enough. And getting on the dance floor, though he'd sworn to Chris and Santi that he wouldn't, had exhausted him.

Mouth dry, he stood in line at the water fountain. Girls and guys with damp hairlines and shiny faces took long drinks. While in line, they talked about how much better this junior high dance was than any at their elementary schools. He nodded his head, although this was his first school dance ever. He would've considered what other firsts were possible, but it was his turn at the water fountain. Bending over to get a drink, he was pushed out of the way.

Her spine curved under her blouse. She held her long hair to her right, so it wouldn't get wet. When he followed the bumps of her spine down her back, his eyes landed on her denim butt.

J O R D A C H E   J O R D A C H E

The eight letters were stitched in cursive on each rear pocket. Reading them over and over again, he felt a chill stepping down his own spine. While the moment of her drinking and him watching happened quickly, he knew he'd be able to slow it down later, like the home movies he watched in the closet.

Frame by frame. Second by second. Letter by letter.

She smiled as she let him get a drink. His fingers grazed hers as he reached for the knob. Water slid down the side of his face as he turned to watch her walk away. He swallowed, trying to get rid of the trapped air in his head. The feeling was too familiar.

With the excitement of the dance still floating inside his body, he decided to follow JORDACHE JORDACHE. Questions gathered in his mind like bubbles. *What's your name? Where do you sit for lunch? Where do you live? Can you teach me how to dance?*

His curiosity was hijacked when his two so-called friends ran up behind him. Chris got him in a bear hug while Santi picked up his polo shirt and pinched his panza. While he tried to break free, they started going on about where'd they'd been for the past hour. He half listened to something about a set of keys as JORDACHE JORDACHE got lost among the other denim butts.

Disappointed, he followed Chris and Santi. He figured one of them had left their stuff in the locker room. The boys' locker room smelled the same after school as it did during the day: like Ajax sweat and Pine-Sol piss. He wasn't sure why this surprised him. He liked PE but hated Coach Latner. Ever since he'd made Ruly run laps in corduroys (he'd forgotten his locker key), Ruly had thought Coach was a "joto." Pancho had said this about Coach before Ruly started at Valle Vista Junior High and without knowing how much of an insult it was, he decided "joto" was a good put-down, much worse than "homo." The lockers in his brain were storing more and more cuss words, and sometimes they rhymed in Spanish and English.

Chris and Santi were in a toilet stall by the showers when he caught up with them.

"What are you doing?" He stood on the toilet of the stall next to the one they were in.

"Shut up. Coach may be outside."

Ruly nearly slipped and fell when he looked over at Coach's office inside "The Cage." Red balls for kickball. Yellow flags for football. Orange pylons for soccer. Green nets for volleyball. Coach sat behind the wire cage while they suited up, as if his sole job was to guard the rainbow of PE equipment. Right now, the locker room was empty and dark. Ruly guessed it was getting late by the low sunlight coming in through the windows. In the hollow space of the locker room, dance music still echoed in his head. When Chris heard him singing, he asked Ruly if he'd been dancing. Ruly lied.

He jumped off the toilet and squeezed his chubby body into the stall with his two friends. He smelled what he thought was the worse fart ever. "Damn, you guys. Did you shit your pants?" He covered his nose and looked into the toilet for any evidence. A burnt match floated in the water. When Santi turned to face him, Ruly saw the source of the smell, a fat cigar. Santi took a deep puff and passed it to Chris. He inhaled until his cheeks puffed out like two tennis balls. He held the cigar out to Ruly. The smoke reached out and coiled around his head. He couldn't say no or risk being a homo/joto himself.

Since the first day of school, when Ruly had met Chris and Santi, they were always daring him to do things. Up until now, he'd managed to pull off anything they'd come up with. He almost wanted to say they should save the cigar for later and go steal some more soda bottles. The change they got from the deposits was enough to play several games of Asteroids and Pac-Man. The nearby 7-Eleven kept the latest video games in the corner by the ice coolers.

The cigar smoke piped its way through his mouth to his throat to his lungs. It must've hit something there. Like a mini geyser, it quickly came coughing out of his mouth into Santi's face. Santi cussed and laughed at the same time. Ruly grabbed his stomach, dropped the cigar, and darted out of the stall. He went to the sink and put his mouth under the faucet. He drank. Coughed. Drank some more.

Chris and Santi came up behind him. They were both cracking up, laughing like when they got him to put a dead lizard in one of the gringos' lockers.

"You aren't supposed to inhale." Chris was hitting Ruly on the back as he leaned over the sink. Ruly wasn't sure if he was trying to help or make things worse.

"Yeah, stupid-menso, you're only supposed to taste it." Santi put his hand in the running water and scooped out a drink.

"Where's the cigar?" Chris kept patting his back like if maybe he'd swallowed it.

Ruly pointed back at the stall and coughed out, "Dropped it."

The three of them peeked in the stall door and looked at the cigar. It floated in the toilet, bloated and brown. A tobacco turd. They started laughing even louder. Ruly didn't want them to be mad, so he wanted to come up with something even funnier. He took a pen out of his pocket and wrote on the stall, FROM COACH'S NALGASS, with an arrow pointing to the toilet. He'd try to come back later to erase it, but right then he wanted his Junior High Best Friends to think he was cool. Not someone who danced. Not someone who was too scared to ask a pretty girl her name. No matter if you had hit her boobs.

With his stomach turned upside down, he sat on the cold tile while Chris and Santi tried to break into Coach's cage. A nervous feeling mixed with the smoke in his gut. He was glad when they finally left the foul-smelling locker room and went into the early evening's fresh air.

C / S / R.

When Ruly had first seen the three letters written on a desk at Valle Vista Junior High, he'd thought of them as nothing more than a coincidence. Kind of like when he was thinking of a cheeseburger and strawberry shake and a Whataburger commercial came out on the TV. But when he saw the letters markered on a bathroom stall and the wall outside the gym, he figured it was by design.

CHRIS / SANTI / RULY

Although he was drawn to the graffiti at school, he hadn't done it. So now he wondered which one of his two friends had. He thought about just asking them, but maybe this was part of an initiation. And if he asked, he might mess up his chances of being included. This actually was a fear of his when he saw C / S by itself, no R, written around campus. C / S could have either been before he met Chris / Santi or a reminder that they didn't need him or his name.

"You have to be careful," Pancho had told him before he entered junior high. "There's lots of cholos, even cholas, who might mess with you."

"Really? Why would they want to mess with me?"

"Cuz, stupid-menso. You're just . . . Just stay out of the way of clicas and you'll be okay."

"Are you in a clique?"

"It's 'clica,' the Chicano way. And, no, I'm no lowriding homeboy. I'm into hot rods."

His brother went on to explain that gangs, like VLK (Varrio Los Kennedys), were sometimes known as "clicas."

When he saw other initials tagged around the school building, he wondered who they belonged to, what clica. Most of the graffiti at and around school was written in capital letters for some reason. Ruly thought it might be a way for gangs to make sure their presence was heard as well as seen.

A T M.

A could stand for any of his classmates: Antonio, Alejandro, Agustín.

T: Tavo, Trinidad, Teodoro.

M: Mario (he knew of at least five), Martín, Mando, Memo, Mundo.

A T M could stand for any combination of these fellow seventh graders.

He was pretty sure these graffitied initials were a guy thing, so he didn't even consider thinking of the girls' names in his class. And he was pretty sure that the gringo kids like Andy, Thomas, or Mark didn't hang around too much outside of class. He never saw them lingering along the rear of the school or in the bathrooms, where most of the initials in sets of three appeared. No matter how many times the poor janitors scrubbed the black markings off the stalls or painted over them on the brick walls, the letters reappeared, as if they soaked back through like the chile colorado stain that never really came off the button-down white shirt he used to wear to church.

In addition to thinking of the C / S and C / S / R sightings as part of his initiation, he tried to figure out what else Chris and Santi might ask him to do. He stayed ready, on his toes, as Dad said when they used to play one-on-one in the driveway. He didn't want to mess up his best chance at being part of a trio. Three Musketeers. Three Stooges. Father, Son, and Holy Ghost. Each of these was famous in a way. Even if you didn't like or believe in them, he figured you knew who they were, right? There was something magical about threes.

As he stood next to Chris and Santi at school, he imagined their respective letters written on their bare chests, like he'd seen when he, Pancho, and their dad last went to a college football game at the Sun Bowl. Since he'd imagined this, he tried to stand on the left of both his friends. If one of them would switch places, or if he somehow ended up in the middle, like in the lunch line, he shuffled to correct the order. C / S / R.

"Thanks, dude."

"Too cool."

Chris and Santi always showed their gratitude for his letting them go first, especially on lunch days when they served fish sticks. Everyone at school knew that they always ran out, so if you didn't want to eat tacos (like most every other day), then you better hustle to the front of the line. Ruly could eat fish sticks anytime at home, so he preferred the school tacos. These came in hard shells and were topped with shredded orange cheese. Not in greasy corn tortillas with lumpy white cheese like his mother made. When he'd mentioned that he liked the ones at school better, Dad had said those weren't Mexican tacos. Those were American ones. Ruly had figured as much, given where they lived, on this side, not across the border. He didn't say anything, since he knew how Dad got about anything to do with the two flags that were displayed in the entryway. While he, his parents, and his brother were born in the U.S., he did like it that Mexico's flag was in three colored sections: green/white/red. The eagle with a serpent in its beak perched on a cactus was also cooler-looking than all those ordinary stars and stripes.

With each grade he passed into, the more he seemed to realize that symbols, like letters and words, meant more than something simple.

Maybe our clica needs a flag, he thought. What would look cool with C / S / R? A lion. Grizzly bear. Three-headed dragon. Which colors? He liked brown and made a mental note to find out what colors Chris / Santi liked. He didn't want to ruin his initiation, so he figured the mascot they chose or whatever flag they designed would come later. He did make it a point to study the two flags *eagle stars serpent stripes cactus* more carefully every time he left the house.

4 Days after the school dance, Ruly hustled down the canal road. Although this time he didn't think he was being chased, like the time Chris / Santi dared him to shoplift at Kmart. Instead, he was the one in pursuit.

JORDACHE   JORDACHE

His mouth itched with every fifth step he took. Just about. And not in the same spot. While his stubby tongue could rub the roof of his mouth, he couldn't get his tongue way to the back, near his tonsils. This forced him to clear his throat, like he'd seen Dad do before. The noise Ruly made was like the disposal in the new house and was followed by him spitting out a big pollo. The snot-saliva bomb shot out of his mouth and flew through the air like the mini jellyfish pictured in his science textbook. It was the heaviest book he was carrying in his gym bag. He alternated the hand he carried it in with every ten steps. His itching mouth and tiring shoulders helped him keep track of how far ahead JORDACHE JORDACHE was on the canal road.

To his surprise, Chris and Santi didn't give him too much of a hard time for having a crush on the girl from the dance. He didn't tell C / S that he'd hit her boob. When he described her, Chris told him that she lived on the next street over from him, near the canal. She'd attended Marion Manor Elementary, and her full name was Norma Rodarte. A name that matched her better than JORDACHE JORDACHE, for sure.

Ruly put this information in his Map Book, a notebook he kept hidden in his closet. One night, when he could no longer close his eyes and picture his old home in Lomaland, he had begun drawing maps and recording everything he could remember.

IMPORTANT ROADS
— Left on Stanford & Right on Yermoland (Best Route to Mini-Market)
— Burgess & Courtland (Bike Rides to Lomaland Park)
— Yarbrough/Lee Trevino to Montana (Family Trips to Cinema Park Drive-In)
— Straight on North Loop, past Zaragoza (Dad's Cruises beyond the city limits)

Ruly always noted the rough illustrations with loose memories of places and references to locations. Poorly drawn pictures represented the landmarks: M-Mkt. sign, Merry-Go-Round, Movie Screens, '57 Chevy.

His Norma Map was the first page he'd added since entering Valle Vista Jr. High. Link Dr. (where Chris lived) was the center, and the school was on top while Ruly's new house was to the right. He drew a thick line for the canal that ran behind their school past his house to the cotton fields in the Lower Valley. This new Map Book entry was a work in progress for sure.

He spent a few days spying on Norma, watching which way she walked, making notes of times and landmarks. He didn't even know if it was spying because it seemed that she knew he was following her. When he would fall behind, his allergies making it hard for him to breathe or his bag becoming too heavy, she'd stop and tie her shoes. She did this often enough. And she also let him know, in a way, that she knew he was close by. Not to his face or through a friend, like he'd considered, but in a candygram.

Every Friday at Valle Vista Junior High, different school clubs sold candy-grams that you could send to someone you liked. Up to that point in the school year, every first period had been torture for Ruly. He never once received a candygram. Sometimes he even wished he'd get a notice to go to the office, like Chris and Santi often did for acting up. Ruly didn't want to be around while others savored their candygrams.

His time finally came. Friday after the dance, while he was hurrying to fin-ish his English homework, Cindy Sánchez, an eighth-grade cheerleader, stood over his desk and asked if his last name was Cruz. He stared at her green-and-white uniform, GIANTS on her chest, and nodded his head. She handed him a lollipop that had a message tied to it with ribbon.

Raul Cruz
Dont Fall
Behind

The candygram wasn't signed, but he knew it was from Norma. "How do you know?" Santi asked when he told him the news. Ruly knew, just by the way the letters were written, round curves that tilted to the right, and the taste of the lollipop, a sweet-and-sour green candy that he made last practically all day.

Santi thought he was out of his mind and waited only one day by the por-tables with Ruly. When Santi saw him making notes and adding to his Map Book, his friend said he was dumb for even having such a notebook. Too much like schoolwork, he said, and ran off to find Chris.

With each day that he followed Norma, Ruly knew he was getting closer. But the thing was, he wasn't in a hurry. Not only was he nervous about catching up to her, but he also began to enjoy the slow pace. It allowed him time to study the canals that ran throughout the Lower Valley. He liked knowing that the canal irrigation system stretched from his current neighborhood all the way to Lomaland. Dad had also told him that the canals all began at the nearby Río Grande. Although his family rarely crossed the bridge to Juárez anymore, he thought it would be cool to follow a canal and see if Dad was right.

Although Ruly initially did it to not be spotted by Norma, he now walked in the empty canal because it felt safe. The dried-up caliche walls stood a couple of feet over his head. He enjoyed the feeling of being almost buried as much as he had when he'd visited Carlsbad Caverns. He'd stopped asking his mom why they didn't take day trips anymore when she said, "Can't you see I'm busy at my new job?" Since they'd moved, that seemed to be her answer for every question.

Each afternoon, for a couple of weeks, Ruly waited till Norma reached the edge of the schoolyard, and then he came out from behind the portable classrooms and hurried to the canal road. Other kids also liked to walk home along the canal after school, but he was the only one who actually crawled down into the empty canal. Walking inside the vacant half tunnel helped him learn to trust his instincts—first born in Lomaland's desert and reawakened in his parents' closet.

While he enjoyed his role as the pursuer, he started to worry that Norma wasn't too happy with their arrangement. He still hadn't been brave enough to speak to her in the halls or the cafeteria. On the Friday when he stopped getting a candygram, he knew he had to do something. But what?

At PE, when Chris and Santi talked about making out with girls, sweat ran down Ruly's back into his butt. His underwear crawled up his crotch. As he'd gotten older, he'd noticed how much more his body got all sweaty in places he never would've guessed. A few of the guys called him "Mojadito" because of the large stains on his T-shirt. He knew this Spanish term because his parents often used it to refer to the men who crossed the river to El Paso from the other side looking for work.

Ruly didn't pay attention to the name-calling until Coach told him to make sure he brought an extra shirt. "Coach homo/joto," Ruly said under his breath every time he changed out of his sweaty clothes in the locker room.

The Monday after not getting a candygram, he was perched at his hiding spot by the portable classrooms, not sure how much time had passed since the last bell. It was as if some moments were going in slow motion and then all of a sudden someone speeded up the film. He couldn't control any of it. Many groups of boys and girls walked by and disappeared down the canal road. No Norma.

As the sun dropped closer to the mountains in the horizon, he finally decided to hurry home. He was real thirsty and hungry, like for a cherry Slurpee and Funyuns, but he talked himself out of going by 7-Eleven.

As he walked toward the canal road, his body pulled to the right because of his gym bag loaded with homework. Since seeing JORDACHE JORDACHE at the dance, he'd fallen behind in all of his classes. After his first seventh-grade report card (4 C's, 1 B, 1 D), his mom had told his teachers at the school's open house to give him extra work. At first she sat with him at the kitchen table, but she soon went back to working late and believed him when he told her that he'd done the work. He had till his next report card before she would learn he was lying.

Any thoughts of walking with Norma, holding hands, and maybe kissing a girl for the first time vanished when he saw that he was the only one still walking home. He decided that Norma must have changed her route away from the canal road. To one that wasn't part of his Map Book.

He'd already spat twice, stopped to pull his underwear out of his butt, and wished he'd left his books in his locker when he reached the canal. What he saw there was as shocking as if he'd seen a shark.

Green-black water rushed through the canal. It reached all the way to the top. Over his head for sure if he'd been walking down there today. While he'd worried about this before, he'd been sure that the watering of the fields happened on Saturdays. At least that's when he'd last seen the green rows of cotton and chile submerged in a temporary lake.

Walking along the canal road, next to the surface of irrigation water, he didn't count his steps or have to clear his throat. The trash swimming in the water accompanied him. A lamp shade. Straw hat. Many plastic bottles. He imagined how all the random objects belonged to the same household. String of Christmas lights. Ice chest. Laundry basket.

When he couldn't stand the weight of his book bag anymore, he sat down on the edge of the canal, the water a few feet away. Although his memory of almost drowning was still a strong one, he'd done this before whenever he found himself around bodies of water. He learned that few suspected that he didn't know how to swim if he risked getting close to the water.

His science book stuck out of his book bag. He opened it to an earmarked page and stared at pictures of different types of algae: prokaryotic algae, eukaryotic algae, green algae, red algae. He allowed himself to imagine diving into the canal water and seeing this world of funny-shaped organisms up close, like one of those scuba divers he'd seen on *Big Blue Marble*. Like making out with Norma, exploring the underwater world was another thing he was sure that he'd never do, especially since he'd never learned how to swim. It seemed certain that the older he got, the less and less he knew how to do compared to other kids his age. Swimming. Dancing. Smoking. Kissing.

Sunlight faded as he sat alone on the canal road. The water kept rushing along, endless in both directions. More trash.

He wasn't sure which he heard first, her voice or the splash. Instinctively, he reached back and grabbed onto the first thing he could, a pair of legs.

When he peered at Norma standing over him, he saw her looking at the canal. She pointed at the water. His science book was floating away like a miniature raft. She jerked her legs; he held on tight.

He stood. She was only an inch shorter.

"I got you," he said.

"You do," was all she said.

She smiled and slipped her hair behind her ears. No time for second thoughts—he kissed her on the lips. She let him.

When he pulled back to breathe, he noticed that her eyes were brown, not a regular brown like the canal road but a color that shined much brighter than their new dining room table.

5   Since Pancho was at work, he had to ask his mother for a ride to Roller King. When she asked if Chris and Santi were going, she appeared surprised when he said he was going alone.

"Is it a school party?" she asked.

"No." He knew his short answer made her more curious.

She got real serious when she sensed he was up to something. "Just behave yourself tonight, Raul Luis."

As she drove away from their neighborhood, he kept changing the radio station, searching for a song that would set the right mood. A beat he would cling to for the rest of the night. A string of disco songs accompanied them on their drive.

When his mother asked if he had a girlfriend, he didn't fully think through what to say. He quickly said, "Yes," and raised the radio volume. Funky music filled the space of the Monte Carlo. His right arm hung out the window. The wind flapped it around like a limp string of chorizo. He was glad that his arm finally seemed to be doing its own thing. He was so caught up in watching his arm wag that he hardly noticed anything else outside the window.

When his mom pulled up to the address he gave her, there was a line outside the warehouse-sized building. ROLLER KING. A neon sign hung under a large roller skate. Flashing lights made the wheels appear to be turning. Seeing other teens, some with skates hanging over their shoulders, all of them dressed up for a Saturday night, left Ruly anxious. Knowing Norma was already inside made him worry more about his sweaty pits. He had resisted bringing an extra shirt like he did for PE.

He was rushing out of the car when his mother called him over to the driver's side. He thought she was going to ask more questions. When he leaned into her window, she handed him some money. He'd almost forgotten to ask. She said 'bye and drove off. Not speaking while sharing the same space was something he and his mother did more and more. As her taillights disappeared he decided that, depending how things went tonight, he would tell her everything or nothing. Keeping secrets and telling lies were easier to learn at his age than dancing or swimming.

Once Ruly was inside, the man behind the counter handed him a pair of skates the color of a worn baseball mitt. They were too big. When he went to return them, he learned that they carried only whole sizes. He kept the shoes, not wanting his feet to be squashed in a smaller size. His right foot, the thinner of the two, kept slipping inside the skate when he rolled out of the lobby area toward the rink.

Waves of music came from all directions. The noise level of the rink was louder than the school dances. He didn't even try to figure out what song was playing. A sheer volume of sound flooded over him. The bass's vibration crawled up his legs and met at his waist, traveled through his stomach, and massaged his heart. His body had never felt this good, at least not with all his clothes on.

The rink was dark and twice as big as the Valle Vista Junior High cafetorium. He slowly rolled around the rink while holding on to the rail. The only lights were the flashing kind from the top of police cars. They lit up the neon green trim that traced the walls of the rink. On the largest wall was a mural of a couple skating. The male looked like Freddie Prinze of *Chico and the Man,* especially with his thick mustache, and the female was a dead ringer for Farrah Fawcett in the poster Ruly wanted from the Fountain Plaza Arcade.

After he had stood by the rail for two songs, his ears adjusted to the volume. More lights came on. A mirrored ball hung in the center of the rink and threw squares of light all over the skaters like confetti. There were about thirty, from his age to about Pancho's. His anxiety about coming tonight grew into excitement. He felt like he was finally understanding what becoming a teenager was all about. This wasn't the boring world that took place at school or on weekends at home with family. And what made it all perfect was that he had a girlfriend. And like he imagined it would happen in a movie, Norma skated up to him at this exact moment.

She said she'd been waving for a few minutes from across the rink but he'd seemed hypnotized or something. He told her his eyes were adjusting to the lights. After they talked for a minute, raising their voices over the music as needed, she took his hand. As great as it was to be kissing at school, holding hands was his favorite part of them walking home along the canal road. She was his trusty guide, like the Indian woman whose name he couldn't pronounce who helped Lewis and Clark.

The outside of the rink was carpeted and had benches where they could sit. The vinyl made a fart sound when they plopped down. They laughed and jumped up to do it again. Strobe lights lit up their teeth when they smiled.

Their hands stuck together by sweaty palms, he asked her if she wanted anything from the snack bar. He'd already spent what his mother gave him on his admission and skates, but he still had his allowance. She said maybe later. He sensed by her fidgeting fingers and biting of lower lip that he wasn't the only one who was nervous on their first date.

The music continued while they told each other how they'd gotten to Roller King. Her sister, Ronnie, was in the DJ booth helping her boyfriend pick records. She had real curly hair and wore a floppy hat like that chubby guy on *What's Happening!!* Ruly smiled when Norma remembered that the character's name was Rerun. Although he saw that Ronnie wore a tight sweater that revealed how much more she had than her little sister, he felt lucky to be with his girlfriend, who wore her hair feathered and off her shoulders like he liked it. Norma took his hand again and led him to the rink.

He'd been so caught up in the music, the lights, and the hand-holding, not to mention how pretty Norma looked, that he hadn't had time to worry about what he was expected to do on the rink. His arms and legs had done fine so far, but skating on carpet was one thing. The smooth surface of the rink, so many people moving in a circle, lights everywhere, was a universe he wasn't sure he could be a part of. For some reason, words like "gravity" and "centrifugal force" kept popping into his mind. He didn't exactly know their definitions, and he was pretty sure he'd failed his last science test.

Since the day his book fell in the canal water, he and Norma had held hands for the whole time on their walks home. Her small fingers inside his stubby ones. While he liked that they talked about TV and how boring school was, he felt most connected to her in the moments when they said nothing. Silence brought them closer somehow in the natural landscape. Now, at the rink—under the influence of flashing lights and loud music—their clasped hands temporarily reassured him that he would be okay. He felt even better when she gave him a quick kiss, leaving the taste of root beer lip gloss on his lips.

She was such a good skater that as long as he held on to her he also was mobile on four pairs of wheels. He even handled the turns. He couldn't cross one foot over the other like she could, but he managed to stay in stride with her. And he didn't think too much about what to do with his arms. With his left hand in hers, he had to move only the right one.

Like at school dances, he studied what others did with their arms. Some waved them over their heads. Others let them hang loosely at their sides. Norma snapped her fingers with the beat of the song. He tried to do this but couldn't find the beat. He hadn't practiced these moves, and even if he had, he'd probably still have gotten them wrong.

After several times around the rink, he noticed his right arm flailing at his side. One moment he was just trying to keep it from hanging still, and the next thing he knew it was flapping around, like it had out the car window on the drive over. His arm swam in little waves as he skated at Norma's side. With his body in motion, swift and confident, he would've sworn to anyone that he also knew how to swim.

Inhale. Exhale. Inhale. Exhale.

After many songs, they skated over to Ronnie and her DJ boyfriend, who were on the elevated platform. The older couple was kissing. This was the best part of being boyfriend and girlfriend, Ruly told Chris and Santi when they asked what he'd been up to.

The DJ was dark-skinned, almost black. From his Afro to his huaraches, he looked like he belonged at a beach party, not a skating rink. Ruly wondered if he even knew how to skate.

"So, you're the one following my sister down the canal road," Ronnie said.

Ruly must've appeared embarrassed, because she said, "No, don't worry about it, I thought it was cute." When she complimented him on his orange-and-brown-striped shirt and new bell-bottoms, he told her that he liked her hat. She let him try it on. He wondered if it would make him a good dancer like Rerun, who was also chubby. Wearing the floppy hat made Ruly look like part of the Roller King group.

When he was invited into the DJ booth, he could see everything. The mirror ball spun over the center of the rink while red and blue lights spun at the corners. He'd thought that it would be more disorienting, but it turned out that he liked the frenzy of it all—the lights, the crowd, the music. He could get lost in it and not worry too much about what his body couldn't do.

He was about to go check out the snack bar when Norma and Ronnie screamed at the first notes of a song. A group of skaters immediately lined up, one behind the other, hands on hips. Norma said they were forming "The Train," although he thought of the bunny hop he'd been a part of at a family wedding. Norma pulled his arm and said they should get out on the rink. The snake of people was already going pretty fast. He decided he didn't want to risk falling, so he motioned for her to go ahead, he'd get some sodas. She and her sister quickly got in stride with the moving line of skaters. He estimated around fifteen people were holding on, several others along the rail ready to grab on.

Near the snack bar, he carefully rolled over to the arcade. He figured he had some time, since he knew this was a long song. He put quarter after quarter in the video games and got caught up pushing the buttons and handling the joysticks—more lights, more noise. Another guy about his age challenged him on Centipede. He easily beat Ruly's scores. He wasn't any better at video games than he was at real games. He had trouble concentrating on more than one thing at a time, as Mrs. Seymour, his science teacher, had written on his report card.

When the DJ called his name over the intercom, he knew he had to get back to the booth. He'd finished one soda, so he bought another large one and carried it with two hands, guiding his butt along the outer rail. The longer he wore skates and moved around, the more poised he became. Taller and faster. If only he could wear skates at home or to PE, he was sure he would not be so "goofy," as Coach Latner had said about a few students, including him, during the last National Physical Fitness test.

Norma and her sister sat in the DJ booth looking through crates of albums. They shared the soda he'd brought. When the DJ asked Ruly what kind of music he liked, he shrugged at first.

"The kind where you don't have to move your arms," he said under his breath. The DJ gave Ruly a weird look and told him to pick an album. There were ten times more records in the DJ's collection than in Pancho's.

Squatting on the floor, Ruly looked through the records, mostly by groups he hadn't heard of. He stopped when he got to one he recognized, and he took Norma's hand when the DJ put on a song from the album. He winked at Ruly as they stepped onto the rink.

The longer they maneuvered their way between all the other skaters, the more it felt as if they'd been doing this every Saturday night. He held on tight and tried to ignore the clock by the snack bar every time they came around that side. It reminded him that he had less than an hour before his mother would come for him. Although his parents had let him come on this date, they said he still had to keep a curfew. His less-than-average grades made it hard for him to argue.

The songs the DJ was playing went from slow to fast to very fast. From how much Ruly had skated tonight, he felt as light as he did when he was underwater. Norma must've sensed his confidence because she let go of his hand. She skated in front of him. JORDACHE JORDACHE. He hustled to stay close behind her firm butt. She was faster than he'd thought she could be all those times he'd followed her down the canal. She even turned around and skated backwards a few times around the rink.

Eventually, his legs tired, and he fell farther and farther behind. Without anyone holding his hand, he veered off course and got lost among the other skaters. Their unfamiliar bodies threw off the rhythm he'd eased into with a girlfriend by his side.

When he saw her go over to skate with her sister and the older crowd, he moved to the outside of the rink and skated slowly. His calves were beginning to ache. He knew he would wake up sore, like when Coach made them run a mile as fast as they could. By the start of the second lap on the school track, he was soaked from head to toe in sweat—a mojadito without a doubt.

Thinking of that hot afternoon, Ruly lifted his arms to see how wet his armpits were. His back was very damp, his crotch sticky.

He was skating behind a group of older girls—their butts firm in Calvin Klein jeans. They joined hands. At first, only a few others joined their chain. Each time they passed him, there were more people holding on. And this chain was moving so fast that the DJ's voice came over the loudspeaker and told them to slow down. They didn't seem to take the warning seriously.

When a popular song always played on KGRV came on, everyone hollered. With his energy as electric as a holiday parade, he decided that when the chain came around again he would jump in. He rolled out into the center of the rink and timed the chain's turns. It reminded him of when he, Laura, and Pancho used to ride the merry-go-round at Lomaland Park. If you didn't time it right, you would fall flat on your face.

Focused on the moving chain, he held his arms out. After a few anxious moments, the guy at the end grabbed him. Ruly stumbled and got ready to fall, but somehow he managed to bring his skates under him. He moved his legs and feet like crazy as the last link of the chain. After a few times around the rink, he spotted Norma standing by the music booth. He half waved with his free arm that was trying to keep pace with his legs.

Mo-men-tum n.—A measure of the motion of a body equal to the product of its mass and velocity.

Thinking of one of the vocabulary words he got right on his last science test, he tried to decide if he should try to get over to Norma. The decision was made for him when the guy who was holding his hand let go. He separated from the chain at full speed.

In-er-tia n.—The tendency of a body at rest to remain at rest or of a body in straight-line motion to stay in motion in a straight line unless acted on by an outside force.

Moving faster than he had ever thought he could, he crouched down, as he'd seen others do. It made him go even faster. He thought about using the rubber stops on his skates but was certain he would fall if he did. Like at the pool where he learned how to drown, he thought of a superhero flying. If his arms hadn't been gripping his thighs, he might have stretched them out in front of him like the movie Superman.

He did his best to aim himself at the rail and head for the DJ booth. Norma saw him coming. She pulled her hair over her ears and held her arms out. As if he was slowing down a home movie, he saw himself rolling into her arms, hugging her, and holding her tighter than he had when he almost fell in the canal. Big kiss at the end.

From one second to the next, he realized he was moving too fast. And there were no buttons he could push to slow down. His imaginary movie was about to come undone. At the last moment he managed to stand up and bring his arms to his side.

This is what he filmed: Leading with his stomach, he knocks Norma through the rails. Arms and legs tangle. He lands on top of her. One of his skates hangs over the rail. Pain crawls up his back. Norma doesn't move. Her hair veils her face. Everything stays this way for the end of one song and the beginning of another one. Ronnie and her DJ boyfriend rush over and stand Norma up. They help her to a bench. Her blouse is torn. Her bra, a pinkish color.

He stayed on the floor outside the rink while Ronnie went to get some ice for her sister. He would've gone but decided it best not to skate any more. This first (and probably last) date was definitely over.

He unlaced his skates and stood in his socks, the sting of blisters on each foot. When he finally went over to Norma, he saw her biting on her lower lip and her eyes watering. This kept him from asking if she was okay. When he heard the DJ say something about going to the emergency room, he couldn't help but look over at the spinning red lights.

As Norma's sister and her boyfriend walked Norma toward the lobby, all Ruly could mumble was, " 'Bye." He didn't get a response. Norma walked away rubbing the JOR stitched on her butt.

When Ruly realized that a small crowd had gathered, he hurried to return his skates. Sneakers half-laced, he went outside and thankfully spotted his mother's Monte Carlo. Pancho was in the driver's seat. Hard rock music greeted Ruly when he opened the door. In the long-sleeved white shirt and black tie that Pancho wore to work, he always looked much older. He sped out of the Roller King parking lot without either of them saying anything. When he stopped at a light, he ejected a cassette. Before he put in a new one, he asked his little brother how it went.

Even in his heavy depression, he readied himself for some other comment, something that made fun of him. In recent years, this was the way his brother had talked to him, asking questions to make a joke. He'd gotten used to it. So when Pancho asked him again, with no smart aleck remarks, he was caught off guard.

"What's up, Gordo-Boy?" he asked, lowering the volume of the stereo. "You look like you just realized that Disco Sucks!" He nudged Ruly and cut his laugh short.

He stirred in the passenger seat, put his hand under his shirt, and rubbed his stomach.

"I fell," he said.

"What?" Pancho lowered the volume of the car stereo.

"I fell, okay?"

"Aw, man. . . . Bad?"

"Yeah, bad. I ran into a girl."

"Yeah." Pancho kept turning his attention from the road to his hermanito and back. "Was she at least cute?"

"Pretty. She's pretty."

"What, you know her?"

"Yeah. She goes to my school. We walk home together."

"What did she say?" He leaned in his little brother's direction. "It was an accident, right?"

Ruly hesitated before answering. He replayed the seconds before impact in his head.

Wheels rolling.

Music playing.

Lights spinning.

"*WHAM!*" in big cartoon letters like on TV's *Batman.*

When he didn't say anything else, he was surprised that Pancho reached over, mussed his hair, and patted his stomach. Ruly was about to return the favor when his brother said, "How about Chico's?"

Ruly thought that maybe a double order of rolled tacos and salty fries would somehow ease the pain centered in his belly. Even before he could nod, he was glad that his brother had already turned in the right direction.

6 While Ruly had begun to accept that he might never return to Lomaland, he still didn't like the new house almost a year later. And since he was avoiding the finger-pointing at school, the hallways of Valle Vista Junior High were an even worse confine. The beginning of his teenage years seemed to be a further reminder that his Gordo-Boy body still wasn't fitting in anywhere. Home. School. Closet.

The best thing about the upcoming summer vacation was that there would be three months to try and forget about the incident at the skating rink. While he hoped Norma's arm would heal in that time, he knew no cast would fix his wounded emotions.

In this second summer in the new house, he'd probably end up doing the same things as when he'd lived in Lomaland. Sleep late instead of doing odd jobs in the neighborhood for extra money. Watch too much TV instead of read-ing any books. Play with Pancho's Pac-Man Atari game instead of joining any Little League team. Make grilled cheese sandwiches and instant mashed pota-toes instead of fixing the flats on his bike. And he did these things while he knew other kids his age dared to step out of their houses.

And having to spend the long summer days without Laura, who was now living with yet another aunt, also made him feel lonely. The last he'd heard was that his cousin was spending most of her time with cheerleading tryouts. She was hoping to be on the varsity squad next year at Ysleta High, and she planned to attend a summer camp at the El Paso Community College campus.

The more time he spent alone, the more he realized how he would always have to be his own best friend, especially since he wasn't hanging out with Chris / Santi anymore. Ruly didn't have whole conversations with himself or nothing like Crazy Bobby down the block, but he did give himself instructions, which he wrote down in his Map Book.

1. Wake up. Go to bathroom.
2. Pee. Flush.
3. Look out windows. Check fridge for notes.
4. Read what chores you have.
5. Wash dishes. Throw out trash. Scrub carpet.
6. Remember you forgot to brush.
7. Eat first.
8. Forget to brush again.

Since he was spending so much time at home, his parents began to think he was behaving himself. Now that he was thirteen, he did sense that they treated him differently. They raised his allowance. They hooked up cable to the big TV in the den. Dad even let him take the wheel of the car on short trips to the store.

While his parents' growing trust in him made him a little suspicious, he fig-ured it had to do with Pancho getting ready to move out. His brother spent most of his time at his girlfriend's or at work, so Ruly was pretty much all his parents had left, he figured. And having open access to his brother's stuff—rock records, mall store clothes, cologne bottles—did make him feel older. Now all he'd have to learn was how to act like a teen, which was why he planned on taking drama classes next school year, his last in junior high.

Unlike Dad's '57 Chevy hot rod, his mother's car was ugly—peeling vinyl top, no cassette player, ash gray paint job. And worst of all, it was a manual transmission. "You have to practice if you want to learn," Dad said about his complaints. "I know, but can't I take Pancho's? He's not using it." The Firebird sat in the garage since his brother didn't want the sun to mess up the Porsche-red paint job.

"No, it's his car. When you work for your own, you can say no to him."

With that quick exchange, Dad handed him the keys to his mother's car and ten dollars. "I saw some cute girls at the 7-Eleven having a car wash. Why don't you drive there and back?"

More than the opportunity to practice driving, the mention of girls was Dad's way of giving him incentive. It was also Dad's way of further introducing and avoiding the subject of sex, his younger son suspected. Even though they'd never talked about sex, Dad indirectly shared lessons by leaving dirty magazines where they were easy to find.

Many times, while alone in the house, Ruly would return to the closet and go through the glossy pages. There was always one pictorial that he focused on, tucked between long articles of who knows what. The settings always seemed to have nothing to do with the naked women posing.

Is a barn supposed to be sexy? he wondered. How does drinking a milk shake at a soda shop lead to sex? What does Dad enjoy more? Women straddling motorcycles? Women draped on cars?

As Ruly carefully drove down their street to the corner, where he signaled, looked both ways, and took a left before coming to a Stop sign, he continued to ask himself what were the connections between cars and girls. The most he could come up with on his own was that the one got you the other. There were probably many other factors in the equation, but that seemed to be the simplest answer for now. Since he didn't have a car, or even a driver's permit, he was certain that having sex was years out of reach.

To make the meaning of intimacy more confusing, the first girl he saw at the car wash was none other than his cousin Laura. She was in a bikini top with cutoffs, and of course, barefoot, the way he mostly remembered her. It had been a long time since they'd seen each other at another cousin's birthday party.

When some high school guy had come to pick her up at the party, he remembered she'd said they were going to a concert. When Ruly asked if he could go, she said he was too young. "Anyway," she teased, "you're a disco skater boy. You don't know how to rock out."

Before he could return the taunt, she'd hurried out the door and into the passenger's side without saying good-bye to anyone else in the family. Laura was good at coming and going, but not staying.

"Look who cruised in," Laura said to the group of girls washing cars.

"Yep, like my fine carrito?" he said as he turned off the ignition.

"Cool wheels, Cuz. . . . Did you take it from some poor viejita?"

Laughter: her gurgling drain of water; his hiccup snorts.

After he got out of the car and hugged his cousin, they kidded some more. Whether it was about someone in the family or something they'd been saving to tell each other, they always picked up from the last time they'd seen each other. No time seemed to pass between the periods when they lost touch. She was more than like the sister he never had.

"Are you a cheerleader now?" he asked when he read the hand-painted signs on the wall of the 7-Eleven.

CAR WASH $5.

SUPPORT YSLETA HIGH CHEERLEADERS.

GO INDIANS!!

"Not yet. I'm still trying out." She pointed to the other girls nearby. "Debra's the one who's helping me get in. She's over there."

"Cool. You'd be a good cheerleader."

"Thanks, Cuz."

She walked over to the girls washing and drying cars. He followed.

"Dee, come here. I want you to meet somebody."

Long legs brought over a very cute girl (*Dad was right*, he thought) and got Ruly's attention before she said anything. She was damp from her braided hair to her flip-flopped feet. The T-shirt and athletic shorts she wore left no doubt that she was a high school cheerleader. She seemed ready to do a cheer for him right then.

Give me an R.

Give me a U.

Give me an L.

Give me a Y.

What does that spell?

RULY! RULY!

GOOOOOOOOOOOOOOO RUUUUUUULYYYYYYY!!!!

He did his best to hide his excitement at meeting a hot high school girl. The fact that his own cousin knew her personally made him think that this meeting was no accident.

In the time Laura took to tell Debra that he was her cousin and that he was going to start at the high school in a year and something unflattering about his taste in music, he'd already imagined Debra in her cheerleading uniform, pompoms and everything. Rather than have her cheering at a crowded stadium, he imagined her somewhere more private, like a movie theater or maybe the backseat of a car. His fantasizing of a personal pictorial was interrupted.

"Hey, Cuz, come back to earth." Laura snapped her fingers close to his ear. "Right?"

When he felt his cousin slap him on his shoulder, he jolted out of his private photo shoot. "Yeah, sure . . . what?"

"I told Dee that you might be trying out for the Drama Club when you get to the High."

Debra stood nearby, wiping sudsy water off her toned body. Her tanned legs and arms were hairless, as smooth as the waxed paint job of the car driving away from the car wash.

"Well, I'm thinking about it . . . but maybe I'll try out for football."

"Football? I thought you said you wanted to act, be the next Chachi."

"Sure, that could be fun, I guess."

The truth was that Dad was the one who mentioned Ysleta's football team at the last family gathering. His uncles had all shared their approval before they turned their attention back to the Cowboys game on TV.

"You'd probably do good at both." Debra's voice was as much of a turn on as the mouth it came out of. She was being supportive, like she must be for all jocks at the High.

"I don't know. Maybe I'll wait a year."

"I better get back," Debra said before she shook Ruly's hand and half walked, half jogged to the next car waiting to be washed.

"I don't know about you, Cuz." Laura stared off at the traffic passing by on North Loop Drive. "I thought you were different."

"What do you mean?" He kept his eyes on Debra, who was now sponging down a car. The details *water sun laughing* of the real scene before him were more than he could record, so they would later be replaced with the airbrushed reproductions he saw in Dad's magazines. His body was experiencing several new urges every minute, it seemed to him. And the loud music coming from the boom box nearby didn't help calm him down.

"You know all jocks are big cabezones. You're not like that. . . . You're more

. . . more sensitive." She moved over and leaned into him. "I thought once you got to high school you'd do something none of us had."

The images of his beefy cousins posed in their respective high school uniforms helped him understand her point. They were good enough guys, but when it came to common sense, they were totally lost. Last he'd heard, Pepito had been beaten up coming back from partying in Juárez and ended up calling his parents in the middle of the night. Tía was embarrassed for her son, while Tío was ashamed of his namesake.

"I don't know. I don't have to decide now, do I?"

"Not really, but you should think about it. Plan for which clubs you want to join."

She went on to explain how during the first weeks of classes there were signs up in the hallways for every club and organization at Ysleta High School.

"I've never been part of a club. Except the Mickey Mouse Club, remember?" Loyal viewers of the TV show, the cousins had sent away for membership cards that came with a coupon for Disneyland that they never had a chance to use.

"Don't be silly. High school is one big club." The tone of her voice told him she was being serious, no laughing, and that this was important. "You can't meet anybody, much less *be* anybody, if you aren't part of something."

The way she described the social scenes in high school, the more intimidating it all sounded. While he'd been anxious about replacing two friends in his junior high clica, he now had several more worries of how he would suffer during high school. Sure, he'd try to keep some friends from Valle Vista Junior High, but there would be kids from at least three other junior highs going to Ysleta High School. He resisted trying to estimate how many new faces that would be.

"You want to meet girls like Debra, don't you?"

His wet grin said more than his only word: "Yeah."

"Well, you'll have to join at least one club," Laura said. "If not Drama, maybe Journalism or Student Council, even FFA."

Every group she listed seemed foreign to him, nothing like the ones he'd successfully avoided in junior high. Whatever they did seemed too much like work, especially FFA. Luckily, he still had enough of his allergies to excuse himself from ever working with farm animals. He wanted to ask if there was a TV Club or a Map Club, but that might disappoint his cousin even more.

"All right, I better get back or I won't ever make it as a cheerleader."

They hugged and said good-bye. As he got behind the wheel of his mother's washed car, he honked. He was glad when Debra and some of the other high school girls turned and waved along with Laura. As if there was any doubt that he would join a high school club, their sparkling bodies guaranteed that he'd do anything to make his fantasies more real than magazine photos.

After he left with a free car wash, he didn't go straight home, as his parents had instructed. He decided to stop by Dairy Queen. The familiar tastes of fried food (burrito and fries) and sweet desserts (dipped cones and sundaes) always calmed him. The settling of the food might help draw blood to his stomach instead of to his confused brain (starting as "Freshmeat" in high school) and his hard palito (cheerleaders washing cars).

While he was very aware that his body was changing with every school year, it felt like all it was doing was getting bigger: bulging stomach, thickening fingers, swollen cheeks. And not in the places he would've liked—shoulders, penis, thighs.

It appeared to be true what he'd first learned from watching the Dr. Goodbody segments on Saturday-morning TV: *You are what you eat.*

Lumpy as his mother's mashed potatoes.

Dark as Little Debbie Swiss Rolls.

Gassy as refried beans.

Hair as puffy as sopapillas.

Lists continued to help him cope, more and more as a teen. Even if he didn't write them down, they were an extension of his Map Book. A way of learning on his own, especially when it came to the geography of his gordito-self.

Raul Cruz

1 Movie star hair. Clothes not from Kmart. A rad car. Real cute girlfriend.

Only those teenagers lucky enough to have these were invited to high school parties. At least that's what Raul thought before he was asked if he was going to a party at a football player's house. He said yes before thinking to ask any of the questions he'd asked himself since he began attending Ysleta High School.

Do all the popular girls go to parties?

Do you really get horny when you drink?

Do they go all the way?

How much is all the way?

He wondered if all sixteen-year-olds had these questions. And how many of them were also virgins.

Agreeing to attend the party was an invitation to a spot that was as far from his house as California or Canada or China. It didn't matter what location on his child globe that he compared it to since he'd never left El Paso, living all his life in the Lower Valley.

This leg of his teen journey actually began the day when he approached Ysleta's head varsity football coach at the end of his sophomore year. His idea was to get one of those numbers nobody ever wants (61, 49, 83), sit on the end of the bench, and think of what kind of toppings to order at Peter Piper Pizza after the Friday-night games.

With a confidence that he'd been building since he left Valle Vista Junior High, he stood face-to-face with the coach and asked if the team needed any help. When Coach asked if he knew anything about grass, he thought it was a strange question that he had an answer for. He said, sure, plenty, in fact. Bermuda. Fescue. Santa Ana. Crab. I have some planted on my back, he wanted to tell Coach, who was scratching the hairs sticking out of his shirt collar like frayed radio wires. "Fine, son, go see Mr. Clay," Coach said and pointed him to the other side of the football stadium. He figured that was where he'd get his shoulder pads and helmet.

He half jogged across the grass field (probably Bermuda) and imagined a voice over the loudspeaker: "Now in at flanker, number 66."

Days passed before he realized that Coach hadn't understood his initial question at all. But getting to be part of the team at any cost was a greater goal than worrying about what position he played.

RAUL CRUZ—VARSITY TEAM MANAGER

Mr. Clay, the head trainer, made his title official by writing it on a piece of masking tape and sticking it on a locker. It wasn't next to the ones holding jerseys or jockstraps, but that was okay. The important thing was that he had a locker under the football stadium, which he'd longed to inhabit since first stepping onto the high school campus two years ago.

INDIAN PRIDE

ONCE AN INDIAN ALWAYS AN INDIAN

He admired the slogans along with the arrowheads and the headdress painted in maroon and white above the large letters that lined the cement tunnel. His five-foot-seven-and-a-half, 167-pound body, as confirmed by Mr. Clay's scale, felt at home in the cavelike dwelling. The cold-mildew smell took him back to family trips to neighboring New Mexico. With a few stalactites and stalagmites and the fluttering of bats, Indian Stadium could be a tourist site like Carlsbad Caverns. The high school stadium's bright lights already attracted many from every neighborhood in the Lower Valley.

The gap between him in the stands and him on the field lessened with each day he served as Team Manager. From the onset, when he introduced himself as "Raul"—not as "Ruly"—he'd stepped into a new skin that was as good as a game uniform. And he wore it as proudly as the one Mr. Clay gave him: one maroon and one white polo shirt, the profile of an Indian silk-screened on the breast; gray polyester slacks with extra pockets for rolls of tape and mouthpieces; and best of all, cleats, size ten, white Adidas with maroon laces. Raul didn't care that they were left over from last season and had to be sprayed with two cans of disinfectant. They made him feel right in step with the guys on the team.

The upcoming football season promised much glory for the Indians. Even before he became Team Manager, he could have told you the names of the star players, their nicknames, their positions, and statistics in past seasons. As a freshman and sophomore, from a seat high in the stands, he'd studied the Mighty Tribe.

Instead of pumping weights to get stronger, or maybe dieting to lose some of his junior high belly, he played the game from a safe distance. He thought of himself as more than a regular fan, although he acted like one. Yelling out during key third down plays. Booing the referees for making bad calls. Patting the players on the back as they entered the stadium for pep rallies. Even spying on them from a corner booth at Peter Piper.

"Raul, bring me some Gatorade."

"Raul, hurry with more tape?"

"Raul, straighten out the sprinklers at the thirty-yard line."

"Raul, touch up the hash marks."

"Raul, pick up my jockstrap. . . . And don't smell it this time."

Although "Raul" was a common name at Ysleta High, "Raul Cruz—Varsity Team Manager," he was certain, would look good in the yearbook next to the other well-known Rauls.

Raul Muñoz, Student Council Vice President. Raul Chávez, *Pow Wow* newspaper editor. Raul Rosales, All-District Point Guard. Raul Venegas, Tribesman Club Sergeant-at-Arms. And most important, Raul Cruz (not Ruly, Gordito, Stupid-Menso) was the guy you invited to parties.

Raul Cruz had always been more comfortable on the sidelines.

Before he took the position officially at YHS, he'd brought towels to his cousin, changed the channels for his mother, fetched Pancho a Coke, handed Dad a tool, was the first one to taste his aunt's hot chile con carne. Even with the girls he liked in junior high, like following Norma for days before he even got her name. And, of course, at the neighborhood pool. Being on the periphery is safer, he'd learned the hard way.

And he was also good at waiting. Not necessarily patient. More like nervous, scared even, hesitant, reserved, for sure. The simple thought of acting too soon, without much thought, terrified him. He didn't just dive in anymore, another lesson learned outside of the classroom.

Although he hated math (like most school subjects that required homework), he was intimate with being calculating. As a teen, he planned out every scene in his head like a movie director before he initiated anything. He didn't care if his worries, his deep-set anxieties, were mostly unfounded. The feelings were very real.

Long before he dared to jump into the neighborhood swimming pool and learn how to drown, he'd felt safe in the wide-open spaces of Lomaland's desert. Sure, he suffered small injuries, plenty of scars to prove it, from playing around with Laura and Pancho and the rest of the neighborhood kids. He even had a nail go through his right calf one time. The rusty metal pierced his boy-flesh when their homemade go-cart flipped over. Tumbling inside of it, he didn't have time to be scared. The pain would crawl out of him later. He was more stunned than hurt.

After he came to a stop in what was left of the go-cart—a crooked wooden frame, missing at least one nail, two out of four tires, and the steering wheel— his thoughts bounced around like socks in the dryer. Fueled by his adrenaline, flashes of his short life passed too quickly for him to think he should be anything but relieved.

In the last scrimmage football game before the start of his junior year, the Indians came back from a two-touchdown halftime deficit and claimed a victory over their cross-I-10 rivals, the Eastwood Troopers. On the bus trip back to the High, as Raul picked up dirty towels and chinstraps off the floor, he found himself at the heart of the celebration.

CheeringStompingClappingCheeringStompingClapping.

Alberto Baca was the one who shouted at him about the house party: "Raul, you're going, right?" He looked at the six-foot-two, two-hundred-thirty-pound sack-machine and said nothing. He guessed he'd smiled when the brown, hairy giant said, "Great, ése, see you there."

Just like that, Raul Cruz was invited to his first high school party.

He'd often wondered how such things were handled. He imagined a series of phone calls, a fee maybe, someone important giving the final okay, and possibly a handshake or a password. But that wasn't how it happened. It was merely a matter of being at the right place. And he'd had no clue how this fateful Friday would change the weekends ahead.

The directions to the house party were less clear than the invitation. Not comfortable asking anyone in the team locker room for the exact address, he sneaked around as the team showered and got dressed. Their nakedness made him careful of where not to look. But it didn't matter if he looked or not, the guys kidded him that he did.

He fit into this post-game ritual by bringing extra towels and sodas for the team. Each snap of a wet towel on his Husky-Sears-Jeans ass and each spray of a soda can on his helmet of thick hair made him feel more a part of their victory. Sticky from soda and sweat, he was tempted to strip right there in the locker room and shower with the team. But he decided not to push his luck, not to mess things up. Instead he would hurry home to get ready. There wouldn't be time for a long bath (a Ruly ritual), so a quick shower would have to do this night, as important as it was.

FIRST HIGH SCHOOL PARTY

— North Loop & Pendale

— Leo's TV Rental

— Near Another Raul's House (Rosales not Muñoz)

— J&R Beer Depot

From the talk in the locker room, he was able to learn that the location of the party wasn't far from his house. The names of Lower Valley streets and landmarks were familiar and not on the other side of I-10, El Paso's longest freeway, where he'd imagined all high school parties took place.

Now all that was left was convincing Pancho to let him borrow his car for a few hours. Since his brother had moved back in after breaking up with his longtime girlfriend, Raul didn't like to bother him. He had to promise his brother to wash his car for the whole month if he wanted to use it. "And you have to do my chores. That includes picking up the dog shit, Gordo." His brother hated doing this and anything else around the house. But as long as he lived at home, Dad said, "You have to pull your weight." Raul knew exactly what that meant but figured his always skinny brother didn't.

After getting a Whataburger Combo #3 (single patty with cheese and jalapeños, onion rings instead of fries, large Dr Pepper), Raul ate while he drove down North Loop Drive. He passed the same streets more than once. He'd hoped there would be a sign, or as silly as it sounded, some balloons and streamers, like he remembered from the parties in Lomaland.

You couldn't really get lost in this part of the Lower Valley—one road led to the next and eventually they all connected. Like the irrigation canals that traced back to the Río, the Lower Valley's roads, paved and unpaved, all seemed to lead back to the High. The trick seemed to be to keep driving. Eventually you'd end up somewhere.

All that was left of his food was some onion rings when, by luck, he spotted lots of cars parked down a dead-end road. He positioned Pancho's car away from the nearest truck to be safe. "I'll beat your fat ass if anything happens to my car" was his brother's form of a good-bye. *What else is new?* he thought as he flipped Pancho off behind his back.

Without the help of streetlights, an early fall moon guided him forward. Even if this wasn't the place of the football player's party, the number of cars here meant something was happening. Maybe another beer bust. For two years now, in the hallways, he'd always heard about keg parties and beer busts. The thought of a house full of strangers would be less stressful than one filled with guys and girls he recognized from the High. Either way, blood pumped like crazy through his heart. He burped and tasted Whataburger Combo #3.

Bringing the guys water and helping them put on their pads was one thing, but hanging out and acting cool were two skills that he hadn't learned. And there was sure to be many here that hadn't had a chance to experience his new identity as "Raul Cruz—Varsity Team Manager."

Flashes of strobe lights shot out from the backyard of the largest house on the dead-end road. When he walked onto the property, he thought he recognized some of the crowd hanging out in the driveway. They leaned against a black Nova he'd seen cruising Alameda Avenue at lunchtime. They passed around a joint. He wasn't surprised that they were smoking pot, another thing he hadn't done by his junior year. From putting away the uniforms and equipment in players' lockers, he knew what many others did at these parties besides drink beer.

The group in the driveway offered him a toke when they caught him staring. "Rockers" would be their designated team. Uniform: jeans, concert tees, long hair. He told them, "Maybe later," in the coolest manner he could. The pungent smell slithered past his face as he walked to the side of the house. A couple holding beer cans had just exited a screen door. He figured that this was as good a place as any to enter.

Velour sofa with brown and red leaves covered in plastic.

Cracked-vinyl recliner, caca-colored.

Slick-brown dining room table with six chairs.

Oil paintings of horses on the walls.

This was a living room for Thanksgiving or Anniversary Dinners, not high school parties, he thought. What most resembled the interior of the first Cruz family home in Lomaland was the smell that crawled up his nose. The shaggy carpet, a familiar shade of brown, under his feet was where this odor lived. He could tell there were dogs somewhere. Three, four, maybe five. Probably locked in one of the bedrooms. The scent of carpet cleaner used to hide dog pee welcomed him to his first high school party. What a trip.

He lingered and appreciated the smallest details of the home's decor: green-glass grapes on coffee table, a conch-shaped ashtray and White Sands coasters on end table, porcelain duck figurines on shelf. As if he was in the closet watching home movies, he imagined his relatives in this room. Cousins in one corner playing Battleship and old maid. Tías and tíos sitting at the table picking at their carne asada and drinking Schlitz. Of course, Freddy Fender or Johnny Rodriguez spinning on the turntable. This room didn't have a stereo, but there was a TV in the corner.

While he'd expected to find a garage full of guys drinking beer and possibly couples dancing at the house party, he'd been cast into a living room that rivaled the Bradys'. Other than his former home in Lomaland, theirs was the perfect TV house, if you were ever to ask Ruly.

After surfacing from a wave of memories, he worried that someone would come into the room and question him, so he escaped down a hallway. The eggshell-colored walls were lined with family photos. He studied them. *Maybe we're related,* he thought when snooping around the room. The narrow hallway hugged his wide body. He walked sideways and tried to not disturb any of the frames. He was almost through to the other end when a girl came down the hallway in the opposite direction. Maricela had attended Valle Vista Junior High, and more recently she'd been in his sophomore algebra class. Most important, she was now a varsity cheerleader.

"Hey, Ruly, how's it going?"

"Good . . . and you?"

He was too distracted by her attention to worry about her calling him by his former nickname. She had one hand on the hallway wall, and the other one held a plastic cup of beer. He knew she'd been partying for a while by the way she smiled. In every class they'd shared, she never smiled. Always staring out the window or brushing her hair. The algebra equations that Mr. Alvarez put on the board didn't seem to interest Maricela. Raul always thought that whatever a girl like Maricela daydreamed about was more important than knowing the answer to $x + 3x = 19$.

"What are you doing here?" She took a drink of her beer. "I've never seen you at a party."

"I know." He shrugged and stared down the hall.

They stood around and said nothing for a long moment. Just as he was going to ask how the party was, someone ran up behind him and pushed in the back of his knees. He buckled and almost fell. When he reached for the wall, he clutched Maricela's arm instead. She did her best to keep them balanced.

"What's up, ése?" The football team's leading tackler, Alberto Baca, clamped his hands on Raul's shoulders. Now Maricela and Alberto—one on his right and one on his left—blocked him in the hallway. Not sure where to put his hands, he shoved them into his corduroys' back pockets.

"Whoooo, yeeaah, helluva game, huh? We kicked those calote gringos' asses."

"Do you mind, Chewie, me and Ruly were talking. You're such a spaz."

Raul avoided eye contact with Maricela. He took his right hand out of his potcket and fidgeted with his shirt collar.

"Give me a break. I gotta piss. I'll leave you lovebirds alone."

"Get out of here, dweeb," Maricela said playfully.

Before the lineman went into the bathroom at the end of the hallway, he pulled up Raul's shirt. Alberto's laughter crowded the hall even more. Raul quickly pulled his shirt back down and hoped Maricela hadn't seen his "Black Hole," as Pancho had labeled his hairy belly button. Every morning that Raul studied his growing body in the mirror, he had to agree with his stupid brother.

A stirring inside his stomach, like a big burp—or worse, a Whataburger fart—made him wish that he could get out of the hallway and back to the living room, where he could look for a hideaway.

Standing in the hall with Maricela, he felt himself sweating big time. His shirt, which his mother had made time to iron, stuck to his round stomach.

In her buzzed state, Maricela had knocked down a photo and was trying to put it back up. He helped her find the nail. The photo of a boy on horse-back was required in all Lower Valley homes, he figured. For a few pesos, you could go and get your picture taken at the Juárez Mercado. Somewhere in his parents' closet, there was one of his brother and another of his cousin Laura. Ruly never had his photo taken since horsehair was on the long list of his child-hood allergies.

"Thanks, Ruly. You're so nice." The photo was returned to its place.

Maricela's eyes were a shade lighter than a football and the layers of her feathered hair were like Farrah Fawcett's, at least in the old poster he used to have. Even if Maricela hadn't been a cheerleader, he would've still thought of her as one of the prettiest girls at the High. As they stood there, nothing being said, he noticed the top two buttons of her blouse were undone. *Bra Beige Silky.* Suddenly, he too felt that he had to pee. He'd finished two sodas after the game and the large drink on the ride over.

"You guys should go find a room." Alberto came back down the hallway.

"Shut up, Ruly and I were just catching up." She fidgeted with her buttons.

"C'mon, Ruly-Ruly, let's get some *sir-vay-sas*." The star player's paws dragged him past Maricela. She pressed her thin body against the wall to let them through. Her free hand, the glass of beer still in the other, brushed against his stomach. Her outstretched fingers snagged his shirt. It rode up to his chest. He was sure that if she hadn't seen his half-dollar-sized ombligo earlier, she'd defi-nitely touched it this time.

"See you, Ruly," Maricela said as she walked in the opposite direction. "Maybe we can dance later."

"Okay." He looked back and watched her walk down the hall. Her tight black jeans made a decision for him: *Even if I don't see her again tonight, I'll do everything possible to meet more cheerleaders this year.* For sure, he would fantasize about the last few minutes the next time he masturbated.

BrabeigebellyButtonBraBraBeigeBellybuttonBraBrabeigeBellybuttonBra
BeigeBrabellyButtonbrabrabeigebellybuttonBraBraBeigeBellyButtonBra
BeigeBrabellyButtonbrabrabeigebellybuttonBraBeigeBrabellyButtonbra
brabeigebellybuttonBra

2   Alberto was Raul's blocker through the kitchen crowded with bags of chips, pizza boxes, plastic cups, and beer cans. Past the mess of an eating area, they slipped out a sliding glass door, like a halfback dive play between center and tackle.

Growing up, he'd thought the backyards in Lomaland were the largest in the Lower Valley. But this backyard was way larger. He couldn't see how far the yard extended, but the disco's lights and small torches on the side of the patio lit up about three first downs of grass. Fescue, it smelled like. Maybe Bahama.

On the left of the yard, the Indian offensive line huddled around four kegs. They nodded in his direction. He resisted the urge to get them some towels and restock the tubs of ice. On his right was the mobile disco. He thought he recognized the Midnight Galaxy DJ from a cousin's wedding. Michael Jackson's latest was playing. Raul still wasn't as much of a music lover as his brother, but it was hard not to know what was popular. The FM stations played the same songs over and over. Pancho also played his cassettes loud on his car stereo.

While Maricela had started Raul's pits sweating real bad and his heartbeat running wind sprints, surprisingly he wasn't totally nervous about the party anymore. He dried his palms on his cords and tried to keep from fidgeting. He wished he had his own personal manager to fetch him a towel or something to drink. His first high school party was already as exhausting as some of Coach's two-a-day practices.

Like tumbling in the go-cart as a child, his emotions hit another dip when he walked farther into the yard. Most of the partygoers stood around a swimming pool. Shaped like an hourglass, it was big enough to hold the football team's first-string offense and defense, maybe even the kicker.

Except for the guys from the team, he doubted others at the party knew him by any of his names. A few swam around and some sat on the edge with only their feet in the water. In trunks, bikinis, and bathing suits, they looked nothing like they did at school. While he'd gotten used to being ignored in the halls by crowds wearing clothes with labels from the newest stores at Cielo Vista Mall, he found them less threatening tonight in their bare arms, bare stomachs, bare legs, bare feet.

In a strange way, he felt he was seeing them, the real them, for the first time. There were even a few belly buttons as large and hairy as his. This made him consider taking off his clothes like he was always tempted to do in the locker room.

He would've given this further thought, but he was more concerned about the pool than who was or wasn't wearing what. From many summers of experience, he knew that if he kept his cool, he'd be okay. *No need to panic,* he told himself. *Just like no one here knows my name, no one here knows I can't swim.*

In a matter of minutes he finished two cups of beer, courtesy of his varsity friends.

The cloud in his head and Midnight Galaxy's continuous strobe lights made this the best feeling ever. Even when he masturbated, that jolt that rose from his hard palito up his stomach, past his throat, and rolled his eyes back was over much too quickly. Tonight's buzz *beer music pool* was sure to last till the end of the evening.

When he saw the first-string backfield begin chasing second and third stringers around the yard and carrying them like human handoffs to the pool, he ducked under the back porch near the sliding glass doors that led to the kitchen. This was the way he had come in and what seemed like the best way out.

Alberto left the keg duties to someone else and came over next to Raul. Another glass of beer made him trust this joker, who had probably started the chaos in the first place.

"You having a good time, Ruly-Ruly?"

He nodded and kept his back to the sliding glass door.

"Damn, this is great." Alberto patted him hard on the back and caused him to stumble. Raul took a few steps forward to regain his balance.

Between more guys raising their glasses and chugging, more people were thrown in the pool. Whether it was real or just in his mind, he heard chanting.

"Indians Number 1!"

"Indians Number 1!"

"Number 1 . . . ! . . . Number 1 . . . ! . . . Number 1 . . . !"

Raul looked through the sliding glass door into the house, where some of the quicker partygoers had escaped. Not everyone had brought trunks or a bathing suit, and like him, the ones who hadn't didn't want to get thrown in with their clothes on. Though with or without the right clothes, the pool was the last place he wanted to end up this night. Despite his buzz, he knew this for a fact.

And things were going so good. He was even about to ask Maricela to dance before some of the guys threw her in the water. At least he was thinking about it. She came out mad, and he didn't see where she'd gone.

He even considered going to the front and seeing if the invitation to smoke a joint was still open. That would surely heighten the cloud in his head. He'd walked in on his brother one time while he and his girlfriend were getting high. They let him stay as long as he didn't say shit. When his brother's girlfriend offered him a toke, his brother had said, "No, he's allergic." Ruly had heard it called "grass," so he probably was.

Not wanting to bring any attention his way, he stayed in the backyard's porch area. Whether it was the pulse of the disco's huge speakers or his fifth—no, sixth—beer in an hour, his senses were too aware of the danger of being thrown in the pool.

The varsity team had definitely carried their gridiron victory to the party, and their fans along with it. Tackles in front of the disco. Bodies passed in the air. Crashing water cheers. Many who scrambled out of the pool were caught and thrown in again. If Coach were here, you bet he'd be yelling, "C'mon, faster, quicker, harder. You play like girlie men."

When Raul saw the team throw the party's host off the diving board, he found himself transported back to the neighborhood pool. The day of his fateful plunge was more than a memory. Any risky situation he faced—the first day of high school, giving an oral book report in sophomore English, lacing up his cleats for two-a-days—was like climbing the stairs of the diving board. Boys and girls encouraging him: "Jump. Do it. Jump." Staring into the bottomless blue. Slow-motion descent.

Even after he'd been rescued from drowning, he was still curious as to what he'd been saved from. The next day that summer, as his cousin Laura, her crush Arturo, and the lifeguard Debbie ate lunch in the office, Ruly had approached the pool again. No one there seemed to remember that he was the boy who had almost drowned the day before. Maybe because he wore jeans, a tee-shirt, and high-tops. And no one noticed when he went to the deep end of the pool and put both hands in the water. He scooped out two palmfuls and poured the liquid over his head like he'd seen a priest baptize a baby on Easter.

His fluid memory evaporated when Alberto took him in a Chewbacca hug and wrestled him to the ground. Even if he'd tried to escape, he knew he was no match for the All-City lineman. While Raul was probably heavy enough to play tackle or guard if he'd had a position on the team, he didn't have the advantage of months in the weight room. Two other players, Mando and Rene, got hold of his legs. They picked him up like one of the tackling dummies they destroyed at practice.

The guys held his legs higher than his head. His butt dragged on the moist grass. He didn't let go of his plastic cup, and so beer spilled on his arm and ran down his chest. His shirt was halfway up his stomach and his belly button half filled with beer. With the growing urge to pee, he tossed the rest of his beer on his crotch. A good cover.

His body swinging like a hammock, the guys counted down from ten.

" . . . nine . . . eight . . ."

His butt scraped against the cement pool deck. He laughed and his mouth opened as if to swallow.

" . . . seven . . . six . . ."

The moon had cleared the clouds, a basketball in the sky.

" . . . five . . . four . . ."

The countdown continued. At least five sets of hands on his fat body.

" . . . three . . . two . . ."

Over the water.

"One."

Over the yard.

His lonja shifted above his waistline like waves of flesh. He laughed harder.

A grunt and the guys let go.

"Zero!"

Blue. Light. Air. Wait.

Too short of a moment. Barely long enough for him to shift his chubby body and clear the edge of the pool. He hit the illuminated water on his side. Left shoulder first. Stomach and butt followed. Mouth closed, eyes open. The chlorinated water stung.

Inhale. (No exhale.)

Unlike the first time a pool almost swallowed Ruly's body, this time he didn't panic. While others had appeared to float in the air tonight, his hang time was short. And his seconds underwater too short to resurface a past mistake at the neighborhood pool.

As a reflex, he pushed himself off the pool floor. When he came up, he spat out water and raised his arms.

A black "5" was painted on the pool's wall. Eyes and nose bobbed above the plane of water. Thank God he was wearing his cowboy boots from his *Urban Cowboy* phase. The group of guys looking down at him laughed and high-fived each other. *As proud as a team should be,* Raul thought. *They should be congratulated. They're winners.* "Indian Pride, Once and Forever." He raised a finger *#1#1#1* in their direction. Some thought he was flipping them off, so they returned the gesture.

Struggling to stay balanced for a good while, his boots sliding on the pool floor, he felt himself pulled by his belt loops. Like a ship hauled by a tugboat, his body floating through the water. When his feet were firmly planted on the pool floor, he turned around to see who'd dragged him to the shallow end.

!RELAX!

The one word that he most needed to hear at this moment was written on a girl's chest.

"You all right?"

He nodded.

She treaded water while he carefully maintained his balance. The "3" on this side of the pool wall let him know that he was safe, for now.

His shirt ballooned. His belly was like a white medicine ball that floated above his waist. He turned his attention from the girl's chest to her face— round and dark, flat nose, a wide mouth. The same face he'd seen three years ago in Mrs. Harris's English class at Valle Vista Junior High.

Julia Martínez. Sat between Aaron Martínez and Sylvia Martínez.

The last time he'd seen this classmate in the hallway she seemed angry. In the water, laughter and music in the air, her face was an earthly moon. A jack-o'-lantern. The lights below the water, on the sides of the pool, made her that much more radiant. It was silly, he knew, but a big-breasted angel had rescued him.

Did I need saving? he wondered for the second time, the taste of chlorine in his throat.

His lifeguard waded over to the side of the pool and handed him a big tumbler from the deck. He didn't know why, but he hoped it was soda, Dr Pepper or RC Cola. Of course, it wasn't. The taste of cheap alcohol was only slightly improved by the Hawaiian Punch. *Jungle Juice*. After hearing others talk about this popular party drink, he'd finally tasted it for himself. Another first tonight. And one less thing he was a virgin of.

He smacked his tongue and wanted to drink some of the pool water. The chemical taste was surely better than Jungle Juice. Julia laughed at the sour face he made. He took another drink to show her that he wasn't ungrateful. He chewed the orange slice that fell into his mouth when he emptied the tumbler.

"I bet you don't remember me." She continued to tread water, although he figured she was also tall enough to stand in the shallow end of the pool.

"Yes I do." He swallowed the orange peel.

"What is it?"

"Julia. Julia Martínez," he proudly said while wrestling with his bulging shirt.

"My last name is Reese now. Julie Reese."

While she floated in the water around him, he kept turning to face her. Midnight Galaxy's DJ announced Madonna's latest single. Julie mouthed the words. Others splashed around and caused waves in the pool that brought them closer to each other. They appeared to be dance partners.

"Where you been?" he asked her.

"Right here, I saw you when you first came in." She pointed to the rear sliding glass door.

"No, not tonight. Since Valle Vista." He gave up trying to flatten his shirt. Hiding his hairy black hole seemed insignificant now. Even if Maricela was still around, she didn't come into his mind.

Julie dunked herself under water and popped back up. Her long hair whipped around. He laughed with each streak of water that struck his face.

"In California. My mom remarried." More whips of hair. "Then divorced. We got stuck with his name."

He wanted to ask her what part of California, another place he'd experienced only through cable TV, but he didn't want to scare her away with so many questions. Instead, he reached over and brushed a wet strand of hair away from her face. She laughed a smile.

He stayed in the pool, away from the football mob. With bodies still flying all over the place, he figured, the water was the safest place at this party. Who would've thought?

So when Julie started to get out, he wanted to tell her to stay. He'd quickly gotten used to her body floating next to his. She made the space his body took up feel more intimate. He didn't pay attention to anyone else in the pool or care too much that some guys were trying to push Alberto into the deep end. It looked like the Wookiee lineman was going to take three others in with him.

As Julie exited the pool, she motioned for Raul to follow. He walked through the shallow end of the pool like the Stay Puft Marshmallow Man in *Ghostbusters*. He felt almost twice as heavy as he climbed the cement stairs. Wet clothes an extra layer of fat. He followed her cutoff shorts and FRANKIE GOES TO HOLLYWOOD T-shirt.

!RELAX!

3 SÁNCHEZ FAMILY CLEANERS
AZTEC LAUNDROMAT
JUAN'S TIRE SHOP
LONE STAR GAS CORP.
LA FIESTA PRODUCE
FIESTA SUPER MERCADO

Of the many times Raul had traveled on North Loop Drive over the years, alone and with his family, he'd noticed that although the names on the business signs changed more than once, their merchandise or services didn't.

Lomaland Drive-in was one such Lower Valley landmark.

The easiest route from his family's new house was to get on North Loop, go straight ahead for less than five miles, and keep an eye out for the flashing lights of the movie marquee.

Lomaland Drive-in's large neon arrow pointed in the direction of Juárez across the border, and the marquee lit up every night, even Christmas and New Year's Eve, like the Fourth of July. The drive-in was to this part of the Lower Valley what Indian Stadium was to those who lived off Alameda Avenue. Each community was proud of its illuminated symbol.

The three-screen drive-in dated back to the mid-sixties. Raul's parents had come here to watch all of Steve McQueen's movies, Dad had said to him when he asked to borrow the Datsun for a date with Julie. Raul wasn't surprised when Dad said the car was messing up again, since he was holding on to that car, it seemed, like he had to the air conditioner and the lawn mower, until the motor completely croaked.

His brother hadn't lent him his car this time, since he'd come home late after the party where he'd been rescued by Julie. "Don't even ask," his brother said when he came into his room. Raul thought about calling Alberto, but his car smelled like smoke. His friend didn't smoke cigarettes. It was just that if the car was driven for a long time, exhaust came in through the cracked rear window.

As a last resort, he called Laura. His cousin's roommate said she was at work. Since he'd entered high school, he hadn't see her much. But they did talk on the phone a few times each month. The last time he'd called, he was happy to learn that she was working at the Dairy Queen on Zaragoza Road.

The other big news was that she had a car. The Chevy Blazer was a combination of rust and dents and blue. Even the tire rims were painted the color of menthol cough drops. The white top was as corroded as the rear bumper and fenders. Laura said her dad, Raul's Tío Manuel, had gotten it for her en el otro lado. The imported vehicle still had Mexican plates. Raul didn't ask her if she thought the Blazer was stolen, like so many other vehicles in the El Paso/Juárez area.

Raul took a chance and made the long walk to Dairy Queen. If his cousin said he couldn't borrow her car, he figured he'd at least get a free ice cream. What he craved was an order of hard-shell tacos and onion rings and then a chocolate-dipped cone to wash away the taste of the fried food. Anxiety about his date with Julie had heightened old appetites and given birth to new ones.

Although he could see only half of his cousin behind the Formica counter, she appeared bigger than he remembered. Her face was as round as the DQ sign, and her red work shirt appeared to be a size too small. He wondered if she'd really gained that much weight or if he just saw her that way. Since his intimate experience with Julie at the party, he looked at every other girl differently. No matter if he knew them or if they were strangers. Lips, breasts, hips, butts—none appealed to him as much as Julie's.

"What's playing?" his cousin asked as she poured chocolate syrup over a sundae.

"Huh?" He was staring at the other DQ girl mixing a milk shake. She was a brunette with a lumpy butt and lips that were too small. Or maybe her nose was too big for her face.

"The movie. What is it?" His cousin sprinkled nuts on whipped cream.

"The new one with Tom *Cruz.*" He laughed at his own pun. "We're brothers, you know."

"Yeah, right. You wish you were Ruly *Cruise.*" She came around the counter. Her big belly rubbed the tabletop when she squeezed into the other side of the booth.

"What's the big deal with this guy anyway?"

"He's cute, you know? And he was practically naked in his other movie."

Raul slurped on a soda, which was nothing but melted ice and brown water, just like he liked it. He'd already wolfed down a steak fingers and fries basket.

"Aren't you jealous Julie wants to see him?"

"Why? I'm the one paying for the movie."

"Don't be dumb, menso. All girls think of someone else when they're with a guy."

He stopped playing with his straw and paid attention, figuring she'd always know more since she was older and more experienced.

"Even when they're, you know, doing it, they think of someone else. Or at least something else—washing their hair, buying new shoes." His cousin smiled as if she'd made a joke. He didn't remember the sound of her laugh anymore. She didn't offer one.

He was about to jump in, but she continued talking. "At first it's fun and your heart won't stop, but after a few times, it's like kissing. No big deal." She stared out the window across Zaragoza Road, where they were building what he guessed would be another convenience store. So many new businesses had already opened since they'd first moved from Lomaland, where there were more tienditas than convenience stores.

He wanted her to slow down, go back, repeat what she'd just said. Nothing came out of his mouth except a burp as she went to the register and rang up a customer. He knew that his cousin had had many boyfriends when she was at the High. And by what she'd said, it sounded like she'd had many more since graduating. Although she'd spoken about sex as if she were speaking about prepping burgers, he knew she would never lie to him. He trusted her. Always had.

Promising to come by tomorrow and tell her everything, he left Dairy Queen in BEBBA. Although his cousin said BEBBA sounded slutty, Raul liked the sound of the name stenciled on the Blazer's driver's side. He wondered if the name was of a woman, maybe a previous owner's girlfriend.

Tonight was special. Tom Cruz or no Tom Cruise.

He'd never been to the drive-in without his family, he realized as he got ready for his big date. When he was a child, they'd gone to Cinema Park Drive-in on Montana Avenue almost every Saturday during the summers. In the big backseat of Dad's '57 Chevy, he would fall asleep during the forty-five-minute drive from Lomaland to the upper east side, where Montana ran out of El Paso toward Carlsbad, New Mexico. Not only did Cinema Park play the latest movies, but he knew Dad welcomed any opportunity to drive his hot rod. Over the years, Dad spent any free time he had working in the garage. And too much money, as his mother complained.

As if Ruly had a built-in alarm clock, he would awaken just as they were pulling into the gravel entryway of Cinema Park. There was always a line of cars with families piled inside. $5/car. He spent this time in line staring at the lights along the entryway. The metal lamps were shaped like a woman's body—wide on top and bottom, thin in the middle. Red, green, and white light came out of baseball-sized holes cut out of the metal. Tiny moons. Plenty of them.

As much as he and his brother asked Dad to park by the snack bar, he always went to the same spot—about midway back, to the right. Dad parked his prized '57 Chevy on the tallest dirt mound, so that it rested a few inches higher than the surrounding cars. The brothers figured that he wanted everyone else to check out his hot rod instead of watching the movie. And they did.

Throughout the night, many men and teenage boys would come by and admire the car's cherry red paint job, and by the way they reacted when the hood was raised, Ruly and Pancho figured all the shiny chrome and black parts were equally impressive. His mother always ended up falling asleep as soon as the second feature began. That was when Pancho led Ruly to the snack bar, their pockets filled with change for the pinball machines.

Those nights at the drive-in with his family had not prepared him in any way for his first high school date. Julie had been bugging him about wanting to see a movie with the young actor with a similar-sounding last name. Raul didn't care if he was cute or not. While he'd learned that many of his classmates went to the new multiplex inside Cielo Vista Mall on movie dates, he was glad to see *Top Gun* on the Lomaland Drive-in marquee.

Since he and Julie had made out big time after the house party, they'd become boyfriend and girlfriend. Neither of them had asked the other, but as little as he knew of these kinds of things, they did stuff only high school couples did. Sit together in the lunchroom. Hold hands in the halls. Wait for each other after football practice or club meetings. He was now Head Team Manager of the basketball team while Julie was involved in the school newspaper, the award-winning *Pow Wow*.

They spent many hours out of school together too. While he thought it a big deal to bring her to his house one evening, his mother hadn't said anything about it. Like so many dinners, after getting home late from work, she simply sent Dad to Pizza Hut. When his mother took the time to ask Julie what toppings she liked (pepperoni and mushrooms), he figured his mother must've just been glad that he'd brought any girl home. "Finally, my Gordito has a novia" was the phrase her satisfied expression seemed to say.

As boys, he and his brother always got a pizza to eat at the drive-in. Back then, he didn't worry about how much one cost. When he and Julie walked into the snack bar and he compared the prices to the amount of money in his wallet, he told her that he wasn't hungry. He mentioned splitting an order at Chico's Tacos after the movie when he bought a small Coke and a small popcorn. "The pizza here isn't that good," he lied when they inhaled the warm smells coming from the huge oven.

Midway through the movie, empty popcorn and Coke container on the floor, he decided it was time to make his move. He'd practiced in the garage when no one was home. With an old tackling dummy Coach threw out, he'd positioned himself in BEBBA's backseat. The much-tackled dummy was a plump substitute for Julie's body, which was chubbier than a cheerleader's.

Confident from navigating in cramped quarters, he whispered in her ear that they'd probably be more comfortable in BEBBA's backseat, where they could stretch out and put their feet up. He'd already slipped off his loafers and she her Pat Benatar boots. "Sure . . . if you want." She didn't take her eyes off the screen.

In the short time they'd been dating, he'd gotten used to them bumping into each other's hips, arms, butts. Sitting on the same side of a booth at Whataburger. Having to stand on bus rides home from the park. And while her breasts excited him like you wouldn't believe, he especially liked it when she laughed and they jiggled like cake batter ready for the oven.

She let out pops of laughter when he put his hands on her butt to push her over to the backseat. "Hey, watch it." She got him back when he threw himself on top of her. His lonja, he'd confessed to her, was his weak spot. "You're in big trouble, Rulllyyy."

She attacked and tickled his belly. Her hands quickly went under his shirt, which never stayed tucked in. She straddled him. Like that night after the house party, things moved quicker than he'd imagined they would.

Although they hadn't gone beyond the point they did that night, he hadn't admitted that he was a virgin. And he assumed from her behavior that she probably wasn't. He found relief in her being more experienced. *What else did she learn in California?* he wondered.

He tried not to think too much while they made out. She'd said he was a good kisser. And that was all he needed to hear, since he didn't think he was good at too many things, especially anything having to do with his body parts.

One thing he hadn't figured out was why, after all that they did in his brother's car after the party, she always kept her bra on when they made out. Even when they were alone in his room—watching TV, listening to the radio, doing homework on his bed. Every time he'd slip his hands under her blouse and reach to undo her bra, she pushed him away and made the excuse that his parents might catch them. He guessed Dad wouldn't care, and his mother was always working late anyway.

When he told Alberto about his drive-in-movie date, the loudmouthed lineman told the huddled team that if this were his chick he would go all the way. As Raul intently listened to the guys talking about sex in the locker room, he was confused by their use of baseball terms for going all the way. "What's third again?" he wanted to ask. "Don't think about it, no mas go for it," Alberto said as he swung an imaginary bat and pointed to left field in the sky. A "home run" had always been another of Raul's sports fantasies. And since he'd always only watched the Tribe's baseball team from the bleachers, he knew Julie was his best chance for rounding the bases. At least that was what he let the guys believe.

4 Raul was still learning how not to be a virgin. After months of dating Julie, he'd used up lots of energy and time thinking of ways to be alone with her. His Map Book II was filled with various notes about making the right moves with his first girlfriend.

MAKE-OUT SPOTS
— Transmountain Road (Pancho says girls love the view from the very top)
— The Trees (Laura often mentioned a Dead End by Border Highway)
— Letterman's Lane (Alberto swore by his "lucky" spot in the desert)
— Main Auditorium (Everyone at the High bragged about what they did behind the maroon felt curtains)

Making out with Julie any chance he got had given him more to explore than he'd ever fantasized about. Physical details of different locations in El Paso were as important as those of his and Julie's bodies. Each was a landmark to reaching his destination.

KISSING

— Mouth (me leaning to right, her to the left)
— Inside of Elbows (super ticklish super fun)
— Breasts (Being J's Baby Boy)
— Neck, Wrists, Palms (Toes one time at LL Park)

Mapping what he'd learned and documenting his limited experience helped him feel ready to forge ahead to his high school summit—*intercourse.*

He'd thought for sure that he would grow tired of masturbating once he got a girlfriend, but the truth was that he did it about the same number of times. Usually when he was bored. With nothing to do, the urge to jack off washed over him, like the giant wave that swallowed the surfer at the opening of *Hawaii Five-O.*

It could be another Saturday afternoon watching TV, possibly *Wide World of Sports,* and his palito would become a boner while a petite European gymnast straddled the pommel horse. Or sleeping till noon after a long night, hanging out on the sofa watching TV or in his bedroom listening to music. Too lazy to get out of bed in the morning, he'd lie there, a pillow tucked between his legs, because it felt good, the door locked, the blinds closed, hands fisted on his penis, he'd stroke it, fantasizing, usually with the help of the posters on his wall: Dallas Cowboys Cheerleaders had replaced Farrah Fawcett had replaced Brooke Shields had replaced Donna Summers.

Over time, he learned that Julie had a much different relationship with her body than he did with his. While he and his gordito-flesh had grown up together, steadily feeding each other's cravings, he thought Julie worried too much about her own loose belly, ample hips, and big breasts. She hid her body under layers of clothes. Even on El Paso's warmest days, she threw on sweaters and jackets over blouses, sometimes one over a tank top and bra. Claiming to never find jeans that fit her right, like most of the other girls at the High, she said she preferred skirts. Black or brown fabrics that covered her knees and some that dragged below her suede boots. She bought these handmade skirts at the Bronco Flea Market. He didn't tell her, but they made her look like one of the Tarahumara Indians who begged on the Paso del Norte Bridge. He hoped, in a way, that she was begging for his affection.

While very attracted to girls who wore short skirts, like the Ysleta cheerleaders he kept an eye on during practices, he found his girlfriend's way of dressing exciting in a different way. There was mystery buried in Julie's extra skins. From their making out after the house party and at the drive-in, he desired what was hidden under a shell of fabrics. He was more than ready to go excavating, lend a hand or two. (Sometimes the thoughts in his head sounded like the stories he read in Dad's magazines.)

Julie seemed to think of her body like a world she wanted to keep all to herself. He loved nakedness more and more and told her, in so many words, that he wanted to share this with her. When she said that sounded intense, he confessed that being naked together, maybe taking a bath, was part of his definition of love.

When she gave him a weird look, he hugged her super tight, for no other reason than to avoid saying anything else.

He decided to call his cousin Laura and ask her advice about the upcoming Spring Formal. She was always good about listening, although she seemed somewhat distracted on the other end. The distance between them was heightened more by emotions than by the miles from his house to wherever she was staying at right now.

"Do you think I should get Julie an expensive corsage?" he asked his cousin. "Or should I save some money for a big dinner?"

"Look at you, Cuz. You're turning into a smooth operator." She always knew how to make him smile. "Well, I think you should definitely be classy whatever you do."

"What do you mean? Do I need to rent a limo like some of the guys are doing?"

"Naw, don't do that. You'll just end up having a bunch of couples in your car all drunk. And someone always pukes."

"Then a not-too-expensive corsage and a nice dinner is a good idea?"

"Yeah, Cuz. Just be your cariño-self. If she likes you, she'll love whatever you do for her."

What he hadn't mentioned to Laura was what he also had planned for after Ysleta High's Spring Formal in the coming month. Alberto was the one to suggest that Raul could use his place on the night of the annual dance. The place his friend called "Mi Casita" was a two-room structure behind his godmother's house. As the devoted Head Team Manager, Raul was granted time in the isolated quarters to spend with his girlfriend. While he'd heard some of the guys boast about *going all night long*, Raul figured that one or two hours was enough time for him to lose his virginity.

With all his advance planning, he hadn't even asked Julie to the Spring Formal. He just assumed that they would go since they were girlfriend and boyfriend. He'd mentioned it to Julie, but nothing official had been decided. And he figured he still had a few more weeks before it was too late.

One of the reasons he hadn't been able to talk to Julie about his big plans was because she'd become more and more involved with the Journalism Club. Her goal was to become a yearbook photographer. The Journalism Room was his girlfriend's new "home away from home" by the middle of the school year.

"You possess a gift for images," Mrs. Kinard, the Journalism Club advisor, had written in Julie's journal, which included magazine pictures she'd cut and pasted for an assignment she titled "Midnight Matinee." Next to photos of the desert under a full moon, she'd written poetic-sounding captions in a purple marker.

MOON MARRIAGE

STARRY STARRY EYES

DANCING DUNES

"Mrs. K. said my writing is more impressionistic than narrative," Julie bragged to Raul one day during lunch at Pizza Hut. While he was happy that she was beaming with pride, many practical questions popped into his head: "Do you even own a camera?" "Who pays for the film and developing?" "Since when have you kept a journal?"

When he did ask her some questions later, he found out that her stepfather had left behind an expensive German camera. Her mother had stored it in the garage with the rest of his things when he was out of the picture.

During last period, hours after school, and even on weekends, Julie followed the head photographer around to school functions and city events. She told Raul that she mostly carried Benny's equipment, giving him the lenses and film he asked for and setting up his tripod and lighting. She didn't mind that she still hadn't shot any photos.

"Mrs. K. said I might get to next semester," Julie shared with Raul. Photos of high school life, many shot by Benny, were framed on the wall above the Pizza Hut booths. Raul and Julie sat under one of a silhouetted couple kissing along the Río Grande levee.

"I'm learning to work in the darkroom, too. Cool, huh?" she said.

"Mmmmmmm," he replied as he chewed his personal pan pizza.

"It's about the size of two closets."

This comparison finally got Raul's full attention. Even without seeing the darkroom for himself, he could imagine it from her descriptions. From the red lightbulb to the hanging negatives to the smell of chemicals. Her sensory descriptions of the Journalism darkroom sounded like the world he'd discovered in his parents' closet that first summer of the new house.

"It kind of stinks, but Benny says you get used to it. I like how almost everything glows." Practically bouncing in her seat, she added, "And we get to turn up the boom box as loud as we want."

He finished his pizza and a slice of hers while she walked around Pizza Hut looking at photos of Ysleta High's student body. There were even some of Alberto and the other jocks Raul served from the sidelines. In their game jerseys, they looked heroic. The camera lens captured the athletes in larger-than-life moments, just as he had witnessed as a fan from high in the stadium seats. As Team Manager, his point of view was now much different. When he noticed Julie admiring a color photo of last year's football district champs, he doubted any photos of the jocks in their dirty and smelly underwear would ever end up in the yearbook, much less on the walls of a public place.

By the middle of basketball season junior year, Raul learned that he was hopelessly stuck on third base. He knew this about his quest to not be a virgin as much from what he recorded in his Map Book II as from what Alberto told him.

"You're missing all the signals," Alberto said between smacking his gum. "Hell, yeah, she's ready, ése."

"You think so?" Raul sipped on a water bottle he'd filled with Mr. Pibb.

"Going home is the only thing left."

They were sitting at the end of the bench during a home basketball game. The lineman was almost as bad a shooter as Raul was, but his friend's size made him popular among all the Ysleta coaches. The Indian basketball team was almost the opposite of the football team this year. They couldn't win a game, home or away.

"I'm telling you, she wants you to make the move." Alberto adjusted his XXL shorts, which kept riding up his crotch.

"What move?" He wondered if it was like the reverse layup an opponent had just made. Start of the fourth quarter: Troopers 66–Indians 48.

"Don't be dumb. You know." Alberto made a fist and pumped it between his legs. "Just take your shot."

Although Raul was closer to the action than most as Team Manager, he had trouble keeping all of these sports references straight. He preferred sticking to one sport if he was going to talk about going all the way. "A home run," that was what he needed spelled out.

Alberto was put into the game when things were getting out of hand. He was Coach Lugo's enforcer, and in a six-minute span, he collected three fouls. Raul smiled as his man-sized friend labored up and down the court.

Final score: Troopers 86–Indians 61.

If he followed Alberto's advice, he figured he'd lose his virginity before the start of his senior year. Like drinking tequila shots in Juárez and ditching classes at the levee, going all the way was one more thing almost every guy he knew had done before him. He wanted to catch up. No matter how much hard breathing it took.

5   Twisted maroon and white crepe paper, black and red balloons, construction paper flowers, and a long banner welcomed Raul to his first Ysleta High Spring Formal.

He found a familiar feeling in the festive space, although this was the first time he'd been to the Fountain Plaza building in years. The decorations almost guaranteed a good time, reminding him of his piñata birthday parties in Loma-land. All that was missing was a papier-mâché superhero. As with those family celebrations immortalized in home movies, he felt tonight would be something he would remember for a long time.

And he'd dressed up for it: black tuxedo jacket, white button shirt, and powder blue bow tie. The owner of the tuxedo shop was a friend of his mother's, so they'd gotten a discount. While his aunts and uncles and cousins never dressed up for any parties in their old neighborhood, everyone here at the annual dance wore tuxedoes and gowns, mostly black and red. A few girls stood out on the dance floor in their burgundy, white, or pink gowns. Many seamstresses worked out of their homes in the Lower Valley. Driving on Alameda Avenue, you always saw signs advertising, DRESSES FOR BODAS, QUINCEAÑERAS, HOMECOMINGS. ¡BUEN PRECIOS!

Julie's dress had been made by Mrs. Macias, a woman known for her Christmas tamales. The gown was long, like all Julie's skirts, but this one was strapless. When she bent over, like she was doing right now, he got a real eyeful of cleavage. Across the dance floor, which had only a handful of couples dancing, Julie was helping Benny at the photo booth. Raul decided not to bother her and hung back as she escorted couples in front of a painted background of red and purple stars. Julie was wearing makeup, a rare thing for her. Her big smile was another noticeable change in her usual appearance. He didn't know if it was the night's party atmosphere, her new dress, or his "secret" for later on that made her look so happy. Whichever it was, it made him happy too.

For the past weeks, they'd barely spent any time together. And more and more, he found himself alone again. The kind of drowning he hated most. A numbness more than panic. She assured him in the halls before class and on the phone that everything was fine. "I'm just busy," she said. "When the year-books are done, I'll have more time. Just give me some room, okay?"

This made him feel somewhat better, but when she ended by saying, "I just need some time alone. To think, you know," he freaked out.

Think about what? he wanted to ask, but he just said, "Me, too. Time. . . . To think."

He had driven to the dance alone in his parents' new used car. Julie had caught a ride with Benny.

Having a girlfriend, he concluded in the last months of his junior year, was more work than he'd ever imagined. It was nothing like he saw in movies or read in Dad's magazines: going from party to party on Friday nights, unclasping of bras, driving at sunset with the windows down, unzipping of jeans, sneaking into places after hours, exploring a woman's fleshiest regions.

Keeping track of so many emotions was almost as tiring as knowing when or when not to call Julie. Last night, he'd called to ask when he could give her the corsage he bought, but her mom told him she was off somewhere with Benny. When Raul asked her where, her mother said she didn't know. He didn't believe her and decided to bring the corsage to the dance. He had it stuffed in his tuxedo pocket, and as the dance floor started to fill up, he still hadn't slipped it on her wrist.

With one hand stroking the carnation, his other one held a glass of punch. It surprised him that no one had turned it to Jungle Juice. As he was about to sneak over and surprise Julie, Alberto came up behind him. Before the dude could put him in a Chewbacca hug, like he always did, Raul twisted away. He'd learned a few moves over the course of the year to show off during the next football tryouts. Other than Coach, he hadn't told anyone he wanted to move from Team Manager to player next season.

Alberto was here with Sylvia, his on-off-on-again girlfriend, and another couple, Oscar and Irene, who'd gone to the restroom. From the looks of Alberto's eyes, Raul didn't need to be told they'd been drinking. Alberto let him know he was right when the jokester led him behind a pillar and pulled out a flask. Raul kept an eye out for any adult chaperones while Alberto took a quick swig and passed it on. Flask to his mouth, Raul felt a warm river flush down his throat. His eyes widened. He took another drink. When the other three came over, they asked Raul where Julie was. He coughed and pointed to the picture booth. The five of them walked over.

There was a long line of their classmates. The girls primped their hair and adjusted their bustlines while the guys popped each other's cummerbunds. All dressed up, these were not the same people Raul had seen in the halls, on the football field, or in the snack bar at the High. It was like they were all wearing costumes for some school play. *As long as you can change clothes for each occasion, then no one will ever know what anyone is really like.* This was a thought that Raul was having more and more. Tonight, the tuxedo he wore did make him feel like he was playing a role. 007, Cruz, Raul Cruz, or maybe Fred Astaire in one of the black-and-white movies his cousin liked watching. Laura lived through the world of TV as much as he did, which made him miss her more.

As he stood off from the photo line, he watched the dance floor come alive, and still more couples were coming in through the Fountain Plaza's front doors. With a slight buzz, he began to strip each person of their jackets, shirts, dresses, slips: hairless and too-hairy chests; small, medium, and large chi chis; ombligos of all sizes (nickels, quarters, silver dollars); pimpled backs and butts. It was easy to imagine everyone naked but harder to focus on the ones who were dancing, arms and legs moving like swimmers out of water. His face grew into a big whiskey grin.

He asked Alberto for the flask and went to the bathroom. A few other guys who weren't on any team but that he'd seen around the High formed a line in front of the mirrors. Corey Hart. Bon Jovi. Rick Springfield. All types and lengths of haircuts were represented tonight. His curly hair was a helmet-shaped tumbleweed at best. He knew better than to try to do anything new with it. He went into a stall, sat down without pulling down his pants, and took long swallows from the flask.

At Ysleta (especially during the first two grueling years of high school), he had a favorite stall in the library's bathroom. He liked the privacy and, best of all, the graffiti—mostly cuss words in English and Spanish. When he jotted down his favorites in his Map Book II, he didn't bother correcting the misspellings.

FUCK the Principle y los Tichers
Susie done it Goooood
El Gumpy C / S

Having learned since junior high that c / s was like a Chicano trademark symbol, he no longer worried that his first initial wasn't included. Last he heard of his junior high friends was that Chris was working at Baskin-Robbins and Santiago was now playing trumpet in the school band.

From inside this stall at the Fountain Plaza, he could hear the music of the disco and people coming in and going out of the bathroom. He read over the stall for anything interesting. All he found was a faint picture of a big boner. He wished he had a pen to add "Suck it!" or "Verga" to keep it from looking so bare. Maybe some pubic hair, which grew faster than any stubble on his face, he'd begun to notice.

When he finally left the bathroom and made it over to Julie, he saw she already had a corsage on her wrist. He figured that Benny had given it to her. Disappointment mixed with the buzz inside his head. The strobe lights continued to mess with his vision. A disco ball spun behind each eyeball. The blinking white lights strung on the second-floor banister reminded him of the Plaza Theatre. When the disco's red siren lights came on, he thought of falling at the skating rink and wanted to run or at least find somewhere to hide on the dance floor.

Dancing was one of those physical chores, like skating and swimming, which he continued to worry about no matter how old he was. Ultimately, he wished that he'd taken lessons.

By the time he finished more of the flask and several glasses of the newly christened Jungle Juice Punch, the Spring Formal was almost halfway over. And he hadn't even spent any time with his supposed date. He went to the picture booth. Talk about bad timing, Julie and Benny were hugging in front of the camera, having their picture taken. *Well, at least I'll save thirty bucks,* Raul told himself as he rushed away. His mother had given him the money and had even said she had a frame all picked out. He made sure Julie saw him before he walked out a side door of the Fountain Plaza building.

The night air felt good on his moist face and neck. *Inhale Exhale.* His head filled up like the balls he was in charge of inflating before each practice. If he fell, like he thought he might, he wondered if his head would bounce. He sat on the sidewalk and stared into the dark sky. The CHICO'S TACOS sign a few streets over was brighter than the few stars. On any other night, he would've been tempted to walk over for at least a single of taquitos, extra cheese, fries, and large Dr Pepper. But the motion of the dance music had taken up residence in his stomach.

He squinted as he looked in the direction of the Lower Valley. The lights of the neighborhoods, including Lomaland, seemed close enough to touch. His present house, a little farther east, was lost on the dark horizon.

When he was a boy living in Lomaland, he and Pancho came to the Fountain Plaza on many Saturdays. If their parents couldn't drop them off, they got permission to take the bus. This was one of Raul's favorite memories of Pancho and Ruly. Although the bus ride took more than an hour, he liked all the turns and stops the bus made.

BUS RIDE TO F.P.
— Bus stops on North Loop
— Bus picks up old ladies with lots of bags
— Bus turns right on Courtland
— Bus turns right again on Burgess
— Bus turns left on Yarbrough
— Bus goes under the freeway
— Bus passes Chico's and stops at Fountain Plaza
(Estimated mileage: ten miles, he'd noted alongside a sketch in his Map Book.)

A few years ago, about the time they built the newest mall in El Paso, the Fountain Plaza building had been temporarily closed down and it had only recently opened as the school district's Multipurpose Center. All the high schools used it for their major functions. While the building itself hadn't been changed much, it would be hard for someone who didn't know its history to remember the movie theater, arcade, novelty stores, and food court. Somewhere among all the administrative offices and conference rooms rested many childhood memories.

Among them was the time he attended a movie marathon of old comedy films, some in black and white. While he didn't know any of the actors and couldn't tell you what the movies were about now, he never forgot how much he'd laughed that day. Not since he and Laura had watched a Three Stooges marathon had he laughed so hard. He and his cousin waited till the very last minute of each hilarious episode before running to pee. That's how much laughter they enjoyed.

Outside the former Fountain Plaza, he allowed himself to think of his cousin on the other side. Last he heard, she was spending more and more time at her dad's in Juárez. Or maybe with some guy he'd heard his mom and tías talking about. From the tone of their gossip, he could tell that no one in the family knew how much fun Laura could be. From the first time he'd seen those two masks outside the High's Drama Room, he thought of Cuz like them. One all smiles and the other all serious. No matter how old he and Laura got, he would always remember their laughing marathons more than any tears.

Draining the last drops from Alberto's flask, Raul wandered the parking lot and tried to remember where the bus stop used to be. As far as he could recall, it was where the security kiosk was now. Like the inside of the building, nothing on the outside appeared the same. There were now parking spaces where Ray's Hamburger House (best onion rings ever) had been torn down. A storage facility, it looked like, stood where Pancho had once hid after shoplifting a Pink Floyd belt buckle from Roxy Records. There were hardly any trees and bushes left outside, just those stupid rocks of a fake desert.

By the time Raul reached the west side of the building, he was tired. His feet ached in his "funeral shoes," shiny black loafers that his mother had bought him when her Tío Lorenzo died. The black socks Raul had taken from his brother's dresser were gathered at his ankles. He took off his bow tie and cummerbund. When he stuffed them in his jacket pocket, he felt the corsage meant for Julie. The damp petals were wadded like tissue.

As boys running around Fountain Plaza, Ruly and Pancho spent most of their money at the Arcade. They dropped quarter after quarter into Asteroid, Defender, Pac-Man, Centipede. He was good on the pinball machines, and his brother enjoyed beating him at air hockey.

The large fountain outside the building was where he had spent almost as much change. His heavy mood lifted for a second when he realized the cement fountain was still here. Although he'd thrown many coins in the fountain, he didn't remember anything he'd wished to come true. Years removed from those wishes, he sat on the cement rim and peered into the dry fountain. Rusty circles spotted its tile floor. Many pairs of eyes stared back at him.

With a faint moon hanging low in the sky, he let himself think about Julie and how she'd messed up his being alone. Before she rescued him at his first high school party, he had a good hold on what he thought he was meant to be. While he wasn't happy being a chubby teenager who spent his weekends watching too much TV, at least he knew what to expect from one day to the next. What was around the next corner. No surprises. No deep drops.

Now, he was still learning how not to be a virgin, and his normal feelings of a year ago were warped by his excitement for Julie's body. Each moment spent making out heightened every nerve ending he had, making him more sensitive to a body not his own. "Fuck, doesn't she know this?" he asked with no one around. He threw the wadded carnation in the drained fountain.

He wished that he could house the feelings of being with Julie within his own body. Wasn't his body big enough to contain two people? This seemed the only way that he would be able to walk back to the car, drive home, and lie alone in bed. Probably fall asleep with his tux on.

He stood, blinked, and felt the floor shift under him. He felt real sick now. The buzz was settling in his head, but his stomach swished around like a lava lamp he once bought at Roxy Records. Like a busted rosary, gold beads saved in a jar of marbles, the lava lamp had been left behind when his family left Lomaland for good.

He loosened the buckles on the sides of his rented pants and headed for the underground parking lot. He passed the building's main doors and heard music and yelling. People were chanting to a song like after a grand slam. Alberto and Oscar and their girlfriends were probably dancing up a storm. "Lucky Cabrones."

In the underground garage where he'd parked, he saw a girl standing by his parents' car.

"Where you been?" Julie asked, leaning against the car.

"What?" He blinked and her image became even blurrier.

"I was worried. When I didn't see you inside, the guys said you'd left."

There were a few seconds of silence and the occasional car drove by.

"Did you ever come here when it was the Fountain Plaza?" He put one hand on the car for balance.

She slid along the trunk and sat next to him. "Yeah, I think my mom brought us to the movies once."

He let her put her hand over his. Her flesh was warm while the car's surface was cold.

"Which one?"

"Movie? Oh, I don't remember. Something sad, I'm sure. She likes to cry at—C'mon, let's go inside and dance. It's almost over." She put her arm under his and pulled.

"I think I'm—" He lunged forward and puked, splattering the bumper of the car next to his parents'. JESUS ♥ YOU and SAVE A DOLPHIN. He didn't know which bumper sticker was more random, so he made up one in his head: JESUS ♥ DOLPHINS.

Julie stood off and crossed her arms, looking like she'd rather be back with Benny, a date who stood upright, under the influence of only the lights and music. Raul gathered himself, unlocked the car, and crawled into the driver's side. Julie followed behind him, pushed him to the passenger's side, and took the keys out of his hands.

He leaned back in the seat. Julie sat quiet next to him.

She looked prettier than he'd ever seen her. He told her this and she said "Thank you" in almost a whisper. With each second that passed, he figured that they probably had nothing left to chitchat about. It was as if they'd wasted all the small talk over the last months. With his eyes closed, he tried to think of what he should do, had done in past moments like this. But like his other plans for how tonight would go, he didn't have a clue as to what was expected of him now.

6   As he got older, Raul spent as little time as possible at home. The simple thought of being under the same roof, much less sitting at the same table, with his parents and older brother bored him. He ate food from the kitchen, he wore clothes from the closet, he threw mud balls at the dogs in the backyard, and while he and Julie had fooled around on his bed, the skin of the house still seemed foreign after five years. It was as if his family was borrowing it from some other family after leaving Lomaland for good.

Alberto was his best bet to escape his family's mindless reruns of domesticity. When his oversized friend wasn't at practice, he was helping his godmother, who was his legal guardian, around the house or working at BigWay Foods, the grocery store on Yarbrough. He joked that he had more sacks off the football field than on. Raul thought it was corny enough for him to laugh at. His friend's wild stories about the fun times they had at work suggested he enjoyed himself there as much as he did at school. And, most importantly, he did have a car to show for his earnings.

"Dude, if I could get a car, I'd never be home." Raul leaned back in the passenger's seat of "Chewie's Cheby." The whole team thought the car's nickname seemed perfect for the Nova, which had at least ten thousand miles for every year it was old.

"Well, shit, get a jale, huevón. You need a job to have wheels." Alberto never hid his opinions.

"Where? I go to school," was Raul's poor defense.

"I've told you that I could get you on at BigWay, si quieres."

"With you? Sacking? I'm not—"

"What, you're too good?" A slight shove from the driver's seat. Alberto's stern look followed by a fat smile told Raul that he hadn't taken his comments too personal. "It's better than all the sniffing of jockstraps you do."

Big laughs filled the front of the car, temporarily quieting the rock station on the radio.

"That's different. Team Manager is for me, I chose it, sort of." He waited for Alberto to pick a cassette and insert it before he continued. "If I work—anywhere—it's like my mother's right."

"About what, Ruly-Ruly?"

"What she tells Dad. How Pancho's more responsible and stuff."

"She's right, your carnal's got a chingón car and he's never home."

"Yeah, but he wears a tie and thinks he's all bitchin'."

"Maybe, but we'll be graduated soon. So, we need to act, you know, what Coach says—" Not finishing his sentence, he fast-forwarded to the next song and said, "Fuck, do what you want, ése. I just know that I like being able to drive around El Chuco whenever I want."

On Alberto's days off from work or as soon as he clocked out on weekends, they cruised all the good spots in the Lower Valley. Letterman's Lane. Cherry Hill. Whatever beer busts they could find. If Alberto was able to score some sixers at BigWay, they were set. Otherwise, they picked one of the many tienditas off Alameda Avenue. There was one in the San José neighborhood that even sold you keggers if you had some kind of ID. It didn't matter what date of birth it listed as long as it looked somewhat legal.

Over the years, Raul remembered many events as if they were TV shows, especially at night, like when he and Alberto cruised around town. The open windows, the wide space of the desert, allowed room for his thoughts to emerge. Some memories played over and over again, like the reruns he watched during the summer. And depending on the events, he didn't mind having to sit through them. At least his memories weren't interrupted with commercials.

Click . . . Click . . . Click . . .

As if he were turning the channels on a TV set, he saw himself at the High, walking down the main hallway after last bell, waiting by the parking lot, trying not to be too anxious. He'd known that school morning that something was going to happen later that day. As if a cluster of emotional clouds had perched over him. And only him. Not even the afternoon sun could burn away the weird sensations.

Julie had said she wanted to meet him after school. While they'd walked home together from the High in their first months of dating, they'd taken separate paths in the days after the Spring Formal. He missed holding hands while they wandered the canal roads dissecting the Lower Valley. After countless walks alone home from school, he was thrilled to finally share these journeys with someone who appreciated the natural landscape. She even liked hearing his stories of chasing JORDACHE JORDACHE in junior high. Whatever detail he offered her, she called it "cute," and that meant that he was "cute," right?

When he saw Julie let go of Benny's hands that day before approaching him in the parking lot, he knew his suspicions were right after all. He no longer had what he thought of as a girlfriend. And as much as he wanted to approach Julie and hug and kiss her, do anything to keep what was about to happen from happening that day, he couldn't move.

"Hey, been here long?" she offered.

"Naw, just a few. Is he going to wait for you?"

"Yeah, we have a yearbook meeting, so . . ."

"Right, when are those coming out?"

"The last week of school, like always. You know that."

"I just forgot."

She still wore layers upon layers of fabric, but a recent change was her hair, pulled back, away from her face. This let him see her full cheeks and hazel eyes that changed shades depending on the light source. He reached for her face and touched a stray strand falling over her ear. She shrank back, as if surprised by his touch.

"Do we really have to do this?"

"C'mon, Raul. You know we do."

"We've hardly seen each other since—"

"Well, you're always cruising with Chewie and the guys."

"And you're always busy with Journalism."

The emotional barrier between them grew with each excuse he used to avoid the inevitable: She was breaking up with him.

"Well, I have to go, okay?"

"Yeah, me too. Mr. Clay needs me to put some equipment away," he lied.

She nodded but didn't say anything.

He wondered if Benny, who stayed a safe distance away, was shooting photos of this moment. "Breakup: Team Manager Gets Dumped!" Would this be the caption in the yearbook? If so, the sad image would be there for everyone at the High to see, to remember years later. What the picture wouldn't show, he thought, was him sweating twice as much as usual. His palms, his armpits, of course, and even his butt crack.

As he turned to go, she tried to hug him, but he pulled away. He knew, as early as that morning, that if this moment played out like he feared, for the worse, that he wouldn't let himself be hugged. As long as he kept his distance, and wasn't touched, then he would be OK. For a while, at least.

He did find some satisfaction in this last act of defiance. And as much as he wanted to turn around and flip Benny off for messing up his best chance at not being a virgin, he kept his sight on the nearby football stadium. The profile of the High's proud Indian mascot painted on the scoreboard gave him an extra incentive to keep his chin up.

Click . . . Click . . . Click . . .

He turned the imaginary knob on his memories as Chewie's Cheby continued its cruise of Lower Valley streets. Near Alameda Avenue and Whittier Drive, he decided he'd looked back too long on that sad moment. While he did think of Julie pretty often, especially when he saw girls wearing skirts and sandals, he didn't like replaying that particular memory of her breaking it off.

As he wondered why Alberto was steering toward the Border Highway, he continued to turn through the channels in his mind. Since his first TV in their Lomaland home only had thirteen channels and no remote control, it wasn't hard to focus on the individual episodes of his memories. And like the stations that would come in clearly from as far as Mexico City while others on this side of the border line were full of static, there were images buried in his mind that were sharper than others. He put his arm out the window and moved it around as if it were an antenna.

Quiet in the passenger seat, he locked onto a memory from the recent summer months that was not as sad as the earlier one. Like an *After School Special*

TV movie, this episode-memory took place weeks after breaking up with Julie. She'd been very right about one thing, that he was spending more and more time with the guys. He never had a chance to tell her that hanging out with the jocks was just as important, if not more, than having a girlfriend. But maybe not as important as learning how not to be a virgin.

In this episode-memory, a bunch of guys are piled into the starting wide receiver's car. Focusing on the small screen inside his head, he sees himself pressed against the door in the backseat. The stereo is playing the loudest it can, windows partially fogged up from all the body heat and the cool temp outside. His bushy head leaves its impression on the window. There's beer in everyone's hands, and even some on their laps from the crazy turns the driver is taking.

"Hell, yeah, vatos," someone yells from the front. Three heads of hair block Raul's vision of the coming road. He knows they are near his neighborhood, but he can't tell how close to his house.

"C'mon, hurry up. I gotta take a piss."

"Hold it."

"You hold it, you homo." A group of laughs rivals the volume of the "Bang Your Head" song coming through the speakers.

"I'd have to get some tweezers, you dick." Groans replace the laughter.

Everyone shuts up as the car comes to a stop. It isn't until the guys pile out of the car that Raul realizes whose house the guys have picked to cover in shaving cream and toilet paper.

Even without any streetlights and the porch light off, he can picture himself standing at the door, ringing the bell, and waiting for Julie to come out. He's passed this house, gone up and down the street many, many times. But, on this night, with a car full of drunk and determined guys, he wants to be anywhere but here.

"Why'd you pick hers?" he asks the guys.

"Fuckit, you'll feel better."

The guys spit out other reasons as they exit the car. He stares at Alberto. They exchange looks without saying anything. Their friendship is based more on unspoken actions, as if one knows what the other is thinking, and if not, then he feels okay making it up.

Raul stares regretfully at Julie's house. Even if he wants to convince the team of guys that this is a bad idea, it is too late. A line of bulky shadows makes its way into position. They move swiftly through the front yard and to the side of the house, like in a commando movie or something. Their athletic throws don't leave a single tree limb bare of toilet paper. The cars in the driveway and the front windows are lathered in shaving cream.

One last time, he eyes Alberto, who is standing near the curb with a roll of TP in each hand, as if waiting for Raul to make the first move. He smiles at his loyal friend, and like he's watched the football receivers at practice, he puts his hands out. Eyes fixed on the throw, he follows the roll of TP in the air and gently catches Alberto's spiral. He resists spiking it in the street and tucks it in his arm. With a large figure running past him, he races to catch up to his trusted friend.

Laughing to himself in Alberto's passenger seat, he considered watching the remainder of the episode-memory from that night when they'd also TPed Pinche Benny's house, but he didn't want his wingman to know he still missed his one and only girlfriend.

When they pulled off the Border Highway, he switched off the TV in his head. It needed to rest, so more pictures could be born, as Dad used to say to his little boy in their Lomaland home.

7   Since joining the team a year ago, Raul had learned what Alberto and many of the varsity guys did when they weren't having good times on this side. They crossed over to J-town. Raul also knew from Pancho and Laura that kids his age, some even younger, from every high school in town started partying on the Strip on Thursdays, all kinds of drink-and-drown specials.

Alberto had said that too many cars were messed with in J-town, so he always parked by the downtown border bridge and walked over. Although Raul worried about being exposed to all kinds of elements, a windy night as well as pickpockets, on his first time partying in Juárez, they made their way over the bridge. Half in the U.S., half in Mexico.

It wasn't hard for the doormen at the J-town bars to remember Alberto. Not only was he a giant among all the patrons, but his even larger personality made him a welcomed customer. Even the Corner Bar's owner, who Alberto had said was an asshole to all the pochos from the other side, showed his crusty teeth in a smile when Alberto filled the doorway of the crowded cantina. And like when they went to the mall to check out the chicks, standing by Alberto's side always got Raul noticed.

From the outside, Raul thought the Corner Bar was nothing more than a rectangular slab of concrete, one door, no windows. It didn't even have signs of any of the drink specials that other places on the Strip, right as you crossed the bridge, advertised to throngs of teens, gringos and pochos alike.

ALL U DRINK / ALL NITE   SHOTS UN DOLAR

SEXXXY LADIES   BUY 1 GET 1 FREE

¡¡ BEST MUSICA, NO PLACE BETTER ! !

In all the time he'd been coming to the Corner Bar, Alberto had told Raul on the walk over, "Nothing's changed." The same bartender, the same wooden sign over the bar, the same vinyl stools, the same missing light fixtures, the same customers, the same lack of girls, the same shoe-shine boys working the place, the same ammonia-smelling piss troughs. Todo the same.

Given all this, Raul wondered why his friend wanted to make this their initial stop on his first trip to the other side. He learned that what had changed in the last year and probably was the reason the Corner Bar did a steady business in the face of bigger bars was the jukebox. Top of the line. The first on the Strip that played compact discs. Four songs for a buck. Random setting. The best in Classic Rock (Doors, Hendrix, Pink Floyd), the latest pop (Madonna, Wham!, Prince), and even a few Mexican heroes (anything by Chente). The shoulder-to-shoulder patrons of the Corner Bar drank to the sounds from both sides of the border pouring out of the large speakers hung high in each corner by wire, todo Mejicano style.

While Raul scored a bucket of beers, Alberto dropped four quarters in the jukebox, just like the ritual of placing the exact change into the turnstiles as they crossed the bridge. Having memorized the corresponding letters and numbers of favorite tunes, Alberto said he didn't have to study the selections in the neon-lit panels. They were automatic, like memorizing the plays Coach called in with hand signals. If Raul had been more athletic, his ability to also make sense of scrambled letters and random numbers might make him a decent second- or third-string running back. At least that's what he sometimes fantasized when he took the field, absorbing the cheers but remaining on the sidelines.

The trickiest part was getting from the tight corner where the bar was to the corner where Alberto had created some space for them to stand. His height made him an easy beacon, but getting to him was definitely harder than any of the team's tackling drills. Raul had seen others in the bar play the tough asshole and throw their elbows out as they pushed through, but he preferred to finesse his way with chin nods and short phrases, like "Wassup, man?" "Totally cool," and one he'd taken from Alberto, "Q'vole, ése." Mostly, he relied on what he'd learned in his first two years at the High: how not to draw attention to himself in crowds. The consequences were too unpredictable.

Alberto yelled something over the loud music as he took the beers from Raul.

"Yeah, this song rocks," Raul offered, hoping that went along with whatever Alberto said. "Bitchin' jams." He didn't bother to tell his excited friend that he only understood less than half of what he said while they were in the Corner Bar.

Did it matter? Alberto communicated best through body language anyway. That's probably what made him a monster on the line. This senior season he was going both ways in many games, and despite the team's losing record, he was getting noticed by junior college coaches. Whether on offense or defense, he posed a threat to the opponent positioned in front of him and even others who dared to try to get past him. The Y stitched on the maroon chest of his letterman jacket and countless patches plastered on his white sleeves did all the boasting that he never did. Even in the J-town bars, guys from other area schools stared at his badges of honor even if they didn't make eye contact.

Raul liked watching others admire his giant amigo. It was like in *Star Wars*, with Han Solo and his Chicano friend's nicknamesake, Chewbacca. Raul knew it was nerdy of him to think so and never dared tell Chewie, who reminded those who weren't his close friends that his full name was "Alberto Agustine de Jesús Baca."

Whether in a space cantina or the Corner Bar, one thing was for sure: hardly anyone messed with you if you stood next to a creature that could surely tear off your arms if you dared to try anything. *They must think I'm also chingón,* Raul thought on his first trip to el otro lado. If they only knew that he was the guy who picked up Chewie's dirty socks and checked over his homework. *I'm no one,* he thought as he drank among a sea of partiers. *At least not by myself.*

They hung out at the Corner Bar for about three dollars' worth of songs from the smokin' jukebox. At least that's how many Raul estimated while he fetched more buckets. He knew the bottled beer was going fast since the ice hadn't even melted when the bartender filled it up again. One good thing about hanging out most of the night at this spot was that the crowd slowly thinned out, taking their beer buzzes to the dance clubs on Avenida Juárez, where the strobe lights spilled out from open doorways.

While Ruly remembered his own first public attempts at dancing in junior high (the fresh smell of the smoke machine and the bouncy rhythms of dance tracks), an older Raul and his high school amigo wouldn't be caught dead in any dance club. Even when they were both dating girls who liked to move their bodies to music, Raul told them that Chewie's best moves were on fourth and short. This football reference always signaled that they would rather take a knee to the gut than step onto a dance floor.

On this night on the other side, they did take breaks from the Corner Bar to clear their lungs of cigarette smoke and BO. The vendors selling taquitos and Frescas up/down the Strip were welcome sights. With a simple flashing of fingers, you let the sidewalk chefs know how many corn tortillas filled with carne asada you wanted. A long spatula swipe across the sizzling griddle hit the small oval targets waiting on paper plates. The boy assistant proudly placed the warm plate in your palm as he took your U.S. bills with the other hand. The heat from the tacos seeped through the cheap dinnerware and let you know how your stomach would feel in a few bites.

Chewie drowned his tacos in the reddest salsita from the containers next to the griddle. Raul preferred the green sauce with plenty of lime. The spice and salt of the meat mixed with the semisweet condiment, almost like the taste of Chico's. Next to American school tacos, rolled tacos in soupy salsa were his favorite. With his first bite of J-town's sidewalk variety, he knew that tacos on both sides of the Río (Bravo/Grande) were cheap and always available. The big, juicy smiles on Raul's and Chewie's mugs declared this as truth. There could be few things better in their teen years than being buzzed and eating tacos in the open air.

After walking the blocks of the Strip, taking in the steady flow of the night's crowd, they bought a cheap pack of smokes from a girl in a horde of child vendors. Chewie said he didn't smoke other than when he came partying to Juárez. And Raul even less. More than half of the pack would probably end up on the dash until it got tossed out with a collection of bottle caps and fast-food wrappers.

"Think we'll come back after we graduate?" Chewie asked Raul as they stumbled toward the border point.

Caught off guard by this somewhat random question, Raul muttered, "Why not?"

Somewhere around midnight, they were in line to cross back, one of their last days of high school awaiting them in the morning.

"Maybe we just won't, you know."

"What are you talking about?" Raul asked, not sure what direction this conversation was taking them.

The steep walk over the bridge back to the U.S. side demanded big breaths and halted their questions and answers. The vehicles waiting on the bridge to cross over made a chorus of noises: rattling mufflers, crying belts, screeching brakes, whining motors.

Mixed with a belly of beer/meat and tortillas/menthol smoke, the hike up the International Bridge's pavement fueled their adrenaline to be crossing over a waterless river.

"So, will we?" Chewie had apparently caught his breath before Raul did.

"Yeah, I don't . . . shit . . . " He stalled, trying to remember where they'd left off before they hit the bridge.

"Shit, what?" Chewie had his hands stuffed in his letterman jacket. He didn't bother looking down at Raul, as if whatever answer he received wouldn't matter.

"What's the big deal if we do come back? The Corner Bar rocks, dude."

"Yeah, probably. I just wanted to see what you thought."

"About what? Coming to Juárez?"

"Never mind. Trucha." Chewie warned that they were a couple of people away from passing through the U.S. Customs.

An agent sat on a stool and randomly checked IDs. The questions on the sign overhead were so familiar to most border crossers that they didn't even bother to read them. Responses to the questions were as customary as saying what high school they attended.

"American."

"American."

Since this official passing from one country to another took less than thirty seconds, Raul didn't know why it left him anxious. The momentum of coming down the bridge, back from his first night of partying in J-town, was now spiked with having crossed over into another part of the night.

"What an asshole." Raul took two steps for every one of Chewie's to keep up as they walked away from the checkpoint.

"Who? That agent vato?" Chewie asked Raul.

"Yeah, did you hear how he gave shit to that older señora in front of us?"

"That's his job. You know, his jale."

"Sure, but does he have to be so tough with . . . c'mon, she looked like your madrina."

"Fuck that. If you take a job, you do it, no matter what."

Raul thought about dropping it, but he sensed that his friend had something on his mind. "Really? That's what you think? That no matter the crappy job, you just do it, get paid, and all's good?"

"I don't know about all that. Shit, I just think that it's not bad to sit on your ass and have the government pay you."

"That's true." Raul thought that his friend's logic made sense.

"I'd get bored too fast and probably would fuck with old ladies just to have some fun." Chewie gave Raul one of his patented nudges with his arm. "Simón, Ruly-Ruly?"

"Totally."

After Raul steadied himself and put both feet back on the sidewalk, he was happy to see his friend smiling. He was worried that something he'd said had deflated the night's party mood. Maybe they'd even been spending too much time together now that they both didn't have girlfriends. Even Han Solo had a few adventures away from Chewbacca, he remembered from all the times he'd watched the *Star Wars* films.

They squeezed through a hole in a chain-link fence, a shortcut to the car. The parking lot attendant didn't bother to come out of his shabby kiosk to check on them. It didn't matter since they'd tipped a kid to watch the car when they pulled in. The kid was one of the many mojaditos who crossed over by other means than the bridge. Raul guessed that they must do pretty good with what they made on tips. Much better than the shoe-shine boys outside the Corner Bar or pobre beggars under the bridge.

Wherever Raul looked on this first time so close to the border, it seemed there were countless exchanges—hands out, pockets picked, coins dropped, bills stuffed. The scene was too much to consider in one night, especially in his state of drunkenness. He reached over and raised the volume. Van Halen's first song off their first record (coolest LP cover he'd ever seen) rushed out of the speakers in the back and helped them peel out of the parking area. A few quick turns put them on the four-lane highway that ran parallel to the Río that fenced El Paso from Juárez. *Or is it the other way?* he asked himself. Many questions felt turned around now that he knew more about what went on on the other side.

A few days later, figuring that the awkwardness they'd had on the bridge had passed, Raul decided to ask Alberto if anything was on his mind. He'd been keeping to himself more than usual before and after practice, Raul noticed. They were sitting in the snack bar area at the High checking out the girls in second lunch.

At first, Alberto put off like he didn't know what Raul was talking about. Raul reminded him about his questions of whether they'd party in Juárez after graduating. Alberto didn't say anything. More surprisingly, he didn't whack Raul with his Wookiee-like arm. His friend's only response was to reach in his letterman jacket, pull out a card, and flick it across the cement table. The card landed near Raul's favorite lunch, a bowl of nachos with chili beans.

SGT. ENRIQUE "HENRY" RAMOS

RECRUITER, EL PASO SECTOR

915-555-2072

The official seal on the business card made it clear that this wasn't some kind of joke.

"I'm thinking of signing up."

"What, the Army?"

"Naw, that's for putos. The Air Force. Flyboys, you know."

Not sure of how to respond, he remembered something from watching *Top Gun* at the Lomaland Drive-in. "You're too big to fly planes."

"I know. But I could learn how to fix them. Air mechanic. Make some real money when I get out."

"How many years?"

"The recruiter said I could do three and see if I like it. There's bonuses."

"Three years? That's almost as much as high school. And you complain about coming here every day."

"It's different. They take care of you. They make sure you can cover your ass."

"Have you told your nina? What did she say?"

"Naw, not till I'm sure. I got a physical in a few weeks."

"You already called the guy. When did you see him?"

Raul learned that one of the men Alberto had been talking to most of the other night at the Corner Bar was Sergeant Ramos. Raul hadn't thought anything about that one guy's crew cut and older appearance. Since he'd never been approached, he never knew that military recruiters staked out the bars and clubs in J-town. But it made sense. Other than on campuses, the Strip was a perfect spot to corner a crowd of would-be graduates. One day they're celebrated in the Sports section of the local paper as "All-City" and "All-

District" athletes, and after weeks of boot camp, they're initiated into the ranks of "America's Finest."

Raul did his best to hide his concern for his friend's future. He was deeply saddened that he'd be losing his sidekick to a whole squadron. Especially now that he felt cool being Ruly-Ruly, Chewie's good friend, his camarada, not only Team Manager.

He handed back the card and took a last sip of his soda before shooting the cup toward the trash can. It bounced off the rim and spilled all over the patio.

"Cruz shoots and misses!"

"Baca with the putback!"

High-fives!

Rauluis

1 Cart collecting was a sentence to spend your afternoon out on the streets—chasing down strays that rolled away, wandered off, or were plain stolen. Next to mopping up some kid's puke in the bathroom, cart collecting was the worst job you could get assigned at BigWay Foods.

He had worked only a few weeks as a grocery sacker, so he couldn't tell whether the supervisor's orders were a reprimand or just another shitty part of the job. All the other sackers snorted and grinned their satisfaction. One cashier said the supervisor didn't like guys from high schools on this side of the freeway, especially from Ysleta. A stocker said that cart collecting was part of initiation, like having to wear a crappy hand-me-down uniform.

The polo shirt was more the color of sweat stains than white. The orange clip-on tie smelled like moldy bread. At least the caca brown vest had LUIS stitched on the breast, a pure coincidence.

Though he'd written his full name, Raul Luis Cruz, on the job application, everyone at BigWay started calling him by his rarely used middle name.

"Luis, carryout on checkout 2."

"Luis, mopup on aisle 7."

"Luis, price check in Deli."

"Luis, cart roundup."

Getting a hand-me-down BigWay vest wasn't exactly like being issued a sports jersey, but it did team him with the other carryouts and cashiers.

The more hours Luis worked, the more he learned that not much had changed since graduation. The only difference was that he now was around guys from other high schools. Riverside, Bel Air, Burges, Hanks, Eastwood, even as far away as San Eli. A mixed reunion. While there were other BigWay stores around the Lower Valley, this one on Yarbrough Drive was the largest. Most of the sackers were his age, the cashiers a bit older, and the supervisor tried to act younger than he actually was.

Luis loosened his tie and walked to the edge of the parking lot. Two carts were toppled over. He stood the metal carcasses on their wheels, backed up and ran toward the carts like a fullback. His shove threw the carts back to the middle of the parking lot. He did the same with two other carts loitering in front of the store. When an old woman wheeled a shopping cart out of the parking lot, he looked the other way. $75 or no $75, he figured BFW Corp. could afford to lend a cart to a viejita. Wrinkled skin gathered at her swollen ankles, and her sweater made the afternoon feel even hotter.

From the company's mandatory and boring-as-hell orientation, he knew how much the local grocery chain lost on a daily basis. "Damaged." "Spoiled." "Stolen." Every few months, a full inventory of the store revealed the losses, the company rep said. None of the employees seemed to really care. Especially the part-timers, like Luis, who made minimum with no benefits. But no one complained to management or talked about looking for anything better. As long as they collected their checks on Fridays—enough for partying, gas, food (in that order)—all was good.

It was way better than still living under the same roof as his parents. That's why he'd embraced an idea his amigo Alberto shared before flying off to the Air Force.

Alberto wasn't worried about anything, he'd told Raul, except leaving his godmother by herself. "She says she'll be okay, but I know her. All she'll do is feed her pollitos and pray." Raul already knew what Alberto was going to ask of him before his best friend said, "Will you look in on her?"

The more they talked about it in the weeks before Alberto left, they decided that, if Raul wanted, Alberto would get him a job at BigWay and he could live in the small house behind Alberto's godmother's. At least until Alberto returned. Because he was going to come back: "Home is Home."

At first Raul didn't know what it would be like living in an old Mexican lady's backyard. Would he have to do chores like Dad made him do? Would he get sucked into any kind of weird situation? Would he have to pay rent?

Alberto didn't pressure him, so he took his time in deciding. When he mentioned moving out of the house to his mother and Dad, they didn't push him one way or another. Dad thought it might be a cool thing he could do for his buddy. "If you're good to your friends, they'll be good to you." He said this with something like a Spanish dicho mixed in.

Raul didn't exactly hear since his mother was going on about him having to get his act in order. Since graduation, practically the second he threw his cap in the air, she'd been on him to get off the couch. "Do something, don't be a lazybones, Raul Luis." On and on she went about him needing to earn his way, like Pancho. It didn't help that his brother kept developing into the perfect adult that his mother imagined: having a job where he wore a suit, earning a good paycheck, and moving in with his latest girlfriend.

Raul's loyalty to Alberto more than his annoyance with his mother helped him make two decisions near the end of that year. He would move into Chewie's Casita, and with his friend's help he'd get hired at BigWay. Raul saw it as part of the same deal, picking up after his camarada, as he'd done during varsity sports at the High. The only difference, as sad as it would be, Ruly-Ruly would be a sidekick to no one.

Luis didn't even want to think about making new friends at this point in his life. And this made Laura's absence even harder. The family network of aunts was his only line of communication to news about his cousin. So after he moved out, he made up excuses to call his parents' for any snippets of news, mostly gossip. The latest being that Laura was working at her dad's car lot in Juárez, maybe living near the bullring with some hombre. Raul hoped that whatever Cuz's life was like, she was safe and would be there, on the other side, if he ever needed her. He trusted she felt the same way.

Having done more grunt work than sacking during an early shift at BigWay, he decided he'd rather stack cardboard boxes in the back room and sweep the aisles than step into the oven of the afternoon heat. He hated the idea of leaving the air-conditioned confines of the store as much as the job of corralling grocery carts.

Still in the probationary period as a "#2" (the company code for when they needed to page a carryout), it appeared that he'd earned himself the title of official cart collector. The store supervisor, a dude who thought himself better than his inflated position, always made it seem like he was doing Luis a favor by sending him outside to round up all the carts he could find in an hour. From the Plexiglas booth at the front of the registers, the supervisor fired off cocky stares to all the sackers and cashiers, earning him the nickname "El BigGüey."

When the asshole supervisor told Luis that he'd spotted a store cart off North Loop Drive on his way to work, he wanted to ask the dude if he was serious. Gathering the metal carts in the parking lot and even in the surrounding apartment complex was one thing. But to cross Yarbrough Drive, go past "the Safari" (the property of a strange local celebrity who collected exotic animals), and look through the empty lots along North Loop Drive was asking too much, right?

Luis took his time collecting the carts. If he was going to have to endure the oppressive heat of midday, he decided to ride it out, make the best of it. And he did. On the far end of BigWay's parking lot, he lined up six carts on a worn, grooved path for the "Ride of Your Life"—a favorite expression of a sacker from Riverside High who was more interested in partying than working.

With Luis's eyes fixed on BigWay's front doors, no supervisor in sight, he put his right foot on the bottom rung of the silver cage on wheels. With his left foot, he pushed off. Both hands gripped the plastic handles. He sailed down the parking lot. The sun-faded paint jobs of cars/trucks/vans/motorcycles parked among open spaces blurred as he gained speed. The hard rubber wheels made a high-pitched rattle. If he hadn't seen other sackers do this countless times, he would've never tried it. The surprised look on a customer's face confirmed his suspicion that it looked dangerous.

Each ride probably took less than thirty seconds. Still, from the standing position (cart collector's cockpit), it was less about time than about distance. Like his childhood rides in the makeshift go-cart, the joyride aboard a grocery cart was over way too fast.

The best thing was that there were always plenty of carts. One Cart = One Ride. One sacker always bragged of pulling off a double (two carts held together), but that was probably a lie. He'd gone to Eastwood, Ysleta's rival from the other side of the freeway, and those Troopers were all full of shit.

By the fifth "Ride of Your Life" this afternoon, Luis had most of it down to perfection: the navigation, the acceleration, the positioning. As if he was a Space Shuttle crew member. What he still hadn't mastered was the stopping. None of the other sackers had been any help, either. According to one skinny vato from San Eli, unless you installed brakes on the carritos then you better wear some good shoes. Luis was glad he'd traded in black dress shoes for black Reeboks early on in the job. Who cared what the company policies said about proper footwear? Not even the supervisor followed the official company dress code, wearing his Austin High letterman jacket when he helped restock the freezers. A has-been loser was what most of the sackers thought of "El BigGüey."

"It's all in how you position your heels," Luis told Susie, a cute cashier who enjoyed watching him do cart sprints. "You time it. As soon as you pass the handicap parking spaces, put one foot down, not too hard or you'll twist an ankle. Put all your weight on both heels, lightly loosen your grip in case you have to let go.

"Hope there's no big rocks, or else." He made a loud *smack!* for effect. "As soon as you've slowed down enough, let the cart cruise to a stop. If you're feeling cool-a-mundo, right before the cart reaches the curb, put your foot back on the lower rung, pop a wheelie, and lift the back end."

"Wow, you've really got it," Susie said, taking a drag on a cigarette during her third break today.

"Yeah, I guess . . . ," he said and tried to act casual, although he liked having a captive audience. And one who was cute, in a Lisa Bonet kind of way, with feathered hair like the chola's he watched from a distance at Ysleta.

"You'll have to teach me."

"Naw, it's only for the pros."

Big smiles.

"Yeah, right, show-off."

"Anyway, you're a cashier, a number 1, not a nobody like us." When she didn't reply, he said, "We're low-life number 2's. We work while you guys have it easy."

"No way. You guys have fun, get to go outside, and we have to worry about the dollars, change, coupons, and other stuff. Like all those WIC cards. And I can't ever remember the codes." She finished her cigarette and looked anxious for another one.

He'd seen most of the cashiers use cheat sheets for the various numerical codes to ring up the fruits and vegetables. One guy even wore it on a wristband like he was a quarterback calling plays.

Why don't you make notes?"

"Yeah, I know. I'm just too lazy."

"I can make you one, no biggie."

"No. Really? That's cool. You're nice."

Days later, after he gave her the notes he'd carefully written down on two sides of an index card, like he'd done so Alberto could remember his blocking schemes, he and Susie, by far the prettiest number 1 at BigWay, went out. It was more of getting a quick bite to eat after work than a date-date.

A Chinese restaurant had opened up near the store. And although he ordered the sweet-and-sour pork and she the chicken chow mein, his taste buds remembered pizza sauce and mozzarella cheese. The sign outside did say CHINA KINGDOM, but the building was a former Pizza Hut, no doubt about it. Bright-colored paper lanterns, paintings of flaming dragons, prints of Chinese characters that said who-knows-what did a good job of disguising its former business. If you hadn't come to this restaurant when it was a Pizza Hut, as his family did almost once a month when they lived in Lomaland, you'd never know that the fish aquarium was where the salad bar used to be or that the gold plastic Buddha was where the video games used to be. He and Pancho had fed many quarters into Pac-Man and Centipede, while Laura was more of an Asteroids fan.

"You like talking, huh?" Susie told him as he pointed out where the objects noted in his mental Map Book once were.

"I guess . . . some stuff."

"I'm more of a listener. Guys like that, right?"

"I don't know. Yeah. But it's better when—"

"My mamá always told me, 'En boca cerrada no entran moscas.'"

After he translated the Spanish in his head to English, he said, "Well, it's hard to eat with a closed mouth."

They both took more bites of food, sharing off each other's plates and mixing the fried and white rice. She liked the hot sauce with the rooster on the label while he liked plenty of soy sauce. The eating part of their date went off like one of his better cart sprints in the parking lot. No crash and burn.

Although he was sure she was flirting with him, all he got that night was a tight hug when they each went home. Nothing more came of his paying for dinner, nothing worth writing to Alberto about. In the short letters he did send, he exaggerated Susie's looks (bigger breasts) and left off any of the small talk that they'd shared during breaks.

A few weeks later, Susie changed shifts to work in the Bakery Department, so Luis saw less and less of her. And since he'd never asked for her number, he figured it was a no go. He still executed his cart sprints, but usually his only audience was the passing crowd of nervous customers who didn't expect the young man who'd carried out their groceries to be speeding past them like a dragster.

"'sta loco," their looks seemed to say.

He'd throw them a casual smile and a half wave to assure them that he would be okay.

Occasionally, during the midmorning to midafternoon shift, he'd have an hour or two to get lost outside the store while gathering carts. Business was usually slow, especially in the middle of the month, and the supervisor was often out back checking in deliveries. This left plenty of time for him to map out his new routes of the Lower Valley neighborhoods.

Even if he'd had enough saved to buy the car he wanted, he thought he would still enjoy walking to and from work. As much for daydreaming as getting exercise.

Beyond the baking-hot blacktop, it didn't take long for him to reenter the world of the Lower Valley. With empty lots on almost every street, the natural playground of his Lomaland years welcomed him back. The sandhills of his childhood neighborhood stood off in the distance. Beyond alfala fields and miles of cacti and mesquite, his parents' first place rested. If you drew a straight line, it was about thirty minutes from BigWay's front doors to his former home.

"But don't expect straight lines where the wind blows," he remembered one of his aunts saying in Spanish. "You change with the desert. You don't change the desert."

He respected the untamed desert enough to stay on the paved roads while cart collecting. The palo verde trees and ocotillo plants made great scenery while he pretended to search for carts to bring back. The surrounding desert was so much more beautiful, especially after a hard rain, than the scenes depicted on the postcards sold at BigWay. Although he'd never seen anyone pay 45¢ or 3/$1.00, there was a man who came by every month to restock the postcards and magazines.

He wanted to write on the stupid postcards that these cacti with the arms lifted weren't part of El Paso's desert despite what the messages said on the front: "Ola from the Pass of the North" and "Things Are Hot in El Paso." The clash of these messages and the real-life scenes he recorded in his mental journal prompted him to make his own postcards. If he knew where his last Map Book was buried at his parents', he would add the sketches that he'd drawn on index cards with colored pencils (School Supplies—Aisle #12).

For now, he put his homemade postcards on the fridge with the magnets he found in the kitchen drawers. Alberto's godmother must have left these depictions of La Virgen along with the countless crucifixes and velas, most empty of wax and wicks, in the house. Unless Alberto was some kind of superreligious dude he didn't know about. Every day that he stayed at Chewie's Casita, Raul discovered more and more objects in drawers, cabinets, closets, and a leather trunk.

At BigWay, the area around the registers was always a mess. Tabloids, candies, holiday specials, travel-size toiletries, some office supplies. So when the store began carrying cassette tapes Luis wasn't happy. Sure, he'd accumulated a decent collection of store-bought cassettes, copies from friends here and there, and of course mixes (his, Julie's, Pancho's, Laura's). But he had his cassettes put away in a wooden holder he'd bought along with some other household items at Kmart. He'd thought about hanging the cassette holder, but it fit perfectly on the dresser, so that's where it was.

The black metal holder the stockers forced into the space between the register and the candy rack was unsteady. Every time a customer flipping through a tabloid tapped the rack, the cassettes seemed ready to tumble over. It wouldn't be so bad, he thought, if anyone bought the cassettes. But there seemed to be the same number of shrink-wrapped cases many weeks after they'd been placed there.

He thought it was a dumb idea to sell any kind of music where people bought milk and eggs, lard and tortillas, dog food and laundry detergent. Whether it was during the Friday–Sunday afternoon rush periods, or when the neighborhood regulars came in to do their weekly shopping, he pretended not to notice the mess they left around the registers. Doing "go-backs" was a close second to mopping up puke on his list of things he hated doing at the store. The items customers didn't want or couldn't afford or that were damaged piled up in carts from opening to closing. It was always too busy to start on go-backs during any of the sackers' shifts, so the piled-high carts always greeted some poor sucker in the last minutes before closing.

The cassettes were a reminder that whoever made the decisions for the store's inventory really didn't know what Lower Valley residents would buy. Boxes of matches—Yes. Shamrock-shaped lollipops—No. *National Enquirer*— Yes. *We Are the World* cassettes—Definitely not. Like many customers he'd seen take the cassette off the metal rack and review the artists, he had little reason to want to buy it, much less hear its songs.

If not for a can of Folgers pressing down on a can of Spam, he might have never known that *We Are the World* had everything to do with groceries and the people who desperately needed them. The cassette ended up tossed in a cart of go-backs. The weight of coffee, processed meat, and vegetable medley (Canned Goods—Aisle #7) tore the plastic wrapping and cracked the plastic case.

From the go-back cart, it was supposed to go to a separate cart placed outside the office door. Although the supervisor wasn't personally responsible for the cost of the damaged items, he always made the cashiers, sackers, and the stockers feel like the money was coming right out of his paycheck. Whenever official-sounding memos were placed next to the time clock, they always attracted written insults. It was worth reading the memo to see what graffiti employees would offer as a response.

BWF CORP SUX

A LA BERGA CON COMPANY POLICY

YOU *ARE* A BIG WÜEY!!!

For once, getting stuck with go-backs paid off. With a stiff push on the heavy Folgers coffee can on top of a tin can pyramid, Luis finished the job of breaking the plastic case. Snapping it open, he took the tape and sleeve that listed the artists and songs. He made sure to cover his tracks by putting the broken pieces in his pockets to throw away on the walk home.

While he liked some other songs by the artists listed, he didn't think he'd heard any of these songs. Like beating out Pancho or Laura for the prize in Frosted Flakes (Cereal—Aisle #9), he felt only half guilty for leaving the store without paying for the *We Are the World* tape.

2   At the start of another summer shift at BigWay, the sun darted in and out of long clouds and a slight breeze pushed in from the direction of the Border Highway. The temporary shade inspired Luis to go hunting for carts. Each block away from the store turned up a toppled grocery cart.

Dead ends. Next to Dumpsters.

Empty lot. Lot. Empty lot. Empty.

Along canal roads and thrown into arroyos.

Under bushesbushesbushesbushesbushes.

He felt like a thief, even though the carts belonged to his employer. BWF CORP was stamped on each wheel. Every time he emptied one cart of trash, he wondered if he might have felt bad if anyone had been around. *Am I taking some bum's wheels? Who collects all this shit? Why do I care?*

At first, working in an area with a high number of transients had made him nervous. He worried that their crappy lives could make them desperate enough to become violent. One of the other sackers, a guy who never graduated from any high school, even carried a pocketknife. That vato said he'd been harassed by some "fucking lazy illegals" when taking out the trash behind the store. That area was a bit scary, especially at night, but nothing major had happened in the time Luis had been working there. Each week that he carried out the trash to the Dumpsters, he felt less like a stranger in this part of the Lower Valley. And it's not like a creature was going to pop out of some weird place like in the movie *Alien*.

While some Mexican mojados hung around the entrances to the store, most positioned themselves at the intersection of Yarbrough Drive and North Loop Drive. Each day, on his walks to work, he saw the same faces of Tarahumara Indian women asking for handouts in the desert heat. An Indian burdened with paper bags of clothes and food items and a baby on her back was not the image he remembered from growing up in Lomaland. His memories were of baseball games at the Optimist Field, after-school trips to Dairy Queen, and riding the swings at Lomaland Park. This part of the Lower Valley seemed depressing, like how he'd felt when he flipped through the black-and-white portraits of Navajos and Apaches in some books Dad ordered from a TIME-LIFE commercial.

"Those wetbacks are criminals, puros huevones." When Luis heard the supervisor complaining, he said nothing. "If I was real culo, I'd call la migra to round them up."

As he endured his supervisor's objections to the unwanted solicitors outside BigWay, he ignored him by thinking of the "We Are the World" campaign and the recent benefit concert all over the news. "It doesn't matter if it's in this desert or one on another continent," he wanted to tell El BigGüey, "poverty is fucking sad."

He recognized this now more than before, when he lived with his parents, always having a comfortable bed, a big closet, and a full fridge.

Although he didn't know if he would send any money to the address listed on the cassette cover, he gave change to the BORDER BEGGARS (as a recent newspaper headline had labeled them) outside the store whenever he had some. He didn't bother getting past the headline to learn more, since reading wasn't part of his day-to-day routine. His opinions would have to do. Whether on this side or on the other, he felt that people in El Paso/Juárez were hoping for the same three things.

Money = Food + Shelter.

He wrote the trinity of words on one of his makeshift postcards and capitalized each letter for effect. A Sacred Heart magnet held it on the fridge next to his favorite picture of him and Laura eating birthday cake at a Lomaland party. He hoped his cousin still had her picture of the same celebration somewhere close by.

Having witnessed his aunts in their respective kitchens, he didn't feel like a total stranger when using the kitchenette at Chewie's Casita. A gas stove, fridge, and countertop took up one side of one room. From his mother's kitchen, he'd swiped a few rarely used items (utensils, cutting board, one pan, one pot) and of course the comal that always rested on the stove, ready to hold heat like a stone lying in the sun. Every time he heated a tortilla or toasted chile on the comal, he remembered Lomaland.

And when he ate TV dinners, he thought of when his family left the old neighborhood for good. The cafeteria-plate-sized aluminum trays also held heat, but they weren't as sacred to him as the iron plate salvaged from a wood-stove. Whether made from ancient hands or pulled from a frozen box, food continued to be a steady comfort, especially now that he lived on his own, and mostly ate alone.

Refried beans	Mashed potatoes
Chile verde	Salisbury Steak
Fideo	Peas & Carrots
Pan dulce	Frozen brownies

Very often, the two kinds of food he liked eating came together. When Dad opened a can of peas and poured them into his mother's leftover arroz. When Pancho doused his meat loaf with salsa, green and picoso. When tíos ignored forks for the stack of tortillas at parties. When Laura craved roasted elotes with queso and lime instead of cans of cream corn (one of Ruly's faves). From his family, who always seemed caught between neighborhoods/homes/traditions, he learned how to consume the best from both sides of the border.

Usually, for breakfast, he scrambled an egg and maybe threw in some wieners if he had any. Packaged tortillas, the extra-thick kind, always flour, crowded the bottom shelf of the fridge. He did miss Dad's olla of fresh pinto beans, refusing to try them from the can. Anyway, this left refried beans a delicacy when he ate out. Like in every neighborhood of the Lower Valley, there were plenty of diners close to where he lived now.

Lunch was the easiest. Sandwiches, if the bread hadn't gone stale and moldy. Tuna, fried bologna, maybe Spam. Doritos, sometimes Fritos. Once in a while, if he felt like splurging, he brought home potato salad (Deli Counter). But fancy side dishes weren't really his thing.

Dinner was on a day-to-day basis. If he worked late, then he swung by Whataburger or maybe the new fast-food joint where a taco stand used to be for a chili dog. Onion rings and a Dr Pepper completed his three-course meal. If he was short on cash till next paycheck, he wasn't against leftovers. And if he was feeling nostalgic, he'd go through the freezer at BigWay and see if any of the TV dinners were near their expiration date. Slightly damaged. Unpopular combos. "Reduced for sale."

On this night, not in the mood for chicken or beef, he took a turkey TV dinner to the register. As he waited in line behind customers he'd sacked for many times, he jammed his index finger into the bottom of the sealed box. He started a small tear and reached inside. The film of the frozen dinner was slippery and cold.

"Hey, vato, how's it going?" One of the older cashiers was giving a customer his change when he noticed Luis standing in line.

"Pretty good. I'm outta here. . . ." He faked a smile and shook hands, pretending like if they were more than coworkers.

"All you buying? Dinner for one?" the cashier asked as he looked for the price on the TV dinner.

"Yep, nothing fancy." He reached for his wallet, hoping the dude would notice the damaged box, not make him point it out.

"Yeah, I know what you mean." The cashier didn't seem to care that there were other customers waiting in his line. "Hey, your lucky day. Damaged."

"Really?" He tried to act surprised, fidgeting with his cash to seem even more casual.

"Let's see, is Rivera around?" The cashier reached for the speakerphone, about to call the supervisor. "Naw, heck with it. You work here. Half price."

"Sounds fair." He took a small paper bag from underneath the counter and bagged his own purchase.

On the walk home, he felt sorry for the cashier. The dude must be in his thirties, although he looked older since he was losing the hair on his head but had plenty coming out of his ears. He wondered what kept guys doing this job for who knows how long. Couldn't be the pay—they were always complaining. Definitely not the benefits—there were none unless you were a supervisor or part of the union guys who stocked.

If he cared to know any of the old-timers, he might ask them if they, too, started right after high school. And before he could imagine the evolution from carryout to cashier to supervisor to manager (like that illustration of Ape to Neanderthal to Cro-Magnon to Modern Man he'd seen on a *Big Blue Marble* episode), he promised himself that he wouldn't be at BigWay for much longer. For now, he'd try to save as much as he could. He hoped Dad would help him pay for a car if he came up with enough of his own earnings.

And although he didn't have a plan for his future that night, he knew in the back of his mind that part of the key to evolving into something beyond BigWay Foods was in the envelope he'd received at his parents' from El Paso Community College. Going to school next academic year seemed like the best option, for now, to avoid premature baldness and hairy knuckles.

Paycheck to paycheck each week, he went farther and farther to round up shopping carts. As long as the sun wasn't too bad, he could hang for hours. In addition to getting away from the customers who moaned about squashed loaves of bread or those guys who were too wussy to carry their own bags of dog food, he saw this unpopular chore as a good form of exercise. The big belly that had slowed him down during high school was now flat enough for him to be able to do more sit-ups every night. Current high: 67. The weights Alberto had left behind were firming up his shoulders and chest.

He started rolling up the sleeves of his button-up shirts, showing off his biceps, like he'd seen the night stockers at the store do. He was in the best shape of his teenaged life. And to think all it took was getting a *Fucking Jale*, as one of the other carryouts always called this work.

As a cart chaser, he had some rules:

1) Bad wheels, no deal.
2) Don't empty personal stuff (clothes, toiletries, photos, etc).
3) If it stinks, keep walking.
4) And grimy, gorilla-sized, homeless vets keep their carts.
(The last one wasn't so much a rule as common sense.)

Every block down North Loop Drive was a snapshot. His mental Map Book now included a list of the shops along North Loop Drive: Bust Stop Burgers, Ivy's Flower Shop, San José Bakery, Aztec Laundromat, Tack & Feed Store, Good Time (the convenience store about to open), Linda's Bar. Every time he passed the Mexican Bakery, the intoxicating smell of marranitos rivaled a price check down Aisle #15. *Dove Dial Irish Spring.* The combined scents of bar soaps had become his latest nectar. No matter how much weight he lost, his body always stored extra senses born in his parents' closet years ago.

Each day, he learned how to focus more and more on the landscape around this part of the Lower Valley. Dried cottonwoods that gnarled toward the canal. Freshly cut alfalfa fields dotted with wired bales. Abandoned truck and car parts in every shade of rust. Symphony of noisy dogs and roosters, sometimes horses and goats. He'd forgotten from his Lomaland years how many people kept farm animals in their backyards.

He would've thought that a person pushing a train of grocery carts down the side of the road would attract attention, but no one seemed to care where he was going or, for that matter, coming from. And every time he passed some-body digging through a trash can or asking for a handout, he considered leaving them the carts and going back to the store empty-handed. He'd learned that as long as he looked busy his supervisor found some other poor sacker to boss around.

One afternoon, curiosity pulled him the farthest he'd ever gone looking for carts. He turned off North Loop Drive, wandered down a narrow road without a street sign, three grocery carts rolling a rickety tune in front of him. At the end of the nameless road, in an open field with more rocks and dirt than bushes and shrubs, he spotted a stove and fridge, both hollowed and rusty like dried cockroach shells. The only other object in view was a sign with a stranger's name.

PETER JOSEPH LEA PARK

There was some other information printed below the name, but he was more interested in what had become of the first, middle, and last name. The E T and R in the first name, the J S E and H in the middle name, and the A in the last name were scratched out. And with a spray-painted S and a stray apostrophe added, the sign had been revised.

PEOPLES' PARK

Unlike his child memories of him and Laura playing on swings, this secluded park in the Lower Valley was populated by a group of adults, mostly men. Enough for a football team's offense. He recognized some of them as the ones he saw waiting for the work trucks on his way to his own job. *So this is where they live*, he thought, as he stepped into the discovered park area.

Layers of clothes, mangled hair, bundled goods. And the smell. It wasn't a bad odor really, like his supervisor complained about the mojados outside the store, but it was certainly a distinct one. When the border beggars managed to sneak into the store and use the bathroom, they left their wet clothes behind. The moldy, pent-up smell reminded him of the Indians' locker room when he would have to pick up after the Friday-night warriors. Many cans of Lysol resurrected the cold-concrete smell. (Cleaning Products—Aisle #14.)

There was nothing clean about Peoples' Park. He doubted if any of the people in the park had stepped inside a grocery store or any kind of business in a long, long while. This outdoor world seemed removed from anything that required order. And he felt very self-conscious about his clean clothes the longer he stared. Leaving two grocery carts by the road, he pushed one toward the center of the park. The wheeled creature helped him blend in. When he saw a paper bag full of trash, he picked it up and threw it in the cart.

With each step, the ground more rocks than dirt, he felt like he was meant to learn about this community. And like he had done on the first day of junior high and high school, he tried to avoid eye contact while taking in a new environment. The key is pretending to look like you know what you're doing, he reminded himself. But he wasn't sure what there was to do here among this group of outsiders. No one was really doing anything but hanging out. In small circles, people talked. About who knows what. Some seemed to be taking naps. A few kids that popped out of who knows where chased a mutt.

He had now outgrown most of his allergies, and the rising temperature of the afternoon helped him make up his mind about trying to blend in even more. He took off his shit-colored vest, BigWay tie, and work shirt. The sweaty undershirt he wore seemed more suited for this space. About to investigate some more, he found his attention was drawn in the direction of the only road leading to Peoples' Park.

Loud music appeared before its source. Organs and horns filled the air over the park in the absence of any clouds. The holy sounds emerged from a pair of speakers atop a lunch wagon.

He made out an outline of some Mexican last name and TORTAS underneath a new coat of white paint, as if someone had taken a bucket of whiteout and made a correction. Otherwise, the lunch wagon resembled all the other taco trucks spotted around town, especially during lunch hour outside the factories like where Dad worked. Sometimes one came by BigWay's parking lot, but he'd never been brave enough to try anything like when he was buzzed and hungry on J-town's Strip.

Coming to a stop on the dirt grounds, the lunch wagon was to the adults in Peoples' Park what an ice cream truck had been to him and his cousins in Lomaland. A small group of women had exited the vehicle and appeared in charge. They were about his mother's age and had their hair tucked under scarves and their necks weighed down by crucifixes. From behind a cart table, the squad of women put out foil containers of what he figured to be food.

As quickly as the truck's occupants had set up shop, the men he'd seen taking it easy, slumbering bodies, and others he hadn't spotted before took the form of a familiar lunch line. Like at a cafeteria, each person got a plate, fork, and napkin. From where Luis stood, he couldn't hear if anyone said anything. He did notice that no one seemed to have anything to drink. His throat was as dry as the dust that rose from people shuffling through the lunch line. He left with a curious thirst to learn more about this location that didn't appear on any map.

3

Over the following weeks, he wandered in the direction of Peoples' Park more than anywhere else. And not only when he was scheduled to work. Days off and weekends, too.

He couldn't have located this Lower Valley spot at a better time in his life. While he loved being out of his parents' house and making his own money, he was getting tired of his routine on days off: sleeping till noon, scoring some fast food, and catching a bus to Cielo Vista Mall. While movie theaters had always been a reliable refuge, he felt less and less like hiding out now. The part of him that felt secure in a dark room was searching for new spaces to grow, like what the desert around Lomaland had been for Ruly.

It didn't matter what day of the week it was, Peoples' Park was always packed. He figured that paying attention to days and time, punching in, punching out, weren't things anyone here cared much about. From the lack of activity, the people in the park didn't seem like they had anywhere else to be. With or without jobs, they didn't appear to care too much one way or another. This mentality affected his own attitude about his BigWay Jale.

In corduroy cutoffs, a T-shirt, and a Diablos baseball cap, he found a free patch of white-yellow grass under a tree that was as beat down as some of the park's residents. Unlike other parks he'd gone to over the years—watching Pancho play baseball at Shawver Park, Easter picnics at Memorial Park, family cookouts at Yucca Park—this park was in desperate need of sprinklers.

Mr. Corral would know how to resurrect this park, he thought. Mr. C., as Raul renamed him in his head, was Ysleta High's head custodian and had maintained the school's football field for generations. Raul had spent many practices listening to Mr. C. go on and on about caring for grass. He remembered something about eggshells and manure. While he missed Mr. C.'s mentoring, he didn't miss the stench of the football field, especially around the fifty-yard line.

When he couldn't locate a drinking fountain or a faucet in Peoples' Park, he found the absence of water suspicious, especially with so many ditches so close by. He suspected that most of the park's residents were probably not born here—native El Pasoans always understood the value of water.

While he hadn't picked up a basketball since the High, he quickly became a star at Peoples' Park. He played mostly against older, tired men, who must've walked most of their adult lives in uncomfortable shoes. Occasionally a young guy would show up, but he never finished a game, since something more interesting always lured him away.

Sitting in a circle of sweaty men, he shared the jug of water he'd carried with him. Today, he'd also brought a bag of fruit from BigWay. The Produce guy was cool and let him walk out with whatever was too bruised or overripe. El Duque was one of the few older vatos at work that he liked to shoot the shit with after he got off. Each time El Duque gave him the fruit, he figured he took him for hard up. He didn't really care what anyone at the store thought about him. The rickety-fence smiles of his new friends at Peoples' Park were all that mattered these days.

"Got any nectarines, amigo?" a man who went by the name of Finn asked.

"Let's see." He dug through the bag although all he remembered seeing were apples, oranges, and some mangoes. At the very bottom, he was surprised to find a peach.

"This do?" He gave it to Finn, who held it delicately in his palm, as if it was still hanging from a tree. "Sorry, it's a little mushy."

"Hell, I've eaten many things that looked worse than this." Finn took a delicious bite.

"Yeah, Ol' Finn looks like he's put more than a few bad peaches in his mouth." This came from another man in the group. Like Finn, he was black. Both must've been somewhere in their fifties. Luis never got the second man's real name, but he'd heard someone call him "Liver." He liked it that almost every person he met at Peoples' Park had a nickname. It reminded him of being around the jocks at the High or the stockers at BigWay.

He wondered how long it would take for him to get a nickname. Anything but "Gordo-Boy." Hell, as far as he was concerned, that chubby schoolboy no longer existed. At eighteen, he was full of energy and muscles. "A strapping young man," one of the motherly women at the park said. He liked the sound of that, even if it sounded like something from a *Green Acres* rerun.

The group sitting near the basketball court laughed about some more-playful put-downs as he went around the circle with the fruit. Everyone put a hand in the grocery bag like it was Halloween. Without his ever having to say anything, no one took more than they could eat at a sitting. No one ever hogged any of the free food. Even Rachel, who had four kids, always took only a piece of fruit for herself. When the group broke up, he folded up the bag and dropped it in Rachel's grocery cart. He'd brought the cart for her one afternoon while he was supposed to be rounding them up, not delivering one to a woman who was once a modern dancer back east, as he'd heard others say.

In the time that he'd been coming to Peoples' Park, he was drawn to a solitary figure. At first he'd dismissed the shadow-of-a-body as quickly as he had the bicycle and cart near it. There were so many cast-off objects (lawn mowers, motorcycle frames, what looked like an air conditioner) in the vicinity that if something didn't move then it was better left alone. The activities of the rascuache community was enough to keep your senses occupied. "Rascuache" was one of those words he remembered Alberto using to describe anything that was tacky but still had value. As with Chewie's Cheby, "rascuache" definitely fit the population at Peoples' Park.

This all changed when he had to take a pee one morning. He thought about searching for a bathroom, even a port-a-john would do. But he was smart enough to figure it out. Without drawing too much attention to himself, he wandered away from the group and headed to the far back of the park. Among some mesquite bushes, he pissed with only the desert vermin to worry about. Or so he thought. Cut short by some motion in a nearby bush, he zipped up and hustled back to the company of others.

When he looked over his shoulder, he made out a definite human shape. The shadowy figure now had a face and moved, albeit very slowly. At first the body became a man then the man became a viejito then the old man became, yes, he was sure of it, El Marito. While it had been years since Ruly first saw El Marito riding his bicycle cart up Lomaland's steepest roads, he was now getting a fresh glimpse of the ancient figure.

Walking backward toward the main park area, he kept his eyes focused on El Marito pedaling away. The disappearing figure moved too slowly to be mistaken for a mirage. Even in the glare of the heat, he knew without a doubt that the man who rode up and down the Lower Valley's hillside neighborhoods all those years was now living on the margins of Peoples' Park. His worries of how the viejito might be doing ("He's got to be like a hundred or something by now," he once told his cousin Laura) were swept away by a strange pleasure of having a familiar spirit around.

"You know Ma-ree-toe?" Finn asked him when he returned to the group.

"I think so." He squinted until he couldn't see the bicycle cart's rear tire.

"He keeps to the trees mostly, but we make sure to keep our eyes on him."

"Has he always been here?" he asked Finn before thinking it might be a dumb question.

"Since I've been around. Some say he's got family in that neighborhood, but if he do, he don't stay with them."

He didn't have to look where Finn was pointing to know it was in the direction of Lomaland. From then on, he would make it a point to also keep an eye out for El Marito. The next time he visited with his parents he'd try to ask questions about people from the old neighborhood. It wouldn't be easy, since they didn't like to talk about what they'd left behind, as many deep feelings as discarded possessions.

LOST IN LOMALAND

Warmth	Lava lamp
Trust	Rosary beads
Connection	Class photos
Celebration	Xmas tree stand

It was several weeks after he discovered Peoples' Park that another stranger approached the gathering spot by the basketball rim. Carrying a box of donated clothes, a young woman went around and talked to each person in the circle.

As he watched Liver and some other men dig through the box, fishing out pants and putting them up to their bony legs to see if they fit, he considered getting up and brushing the dirt and dried grass off his clothes. His hair was crammed under his favorite cap, with a pitchfork insignia. He'd been rolling around with Rachel's youngest son, a playful blond boy who liked grapes. And after an afternoon of summer basketball, he was certain that he smelled like all the others, although he was the only who had easy access to a shower.

Fidgeting to make himself look presentable before the good-looking young stranger came over, he didn't notice others in the circle watching him. When he caught them staring, he could only smile back at them. Rachel threw him a damp handkerchief. He said thanks and wiped his face. The handkerchief smelled like baby lotion, and he figured it was the one he'd seen the mother use to wipe her baby's drool. He didn't care.

Like with every first time he met a girl he found pretty, his body betrayed him. Sweaty armpits, gurgling stomach, unsteady legs. When the young woman came around to him in the circle of homeless men and women and held out the donation box of clothes, he simply shook his head. The truth was that despite his shabby T-shirt and paint-stained shorts, no socks, and canvas high-tops, he didn't need any clothes. He had plenty at Chewie's Casita and a full closet at his parents' house, unless his mother had cleaned out his room.

When the young woman walked off with her box, a chorus of cackles came from the group. They didn't have to say anything for him to realize that he'd messed up.

"Yes, I'll take what you're offering," was what he should've said. "I'm in need."

The last thing he saw was purple toenails. They peeked out from a pair of sandals that had BIRKENSTOCK on the side. By the foreign name, he figured that they were probably expensive, although he thought they looked like ordinary huaraches. His eyes got as far as the young woman's firm calves before he noticed Finn watching.

"Name's Elena," Finn spat out between chuckles. "She's come out once or twice this summer. Think she goes to one of them big colleges in California somewhere."

He wanted to ask more questions of the old-timer, but he allowed himself to simply take pleasure in her name.

Elena. Right number of letters. And an "a" at the end.

One night, not too far back, when he couldn't sleep—feeling alone more than lonely—he discovered that all the girls he'd ever cared for had names that ended with the letter *a*. A small but significant detail that he mapped in the dark, like stars in a private constellation.

L—a—u—r—a

N—o—r—m—a

J—u—l—i—a

Now, possibly one more.

E—l—e—n—a

The group at the park was getting ready to go their own way when someone touched his shoulder and brought him back to the present. He turned his head expecting to find one of Rachel's kids asking for gum. Instead, he found the smell of detergent brushing against his face. When he took hold of the shirt, he saw Elena behind it. He couldn't stop staring at her eyes, the flecks of beige in a deeper brown. A scar on her calf, an upside down P, was the second intimate detail that he recorded.

"I thought this might fit you." She looked down at him.

He said nothing. A young woman's voice here at the park was new to him. He got up on his knees. His heartbeat sent indecipherable Morse code messages to his brain. He almost began praying the "Our Father" since it was one of those things he could recite without thinking.

"Large. Is that what you wear?" She now held the other sleeve of the shirt. It was as if they were getting ready to play tug-of-war.

Somehow, he got his neck muscles to work and nodded.

She put her hand out and helped him to his feet. When she pulled on the shirt, he let go. She moved behind him. Rather than disappear as suddenly as she'd appeared, like a midday mirage, she held up the shirt so he could slip his arms into the sleeves.

"Yeah, thought so. Mark's a large and you look about his size." Her voice slipped through his ears as he told himself not to drown. *Breathe, menso. C'mon, you can do it.*

As quick as he'd felt light on his feet, that's how fast he swallowed a pit-sized lump. "Mark's—your—boy—friend?" he stammered to connect words into his first sentence.

Elena took a second and smiled.

"No, Mark's my brother. He's back home in San Jose."

He straightened his shoulders in his new donated shirt and asked, "How do I look?"

"Great. You look good." She looked him over as if they were shopping at the mall. "I knew you would. It goes with your color."

There was another silent moment before she put out her hand. "Hi, I'm Elena, by the way."

"I'm Luis. Raul Luis," he uttered and exposed the palm of his outstretched right hand.

"Is that like Bond, James Bond?"

They shared a laugh while their hands were clasped.

"Yeah, I guess so." He fussed with his cap and smiled with his mouth open, pulp between his teeth from the orange he'd shared with one of the kids.

Elena glanced behind her. The other volunteers she was with were boarding a van. She moved her shoulders in that direction, although her fancy huaraches remained planted in the park's caliche. He had an urge to get back on his knees and clutch her ankles. This instinct-memory rooted to the nearby canals filled with water. He would've licked his lips, but his mouth was as dry as the park grounds.

"Well, I guess I'll see you." She walked backward.

"Okay." He knew from years of similar opportunities that he should do something. But what?

"'Bye, Luis, Raul Luis." She waved.

He extended his arms and fidgeted with the ends of his shirtsleeves. "When can I see you again?" came out of his dry mouth.

She stopped and said, "I'm not sure." She didn't come any closer.

"How about next week?" He rocked his arms like a bird testing its wings.

"Well, it depends."

He managed to unglue his lips and said, "All right."

"I'm not sure if we'll be here or not." She turned when the driver of the van honked.

He said nothing as his arms fell still.

He knew the moment was slipping away, running through his fingers, like when he dug holes in Lomaland's desert because Laura said it was good luck to bury lizard tails. An ofrenda. All these years later, believing in the sacred ritual, he hoped he'd buried enough ofrendas for a date.

With Elena getting farther away, a chill crawled under his skin. And it had nothing to do with the sun setting in the horizon.

He was walking to get his basketball and leave the park when Elena ran up to him. She took his left hand and unlocked his fingers. On his palm, she wrote her name and seven numbers. "Call me, Luis, Rauluis."

He made a tight fist as he watched her hurry to the van. As it drove away, he looked around Peoples' Park. The circle had broken up. Only a few bodies remained asleep under naked trees. He thought about looking for Finn along the Lower Valley's intersections, so he could share his good news, but he decided to go home and bathe. He would be sure to write Elena's number down before water washed away the ink.

4. The rhythms of past parties, family weddings, and holiday celebrations left him excited about being at the Ysleta Mission Fiesta. This was the first time he'd come to the street festival without his parents, brother, or cousins.

He enjoyed the live music coming from the outdoor stage while he waited for Elena. When he was growing up, his family had driven through the neighborhoods around this intersection of Zaragoza Road and Alameda Avenue many times. His mother's Tía Nivia lived close by the Ysleta Mission before she died several years ago. His great-aunt always had candies around the house, which smelled like Christmas trees all year long. Probably Pine-Sol Air Freshener (Cleaning Products—Aisle #14).

Like many family members on his mother's side, Tía Nivia was buried at Mount Carmel Cemetery, a few miles south of the mission, close to one of the border bridges. He wondered if all the families attending this fiesta had lived their whole lives here, never leaving, only to make their final resting place a short drive away. The older he got, the more he seemed to be learning how to appreciate the importance of roots, multiple generations sharing common ground.

The Ysleta Mission Fiesta was an annual highlight for the communities in the Lower Valley. The Tigua Indians of Ysleta del Sur Pueblo organized the event on their small tract of land in Lower Valley El Paso. An old adobe mission served as their church. While he remembered Tía Nivia saying the Indios had lived here for countless decades, it seemed that no one really noticed them except when they had some kind of celebration. It had been many years, probably not since they lived in Lomaland, that his family had even attended anything having to do with the Tiguas. What he remembered most about those trips were the matachines. He wondered if he'd see any of the Indian dancers tonight. And if he did, would they be as scary and exciting as he remembered? He peeked around for any sign of matachines. Maybe inside the fiesta grounds.

"Hey, Rauluis, looking for me?" Elena surprised him from behind. "I've been calling your name. Didn't you hear me?"

He wondered which of the names he'd ever answered to she'd been using.

Ruly Raul Cruz Luis Gordo Menso. When he'd answered Elena at Peoples' Park that his name was "Luis, Raul Luis," he'd been renamed once again.

"Rauluis." He loved how it came out of her lips in one breath.

When he turned, he found himself in an instant embrace. Elena was dressed in shorts and a casual shirt. Just like him, except she wore her Birkenstocks. He didn't even know if they sold this type of shoes in El Paso.

"The music is loud," he said after she let go of her hug. "I was watching for you."

"C'mon, let's go in. I'm excited to see what's inside." She walked a step ahead of him toward the ticket booth.

When they got ready to buy their tickets, she already had money out. Before he could reach his wallet, she'd already paid for them. He thought nothing of it at the time, since he was nervous, and thanked her as she led him by the hand toward the amusement rides.

The flashing lights made the fiesta more than a regular visit to an old adobe church. From the poster he'd seen at BigWay, that was all he'd thought it would be, one of El Paso's missions celebrating its saint's day. Other than wanting to have fun, as he'd promised Elena on the phone, he had one goal in mind: Eat plenty of gorditas. That was his ritual at church kermesses since he went to the big one in San Elizario as a boy.

He and Elena rode a few of the fiesta rides, which he was glad were more flash than fearsome. The Ferris wheel gave them a chance to talk. Whether it was the festive mood of this first date or her natural personality, she talked way more than he did. While his voice seemed to get lost in crowds, he envied people that could be heard in public settings. As if the energy of those around them gave them more to say. Laura was this way. Too bad his cousin hadn't returned from the other side. His cousin's absence was further underlined by the stands selling corn on the cob with lots of chile and lime.

After walking through the Tigua Cultural Center, which reminded him of a mini museum, he asked Elena if she wanted in on a secret. She finished reading a description of an Indian pottery collection and said, "All right, what is it? Is there some hidden treasure buried underneath the mission?"

"You'll have to wait and see." He put his hand on the small of her back and guided her toward the rows of food vendors.

ENCHILADAS/TACOS/FLAUTAS
NACHOS & HAMBURGERS
CORN DOGS TURKEY LEGS
FRENCH FRIES WITH CHILI-CHEESE

There were so many combinations to choose from. And they didn't have to go too far for him to find what he considered the treasure of fiesta food.

"See her. How old do you think she is?" He was pointing at a woman leaning out of a booth.

"I don't know. Maybe as old as my mom. Why? Do you know her?"

"Okay, let's try another one."

At the next gordita stand, he asked again, "And her? How old?"

"What does this have to do with the gorditas? I'm hungry. Let's just order."

"Just guess. Older than the last one we saw?"

"Probably." Elena gave him a curious look but allowed him to lead her to another two booths.

At the last booth in the far back of the fenced-in area of the fiesta grounds, he raised his arms, like a sailor who'd just spotted solid land after months at sea.

"This is it." Hands raised to the star-filled sky. "We found it."

She chuckled and said, "What was wrong with the other gordita stands?"

"Look, over there—see that viejita in the blue dress?" He tugged Elena toward him, so she could get a better look. A mestiza woman stood over a makeshift stove, hands as small as the corn patties she flattened before dropping them in hot oil.

"Last time, I promise: How old do you think she is?"

"I don't know, maybe eighty, big-time viejita."

"If we're lucky, she's a hundred." They laughed and got in line. He asked for three orders from a teen girl, who stood before an adult woman, who spoke to the viejita gordita master in Spanish. A trinity of generations, the passing down of recipes from annual festival to annual festival to annual festival.

This time he paid, although she insisted she could pay. He let her buy the largest fresh lemonades they could find.

They ate without talking too much. Since the bleachers around the stage area were already full, they sat on a short rock wall and listened to the music. Mostly Mexican music, like the rancheras from Juárez radio stations, filled the air while the crowd swelled. He knew from the poster at BigWay that a rock band Pancho used to worship was the main act tonight.

He didn't have to ask her if she liked the gorditas. After big bites, she licked her fingers. Even when the salsa, probably also made by the viejita, burned their lips, they didn't hesitate to add more to each patty of meat-cheese-lettuce-tomato. They sucked on ice to try and relieve the burning sensation.

Her appetite was infectious. The more she laughed, talked, and ate, the more he liked being with her. While he hadn't dated anyone seriously since Julie his junior year at the High, he had gone out with other girls who seemed too worried about their weight to enjoy everything on their plates. He thought a girl was right for him if she got as excited about Chico's Tacos as he did. *Take it slow,* he told himself, *don't rush things.* Chico's would be a good second date.

"What should we do now?" Elena wiped her mouth with her hands and scoped out the Ysleta Mission Fiesta grounds. "Wanna try to win a prize?"

He'd seen the game booths and hoped she wouldn't have paid them any attention. Throwing rings around bottlenecks or dimes into dishes was harder than it looked. And now would he have to embarrass himself trying to aim a football? Pretending to be athletic was another thing he hadn't done since leaving the High.

They ended up standing around for a few songs of the rock band. He knew the band had some hits they were saving for the end of their set, but he let Elena convince him that they should leave. Old rock music is full of clichés, she said when making fun of the aging singer with a receding hairline and the middle-age gut of the lead guitar player. He agreed with her, although he found their long hair and stage strutting as cool as the first time he'd gone to a concert at the Coliseum with Alberto. Flashing stage lights still reminded him more of pinball machines and skating rinks than marijuana smoke and drunk bikers. Many of these dedicated rockers were in attendance.

The loudest thought playing in his head as they left the Ysleta Mission Fiesta was that he'd never met anybody who spoke her mind with such confidence. At least not anyone his age. She made him feel grown-up without being boring or condescending. His parents, his work supervisor, especially all his teachers, had left him wondering if being an adult meant that you stopped having fun.

Warmed by the gorditas he'd eaten and excited about holding hands, Rauluis's first date with Elena made him think that the last months of his teens were going to be great fun.

"Okay, Señor. What's next?" By the way she bounced in her Birks, what she'd earlier called her sandals, she appeared ready for anything. "Wanna go dancing or swimming? How about cliff diving?"

The first two left him real nervous. But her laughter signaled that she was joking more than trying to alarm him.

"Well, it's probably too late for cliff diving, but if you want, I can take you to the mountains tomorrow and see what happens."

"Sounds like a plan." Totally by surprise, she gave him a light kiss on the lips. He managed to run his arm behind her and brush her lower back before she skipped away.

They walked for a few blocks from the Ysleta Mission along Alameda Avenue, peeking into storefront windows. Other than a stray dog or two, they had the sidewalks to themselves. Although the last time he'd cruised these streets was during lunchtime in high school, traffic seemed slow for a Friday night. Everyone in the Lower Valley was probably at the Ysleta Mission Fiesta.

Stopping by a used-car lot, each picking from their favorite colors (hers = blue; his = brown), he didn't mind too much that the list prices were more than he had saved up. Thrilled to be walking side by side, a coolness in the dark streets, he got even more pumped up when she asked if he wanted some dessert.

Earlier, when he'd asked what she did for fun with her college friends, she'd mentioned hanging out at coffee shops. He remembered her colorful descriptions of Telegraph Avenue, the main street by the university she attended in California. From what he imagined of her life at Cal, there were more bookstores and cafés on one street than in all of El Paso. At least in the Lower Valley and on this side of the freeway.

Since they were nowhere near the local university, where surely students drank coffee at cafés, he searched his mental map of Alameda Avenue for a good alternative. He listened to her talk about how much she missed her brother and little sister while he scanned the block ahead. When he spotted the fire station, his mind's eye zeroed in on Hamburger Inn #12 after the next light. He'd never had coffee there, but he knew they were open 24 hours, like the other Hamburger Inns in town. He was happy to see the word COFFEE written on the window next to MENUDO and BURRITOS. *Good signs come in threes, right?* he thought to himself.

"Imagination" was one of those words that he knew about before he learned its definition in school. Whether it was trying to understand the Spanish sermon at Mass or trying not to be bored in the backseat on family drives, mental pictures forever played behind his eyelids, curtains that dropped like the red velvet ones at the Plaza Theatre in downtown El Paso.

Everyone in his family often reminded him of how he was the one who fell asleep whenever they drove for more than twenty minutes. Trips to Carlsbad Caverns. Cinema Park Drive-in. Downtown Plaza. *Sleep Sleep Sleep.* And although he wasn't ever alone, always sharing the backseat with Pancho, sometimes Laura, he managed to curl his gordito-self into a fetal position.

"I'm a side sleeper," he told Elena at this point in their conversation.

"Really? I figured you for a back sleeper." Elena sat across from him stirring her coffee. "Guess what I am?"

"Two pillows. Maybe three. And side. Left side."

"Hey, how'd you know that?" Her teeth grazed her bottom lip when she smiled.

He shrugged. "By the way you walk," he joked.

"What, are you Indian or something?"

"Huh?"

"I read somewhere about Indians who can tell everything about a person by their footsteps."

"Well, my mother used to say the Cruz ancestors were 'puro Indio.' Maybe there's poquito in me."

"Cool." Elena sipped and wiped her lipstick off the rim of her cup. "And it's only two pillows, but I got this huge stuffed dog that's as big as a pillow."

"What's his name?"

"*Her* name's Blackie."

In the next moments of silence, when he took a bite of an empanada, he tried to trace back how he'd gotten to talking about ways of sleeping. He wondered if it had anything to do with the shapes outside the Hamburger Inn. He knew from cruising late at night past this diner in Chewie's Cheby that underneath the rags-trash-cardboard were homeless people. He wondered if it was anyone he'd seen at Peoples' Park. When he also saw a grocery cart on the roadside, he resisted the temptation to check if it had BWF CORP on the wheels.

"Wanna know another secret?" He turned back to her from looking out the window.

"Another one about gordita ladies?"

"Naw, better."

"Really? Or are you being a tease on our first date?"

He liked the promise of the last two words, "first date," as they got repeated in his head.

"All right, but if you ever meet anyone in my family, especially my cousin Laura, you can't tell them. Promise?"

When she said, "I swear," a dribble of brown liquid slipped out of the corner of her mouth. (Muy cute.)

"I wasn't always asleep." He put his elbows on the Formica table after confessing his secret.

"What do you mean?" She squinted her eyes like he'd seen her do earlier when he rushed through the whole thing about the gordita ladies.

"On all those trips in the car." He paused for effect. "Most of the time I was faking it." Longer pause. "I'd even snore at times to fool them."

"Really? Let's see."

"What?"

"Fake snore. C'mon, do it." She came over to his side of the table and nudged him.

He gave her a second to say that she was joking, but she didn't. And as if out of some nasal cave, he snored real loud. He was as surprised as she was when he did it a second time and a third time.

The sound he made was more like a pig than like anyone faking sleep. Saliva escaped out of his mouth. (Not muy cute.) When he didn't find a napkin in front of him, he used the back of his hand.

She sat back and laughed hard, so hard that she started coughing. He repeated the awful sound. They both had their mouths wide open at the same time. He didn't take notice if anyone was staring. At this late hour, there were only a few people seated in the tables around them.

After composing herself and drinking some water, she asked, "Why'd you fake it?"

"I don't know. Something to do. A game," he said. "My brother never wanted to play around, so I just figured I'd close my eyes."

"Wasn't it hard? What would you be thinking?"

"Naw. Mostly I made up things."

"What things?"

"Stories. Cielo Stories."

"Heaven? Sky?"

"Not really. More like home movies. Usually boring stuff. Stuff me and my family did. You know, going to the tiendita, going out for pizza. Day-to-day stuff."

The man from behind the counter came over with a pitcher of water. He asked if they wanted refills. He was drinking a Coke, so Luis knew he'd probably come over to check out Elena. He would've been jealous, but this Mexican guy was fat, like the Lucha Libre men that always lose. And, anyway, he'd never been on a date with a girl pretty enough to draw stares.

"The thing was that I heard a voice in my head reading a story." He continued talking even before the wrestler-waiter left. "I decided it was a voice from above somewhere."

Maybe because of their earlier walk through the mission church, with its soothing smell of adobe bricks, he thought of El Paso's Christ the King statue. Like the missions in the Lower Valley, Mount Cristo Rey was one of the holy places his relatives always talked about. They'd told him about their hikes up the Sierra during the annual pilgrimage years before he was born. Like his first and middle and last names, yet another trinity, the mud brown color of his skin, and speaking Spanish alongside English, he'd inherited an awareness for religious landmarks.

He considered telling Elena that maybe the limestone figure on the west side of El Paso talked to him, but he thought that might make him sound crazy.

"A narrator. Omniscience." She pushed the full cup of coffee away and took a sip of his soda.

He kind of knew what the first word meant but had no clue about the second one. For a second, he worried he'd come off as dumb, so he just nodded. He pulled his shirt away from his underarms in case his nervousness got the best of his sweat glands.

"You know when in a story the story is being told by someone who knows everything. That's an omniscient narrator."

"Oh, yeah. I think I remember that from an English class senior year." This was mostly a lie, since all he remembered from that class was Mrs. Mora's painted toenails, which were as red as her lips.

"Do you read much?" Elena now sat sideways next to him. She must've reapplied her lip gloss when he wasn't noticing. Her lips weren't red, but they did look watery.

"Magazines sometimes. I'm more of a TV guy." He slurped more melted ice than soda.

"We'll have to break that bad habit."

This sounded like something his mother would say, and he didn't like the woman who he wanted to kiss for a long time sounding like a pushy parent. And as much as he was falling for Elena this first night, he knew it would take something special to break him of his TV watching.

Long after they'd said no to several refills and the waiters had changed shifts, he'd learned more about her than he had divulged. She said she preferred that people know as much about her from the very beginning. That way if they didn't like something, there wouldn't be any problems later. He thought of that as another thing that adults would communicate.

This must have something to do with her helping raise her sister, he considered. From what he'd picked up, her parents were divorced and her mother was out a lot, so being an older sister meant more work. In his head, he saw Pancho nodding and saying, "See how much trouble it is to be an older brother, Gordo-Boy?"

During the walk back to her parked car near the mission, they held hands and said very little before they began making out. While he could've continued kissing her through sunup, which was probably sooner than either of them knew, he let her go get some sleep. Although she hadn't mentioned it tonight, he knew she did service work on Saturday mornings.

She offered him a ride home, but he told her not to worry about it. He didn't mind walking. As soon as her lights cleared the parking lot, he headed for the canal roads that snaked their way through the Ysleta neighborhoods, from the mission toward the High, parallel to the Río. Darkness surrounded him from all sides except for the occasional light in someone's backyard. He walked and half ran most of the way, like he had done countless times to and from school. As steady as the canals did during irrigation periods, his body flushed pure adrenaline after his first date with Elena.

5   He didn't think twice about lying to Elena so that he could spend a whole day with her. Well, it wasn't a full lie since he had done some community service as part of a recycling project in elementary school. At least that's how he thought of the Saturdays when Dad had driven him around Lomaland collecting glass bottles and aluminum cans. Although he'd only made about ten bucks for the school project, he remembered Dad took him out for breakfast at the Bus Stop Diner. More than words, full plates of eggs, papas, and beans sopped up with flour tortillas had said Dad was proud of him.

As the van with Elena and the other college students in the Hands United program drove through south El Paso, he craved the taste of a burrito de huevos con chorizo. And there were plenty of places that they'd passed on the trip down North Loop Drive to Alameda Avenue to Paisano Drive. As if she read his mind, Elena handed him an apple. He took it, although it would probably only make him hungrier for burritos that dripped down his forearm.

When Elena had mentioned that her group was going to work at Armijo Park in Segundo Barrio, he vaguely remembered that part of town. When she pronounced "barrio" with the full rolling of r's that always tricked his tongue, he decided he'd find a way to tag along. Since meeting her at Peoples' Park, he'd thought of nothing else but how to spend more time with this Cali Girl, as he'd referred to her in his last letter to Alberto. His high school buddy was now stationed somewhere in the Middle East. The spelling of the city's name on a postcard was as foreign as that part of the world. "Ruly-Ruly, you think its hot there . . . its HELL here. Stay Cool."

"Hey, give us a hand." Elena and another volunteer called to him as they were taking tools and supplies out of the van. He'd been distracted by a mural on the side of a tiendita. La Virgen de Guadalupe's face had somehow kept its shine while the wall around her weathered away. The sweet smells of pan dulce followed customers out of the tiendita and put him in a familiar space. Segundo Barrio welcomed Rauluis into its flesh, warm and brown, just as Lomaland had done all those years of his childhood.

"You like Her too?" Elena asked as they walked past the tiendita toward the park. They both looked over their shoulders at the fading mural.

"Oh yeah," he said. "She's like heaven."

"Yeah, I know what you mean."

He wished they weren't lugging tools, so that they might hold hands like they had after the Ysleta Mission Fiesta. Although he knew she was counting on him for physical labor, he thought of today as more of a daytime date and not simply as work.

Allergies or not, he did as she did and got on his knees. Marcos B. Armijo Park was infested with weeds, worse than any he'd seen at Hutchins Stadium, almost as bad as Peoples' Park. He wanted to suggest that they just set a match to the dried grass like many used to do to their yards in Lomaland. Somehow, he knew that wasn't what the Hands United crew was all about.

Checking things out, he witnessed Segundo Barrio coming alive this weekday morning. Adults walked toward El Centro, downtown El Paso, each of them carrying a bolsita of some kind. Kids trailed carrying their own loads. He smiled when they stared. They kept walking. With each barrio resident who passed, he couldn't help noticing how different they looked from the blond-haired and light-skinned student volunteers. Here, the college students were the minority. Other than him, Elena was the only one who might pass for a local in this neighborhood. Still, he was thankful no one asked him any questions, especially in Spanish, which is mostly what he heard in Segundo Barrio.

After a tiring morning of the outdoor work he'd escaped doing as an allergy-stricken boy, he walked over to the park's poor excuse for swings. Everything was run-down. The merry-go-round. The slide. And all that was left of a rocking horse was a large spring with a crumbled cement hind. This park sucked. Compared to Lomaland Park, where he and Laura had spent many summer days, Marcos B. Armijo Park was more of a junkyard. It would take more than one day to get this place looking decent.

Elena and another student brought him some water. He was so thirsty that he could have cared less that he was covered in sweat and probably smelled like a homeless person. Elena still looked good even in a sweaty bandana and clothes covered in dirt.

"Who's that?" asked the student volunteer.

He and Elena both turned around to see what her friend was asking about. The profile of a man was painted on a nearby wall. The three of them walked across the street to get a better look at another of the neighborhood murals. There seemed to be one on every corner in Segundo Barrio.

Elena nudged his elbow as she studied the mural and took a sip of water.

He assumed that she expected him to know, so he tried not to look like a total menso in front of his potential girlfriend.

He glanced back up at the giant head that looked over Segundo Barrio's Park. The brown-skinned man looked familiar, confident and hardworking, like a photo from the Cruz family album. But he didn't know of anyone in his family who had done anything that great to earn themselves a mural.

He quickly studied the images surrounding the man's face for clues. A black eagle against a red background. A row of grapevines. And what looked like another picture of La Virgen, this time on a flag, a procession of people marching behind the sacred image.

"He's some kind of priest . . . don't remember his name. But I think he founded that big church." He pointed downtown, in the direction of Sacred Heart, where his brother had done his holy communion.

"Stop kidding around." Elena took his hand and they stepped back to get a better view of the mural. "You know that's Cesar Chavez, head of the UFW."

As Elena explained to her college friend who the man in the mural was, he listened more intently than he ever did in school. When she mentioned the grape strikes and that Cesar Chavez fasted like a man named Gandhi, she helped him understand why they had painted this man's face on such a tall wall. He might have figured out the symbolism of the eagle on his own. Still, he didn't want to turn her off by admitting how much he didn't know from books.

As they walked back toward the park, he felt he was being watched. He wondered why no teacher had ever bothered to teach him about Cesar Chavez and the UFW and their place in his people's history. If it hadn't been for his grandparents taking him to church, he wouldn't have learned about La Virgen either.

Rather than get mad at how much time he had wasted in school, he looked forward to learning more from Elena. She had a way of teaching him things without making him feel dumb for not knowing. It was a gift. And if she decided to become a teacher, like she said she might after college, he was certain she'd be great at it.

When they got ready to leave Armijo Park later that afternoon, he was surprised at how much better it looked. While it still could use newer swings and more trees, at least all the trash and weeds were gone. They'd even built a wooden swing set that some little kids were already using. He felt good about his contribution and thought he might go out with Elena's community service group again. For certain, he would meet them at Peoples' Park each chance he got.

On the ride back to the Lower Valley, he leaned against Elena in the far rear seat of the van. They both smelled bad, so he didn't worry about that. Whether it was his feelings for her or that he was more tired than he'd ever been from cart collecting, his body relaxed itself against hers. The rhythm of the drive further coaxed him to close his eyes. One second he was looking at the sights along Alameda Avenue and the next he was out.

"Hey, sleepyhead, we're here." Several minutes later, Elena shook him awake. The first thing he did was check to see if he'd drooled on her shoulder.

"We're here. You're home." She pointed to the BigWay parking lot where he'd been picked up. "Boy, you conked out fast. Told you it would be a hard day's work."

As they got out of the van, he kept hold of her hand. When she pulled it away, he felt embarrassed and said, "Sorry."

"Your hair's everywhere," she said as she ran her hands through his bushy mound.

"Yeah, I know. I need a haircut." He did his best to try and flatten it, but he knew it probably resembled a football helmet.

"Naw, don't cut it. I like it a little thick. It looks like Cesar Chavez's." She reached in to give him a hug as they were calling her back to the van. He went limp in her embrace. Combined with his fatigue, her strong hug made him feel like being in warm-hot bathwater.

Later that night, experienced at being alone, he settled into bed with the TV on. The fan in the corner turned and cooled the room enough for him to be comfortable in a pair of briefs. He hadn't bothered to dress after showering. He had no plans.

Like the excitement that had washed over him in the shower, each time he thought of Elena at the park, sweaty neck and tank top, a surge of blood rushed away from his head and through his heart. And it didn't help that a babe in short shorts and a tank top appeared on a TV rerun. Her outfit left little to the imagination, and yet he imagined every part of her body. Big breasts. Smooth belly. Full butt.

He replaced the fantasy of the actress with one of Elena. Their third date (he considered the cleanup at the park date #2) wasn't for a couple of days, so he had to find a way to not get worked up. A few weeks ago, he wouldn't have hesitated to jack off, but he wasn't in that kind of mood. Yes, Elena got him excited like no one since Julie, but what drew him toward this college coed was alive in areas other than just his crotch.

Eventually, the strong feeling for release crawled up to his stomach and left him hungry. On the comal, he prepared himself a grilled cheese sandwich, adding pickles (Ruly's fave) and tomatoes with pepper (Cuz's secret ingredient). As he waited for the bread to brown and the cheese slices to melt, little things Elena had said earlier kept flashing in his mind.

Working out here means something.

Communities make us who we are.

Symbols always matter.

You have Cesar Chavez hair.

Like the words of wisdom printed on the magnets Alberto's godmother left on the fridge, he tried to memorize these phrases. He thought about writing them down once he finished eating.

The one about his hair was silly. But it did mean something, he told himself, that she'd noticed this detail. And to compare it to the UFW leader on the mural in Segundo Barrio must mean Elena had definite feelings for him.

As much as he remembered, his family's encyclopedia set was still at his parents' house, probably packed away in some closet. His mother fought off clutter in her house like Dad declared war on the weeds infesting his lawn. He would make a special visit to his parents' to search for the letter *C*. It didn't seem like a coincidence that "Cesar Chavez" was probably listed in the same encyclopedia book as "Chicano." This related word, he remembered, was one that Alberto had used to describe himself more than once during high school. He decided he would bring that single encyclopedia book home. Hopefully there would be a picture of the farmworker organizer (and maybe one of a Chicano) that he could study.

Washing down the last bite of his grilled cheese with a glass of Dr Pepper, he went to the bathroom. He ran his hands through his bushy hair and smiled at his reflection in the mirror. He would recognize Cesar Chavez the next time he saw his face.

His arrangement with Alberto's godmother was perfect. The kind viejita was either at church, which was all the time, or visiting her grandchildren in Chihuahua. It was rare that she came over to check on him. Around the first of the month, he just slipped an envelope under the back door. It was more of a gesture than an arranged rent payment.

The apartment complex where the Hands United group was staying for the summer was not close to Chewie's Casita in the Lower Valley. Other than the shitty apartment Laura had once shared with a friend, he'd never spent much time at any rented property. He wasn't sure if he'd like living among so many strangers.

Over the next few weeks, there were more date-dates with Elena than just times hanging out. While he enjoyed any time they spent together, he wanted more than to be just friends. Especially since she was only here for the summer. Because he hadn't been in a relationship for some time, he wasn't sure how to go about starting one with Elena. Nothing he rehearsed in his head sounded good.

Like with his last girlfriend in high school, it was Elena who helped take things to the next level one night when he'd caught a ride from a coworker to her apartment.

"Okay, I know it's going to sound goofy, but I came up with some questions."

He tried to act cool and was glad that her assigned roommate had left after only a couple of days in El Paso. The heat had proved too much.

"Questions?" he asked, sitting at her desk like a star pupil. "Like a quiz?"

"No, more like a questionnaire," she said. "For fun. We did something like it in my Human Psychology class."

He swallowed and felt his underarms get sticky. He spotted a cup of pens on the desk but didn't reach for one, figuring he could give his answers orally.

"Number 1: What's your earliest memory?

"Number 2: When have you felt most alone in the world?

"Number 3: If you had one day to live, and ten dollars, what would you do?

"Number— Sorry, do you want me to ask you one at a time or all of them at once?"

He was still thinking of her first question and was reaching for a pen when he replied, "Doesn't matter. Pick one and we'll start there."

"Okay, let's get to the last one, number cinco," she said, "although it was the first one I came up with."

He heard her take a deep breath as if she was preparing for some awful response. This made him wish he'd had some time to study, something he never did at the High.

"How many girlfriends have you had?"

"That's easy," he said as soon as she finished the question. He held up the pen in his hand. "One."

After a few seconds, she went over, sat on his lap, and kissed him. They laughed a little about how nervous they'd been. When he asked her to repeat the other questions, he was somewhat relieved that she said they could wait. Really, she told him, she only wanted to know the answer to the last one she asked.

Although Elena never got around to asking her other questions that night, he carefully thought of his answers before he fell asleep in case she ever did. It was kinda fun to write them down in a Big Chief tablet he'd swiped from Big-Way (School Supplies—Aisle #12).

> Answer #1—Waking up in Lomaland. Everything dark except for one bulb in the other room. Not scared.
> Answer #2—The day Laura moved out. Not telling her to be careful.
> Answer #3—For sure, eat as many gorditas as possible. Maybe go to Lomaland Park and spin like crazy on the merry-go-round. Play King of the Mountain with Cuz one last time.
> Answer #4—(What could the question be?)
> Answer #5—Julia Martínez. (Wonder where she is now?)

He thought about coming up with his own questions or even asking Elena to answer her own, but that seemed too unoriginal. He preferred figuring out personal details by paying close attention when she spoke and noting them in his Big Chief Map Book.

ELENA
Family: Filipino and Mexican ("Mestiza"?)
Fave Foods: Lumpias, Fideo, Everything Bagels
Fave Bands: U2, Red Hot Chili Peppers, Simple Minds
Fave Books: *House on Mango Street*, *The Metamorphosis*
Birthday/Zodiac Sign: May 12/Taurus
Middle & Child Nickname: Sharon & Pare

And whatever he didn't know or yet understand about her, it would be fun to learn, he told himself.

Between her service work and his shifts at BigWay, he spent as much time as possible at her apartment. He never asked her if he could stay over, it just worked out that way. So he wouldn't have to bum rides or bother his parents for one of their cars, she even let him borrow hers, which she had brought from California. This was a good thing, since Laura was still on the other side. While he wondered about how his cousin was doing living in Juárez, he also missed borrowing BEBBA whenever he needed to get around. He hoped that the next time he saw his cousin he'd be able to hold up two fingers for his number of girlfriends.

6 The best memories of childhood were about when he felt safe. And he felt that most of them still lived at his Lomaland house.

A blanket. Even on the hottest days. A thick cotton cobija that covered him from the soles of his feet to the top of his head. This is how he slept most of the time, shrouded under covers. Breathing wasn't hard after years of practice. Whether he took short breaths or he somehow had trained his lungs, he could fall asleep breathing only the air that slipped through the thick fabric.

As important as warmth, darkness led him to sleep. From the navy blue curtains of his Lomaland bedroom to the blinds at the new house in Valle Vista, he made sure he had a light-free room to sleep in.

Eyes open, seeing complete black, coaxed his eyelids shut. He'd slip through darker and darker passages, never knowing where they led. One thing he did know was that the longer he slept the more protected he felt.

Initially, after he moved from Lomaland, he thought the comfort of darkness might be rooted in his family's past trips to Carlsbad Caverns. Those ancient rock dwellings in New Mexico. But when he accessed those mental images of him, his parents, and Pancho or Laura, walking down seven stories, he realized those were the wrong journeys. His skin remembered how much colder it got the lower he went.

Lomaland's comal-like heat rested in the memory images he hugged under covers. As a boy, a bowl of cereal in hand, *Big Blue Marble* on TV, and sitting on his parents' big bed was the best way to spend a day faking being too sick to go to school. As a teen, he only cut back on hours of TV watching to sneak in time for other images, like the ones in Dad's adult magazines. And now that he lived on his own, he remained under the covers, breathing steady, lying perfectly still, eyes shut for fear of allowing in any light of a new day.

One thing that did stay constant over the years was that most mornings passed without his participation. He wasn't due at work until late in the afternoon. Today, he and Elena had decided to take a day off from seeing each other. Over the last few days, they'd spent most of their free time together. She was a morning person, the worst. Weekday or weekend, she was up by 7 A.M. He hated that she could "rise and shine" like all those TV commercials of coffee/

juice/cereals (Aisle #6/Aisle #8/Aisle #9). Okay, maybe he couldn't *hate* anything about her, but she did make him more self-conscious about the things he did alone. And how they were different from the things he did with her. Like something as simple as washing clothes. While in the first weeks that he was in his own place he had to practically force himself to wash on a regular basis, he eventually worked out a routine.

There were countless Laundromats in the Lower Valley, including one down the street from Chewie's Casita, between Lola's Pawnshop and Sal's Upholstery Repair. He walked to the six-washer, eight-dryer Deluxx Laundromat, pockets full of quarters—extras for the video games and vending machines—a pillowcase in each hand, whites mixed in with colors. The fragrance of fabric softener greeted patrons from around the immediate neighborhood.

Occasionally, if he went on a Saturday morning, there were others there alone, mostly women. When he first moved to this neighborhood, he used to think that maybe, just maybe, this would lead to a sexual encounter like those in Dad's magazines. But if he did manage to get the attention of any women, he was met with "Get lost, creep" and "¿Que quieres?" stares. He did get a phone number once, but it turned out that she just wanted someone to care for her lawn.

Week after week, he'd tried to get the most wear out of his clothes without having to wash them. As soon as he got home from BigWay, he would take off his pants and shirt so they wouldn't get dirty. One of the best things about working at BigWay was that he wore the same types of shirt-vest-tie-pants every day. No worries about varying his wardrobe. And as far as socks and underwear, trips to Kmart kept him well in stock. If for no other reason, he missed living at home where his mother always did the laundry.

Although it was one of those chores he had never imagined himself being responsible for, washing clothes with Elena was nothing like washing clothes on his own. He could pick any step of washing, drying, and folding, and everything she did was nearly the opposite of how he did it.

At Elena's apartment complex, the washers and dryers were all located on the ground floor. While she dumped out her washed clothes on her bed and immediately began sorting through the piles, his job was to continue hauling up basket after basket after basket. Since there were only a few washers, and sometimes one was busted, he spent much time running up and down the stairs.

Elena was religious about separating her clothes, not only by color but by fabric too.

Cotton ... Polyester ... Denim ... Poly-blends ...

Silk ... Rayon ... Corduroy ... Fleece ...

Up and down. Three loads in the washers. Two loads in the dryers.

Up and down. Two loads in the washers. Three loads in the dryers.

Load. Sort. Repeat.

He told Elena she was giving him the best workout since running stadiums with the varsity squad at the High. After taking the remaining quarters, she carried the last of her closet, it seemed to him, out the door in search of an open washer.

Exhausted, he threw himself on the rug in the middle of Elena's bedroom, afternoon sunlight blocked out by thick curtains. He dozed off. The absence of noise—no music playing, no kids running, no cars idling—at this apartment complex helped cradle him to sleep. More and more, it was during brief naps that he dreamed the most, like after a long day of cart collecting, waiting for Elena to call. Quickly snoozing off, he found that his subconscious matinees were full of recurring images.

Church lady gorditas

Desert bonfires

Tío Pascual's hands

Flat on his back, drool rising in his gums, arms and legs thrown out to the side, he witnessed these dream-images *pulses of sand-covered skin* before being yanked to the surface of being awake.

"Raul, Rauluis, come on"—a woman's voice. Laura's? Mother's? Girlfriend's. "Rauluis, give me a hand."

Before he could speak, startled and dazed, his legs got tangled in Elena's when he tried to get up from the floor.

Two baskets of clothes, one on top of the other, came tumbling down.

Heat washed over face and neck and arms.

The too-familiar sensation put him back in his interrupted dream.

Cristo Rey Mass

Chugging with Chewie

Cuartito of tools

While these memories of people/places were spread out over years like a mental mural, they came together in the few seconds when warm laundry spilled over him. He might have been able to hold on to the sensation longer if he'd been alone, but Elena had other things on her mind.

"Damn!" She looked down. He smiled behind a warm CAL sweatshirt.

"They're clean." She removed the sweatshirt. He couldn't hide his grin. A serious look consumed her face. The more he tried not to, the more he cracked up.

"You think this is funny?" She pulled her hair back and put her hands on her hips. Her tone matched her body language.

He thought better than to answer and swallowed the last bit of heat from the dream images before he crawled his way to a chair. Elena was on her knees and throwing her once-folded clothes into the baskets. By the way she crumpled her shorts, tees, and towels, it was obvious that she was upset.

The heavy breathing she made, mouth closed, nostrils wide, was a sure sign that she was getting angry. He considered volunteering to wash and dry her clothes again, even if it took all day. Instead, he was moved by a feeling that formed in his mouth then sped past his throat through his stomach to root in his crotch.

"Arms around waist, drive your opponent down," he remembered Coach always preaching. Lucky for him there was a pile of towels, thick and terry cloth, to soften their fall. They landed on their sides, her right, his left. Fans would have cheered his tackle.

As if he were handling one of the tackling dummies at practice, he rotated his body and straddled her. All the while, her breathing became heavy. She tried to get her arms out from under him, but he had her pinned. She cussed. And while she only used three of the numerous cuss words he knew, she had a great way of making new combinations.

Damn-shit-hellshit-damnhell, Rauldamnluis, shit.

She seemed angrier about the mess they were leaving than about being tackled. Pumped up, he made another quick decision and targeted the first sight of exposed flesh. He kissed her stomach. Moist mouth on hairless skin. Her open-handed attempts at slapping his back became a pulling of his hair. He grabbed her waist. Fingertips moved to the hem of her gym shorts. He kneaded the muscle of her thighs as he moved to kiss around her belly button. She squirmed like crazy. Her hard breathing turned to steady whimpers.

As quickly as she'd walked in the door and spilled two baskets of warm-hot laundry over him, they were now tangled in each other's clothes. She pulled his T-shirt over his head. Her tank top came off next. She helped him pull her shorts and panties off her hips, down her legs, tossing them with the other piles of clothes on the floor. When he saw her reach behind her and unclasp her bra, he knew that she had, for the moment, forgotten about the lost loads of fresh laundry.

After a bout of kissing—mouth-to-mouth, mouth-to-neck, mouth-to-shoulder—he would've continued making his way down her body, eager fingers leading the way, if she hadn't taken charge. With a sudden burst of strength, she pushed him to one side, threw her right leg over, and straddled him.

She unbuttoned and unzipped his jeans. Underwear came right off with them. Other than socks, they quickly ended up naked on a floor blanketed in clothes—some clean, some dirty, some to be rewashed.

The week after having sex on top of Elena's laundry, he went to meet her at the university library, where she was researching paper topics as part of her community service project. He traded shifts at work with another sacker, and when that guy asked if he was sick or something, he figured that he looked anxious. Truth was that he was horny. And now that he and Elena were doing it practically every time they saw each other, the possibility of having more sex was at the center of his thoughts.

When he was at work, the young women he used to flirt with now seemed silly compared to Elena. The female customers, even some of the older women he had thought were sexy, now went unnoticed as they pushed their carts up and down the aisles. All his wants and energies were focused on spending as much time as possible with Elena, preferably with no clothes to worry about.

He even considered quitting his job, living off what he was saving for a car, and asking if he could help with her community projects for the rest of the summer. But he decided that probably wasn't the best thing to do. "You don't want to scare her away," he told himself, a warning every time he wanted to call her. He'd even been busted once at work when he snuck down the block to use the pay phone in the middle of a shift. His supervisor gave out warnings every day, so he didn't worry too much when El BigGüey handed him the carbon copy of the disciplinary report.

But all that didn't matter as he walked onto the university campus and made his way through the directions Elena had given him. If he hadn't had doing it with Elena on his mind, he might have taken time to imagine himself taking classes, like the students walking in and out of the buildings there. He figured there were more students his age sitting in classrooms and learning something important right now. If having to take classes at the High during the summer was a drag, they seemed even more of a chore if he was going to college.

He managed to find the library without too much trouble. The sign was next to a tall, pointy sculpture, exactly as Elena had said. She was waiting on a nearby bench, reading and relaxing, some of her favorite activities, he'd learned. As he walked over to her, he was eager to take her in his arms and kiss her, right there in front of the other college kids. Instead, she was the one who rushed over after seeing him. She kissed him, no reservations about being affectionate in a public place. He took a book bag from her, let her take his hand in hers, and they walked toward another building on campus.

Happy to listen to her paper ideas for her community project, he didn't notice where she'd led him until they passed through a door and reached a desk. A woman in a blue smock sat behind a pile of papers and stacks of pamphlets. A nurse. His first clue that this was the university clinic. Before the nervous feelings he had for doctors' offices resurfaced, he took the seat next to Elena. She filled out some forms while he scanned the room. It was pretty bare except for some posters and a TV set turned to the news.

"Are you sick?" he asked her without looking over to see what she was writing down.

"No, not really."

"Are you going to see a doctor?"

"Probably just a nurse."

"Oh. Okay." He felt a bit relieved that this wasn't a visit that might mean some kind of bad news. The thought of his new girlfriend having any type of illness was scarier than the blue-black, achy lungs on the anti-smoking poster. SMOKING IS A LOADED GUN. Still, that approach was way more effective than the SAY NO TO DRUGS posters he remembered from the halls at the High. Of course, his classmates had written "Yes" over "No" on every poster.

As they waited for her name to be called, they held hands and glanced at the news. Although various reports from around the world flashed on and off the screen, he wasn't paying any attention to anything outside this room. Elena appeared equally spaced out. They didn't talk.

When he heard her name called, he was surprised that she didn't let go of his hand. And he was even more surprised that he followed her behind the reception area down a white hallway that also had posters with more serious medical conditions. Diabetes. Heart disease. Skin cancer. It was like a Health Haunted House. Every message he read seemed to be a warning against what might be waiting for him inside the door they entered.

A woman in a white lab coat sat on a stool and asked them to sit on two chairs opposite her. He wanted to ask what he was doing here, but he felt that he should stay quiet until spoken to. This strategy had been pretty successful during high school classes.

"So, what brings you into our clinic?" The nurse smiled big front teeth.

"Well, I wanted to come in and see what we could use, you know, for when we have sex." Elena said this all in one breath and sounded like she'd practiced it many times.

"And this, I see, is the person you are having sex with."

When both women looked at him, he didn't know which of the things running through his head was the right response. He chose to stay seated, not make a dash for the door, and simply lifted his hand from his lap and grinned. As if to say, "Guilty as charged. . . . Yes, I'm the guy she's doing it with."

The nurse went on to ask them questions about what they'd been doing sexually. After the first couple of questions, they got easier to answer. He started to feel a bit more relaxed when the nurse didn't make him feel guilty. It wasn't like she had asked him how long he'd been jacking off.

The session at the university clinic seemed to be winding down when the nurse reached behind her and grabbed a plastic model off a table. She held it firmly with two hands and kept talking to them. When she turned her attention fully to him, he freaked out. Like the time his mother walked into his room when he was looking through one of Dad's magazines. While she didn't say anything, he knew she'd seen it when it disappeared from his hiding place in the closet the next day. At least he'd still had on his shorts and his palito wasn't fully hard when his mother busted him.

"Give me your hand," the nurse said as she reached out to him.

"Excuse me?"

"Your hand. Let me show you something."

"Put your fingers like this," she said and gathered her three middle fingers.

When he did as she told him, she pulled his hand forward and slipped them inside the plastic model.

"See how it curves, how it's not a straight cavity?"

He nodded and let himself be led through this lesson in the female reproductive system. *Vagina Labia.* The vocabulary became more tangible the deeper the nurse guided his fingers. *Clitoris Vulva.* There seemed to be a new term for each minute the nurse kept talking. *Urethra Cervix.*

"You have to know where your penis is entering. Your partner will respond to your movement. Learn to trust each other."

While he felt real lucky to have seen more than one naked woman in his life, not only pictures in magazines, looking at the internal view of a woman's pelvis changed everything. Although the model was plastic, it was soft and real close to what he'd felt before. A long period of time seemed to pass, although it had been only a few minutes since he'd experienced a more intimate understanding of a woman's body.

And while none of the words for his own sexual organs had been used, they now seemed to have different meanings too. As if his penis/palito and testes/huevitos were meant for something more than to simply make him feel good.

The nurse asked him to wait out in the reception area while she talked a little bit more to Elena. With no one holding his hand, and it free from the warmth of the plastic model, he did as he was told. Rather than sit and pretend to watch TV in the waiting area, he checked out some of the pamphlets at the front desk. Most of them were on diseases that affected organs no nurse had ever revealed to him. He didn't smoke, didn't know if high blood pressure ran in his family, and his ethnicity didn't rank high among skin cancer patients.

He did decide to take one on STDs and HIV/AIDS. From the text on the front and back covers, he decided that there was so much he didn't know. And while he wouldn't have come into the university clinic on his own, he was glad that he'd met someone who was smart enough to bring him along. Before Elena came out to the reception area, he also reached into the fishbowl of condoms. He grabbed a handful of different colors and stuffed them in his pockets. The woman behind the counter gave him an approving smile.

Walking out of the clinic, he didn't know what to say or if he needed to say anything. His mission to come to see Elena on campus and maybe get lucky had changed. He'd never planned for anything like this.

"Are you mad?"

"About this?"

"Yeah, I thought about telling—"

"No, don't worry. I'm not mad."

"Really, I wanted to tell you, but I didn't know how . . . and then we were there, and everything just happened."

"I know, really, it was wild." He loosened his grip on her hand.

"Like *bad* wild? Or *good* wild?" She squeezed his hand.

"All good, and look what I scored." He took out the condoms.

"Whoa, that's a lot. What do you plan to do with these, señor?"

"I don't know. Maybe make balloons. Hand them out at work."

"Oh, well, I thought you might want to share. You know, with your girlfriend."

"Okay, you can have two. But not the blue ones. You know that's one of my favorite colors."

They joked some more while they walked around campus and stopped at the snack bar to get some chili dogs and cheese fries. They both had big appetites after their visit to the university clinic. There didn't seem to be a need to go over what the nurse had said. While he might not remember every word she used, he would never forget the tactile lessons. His hand remembered where it had gone, and his mind had made note of each inch that corresponded with his sex partner's body. He hoped to dedicate as much attention to her as he had to examining his own birth-map.

7   Rauluis had to pay up. Elena was super nice, but she wasn't letting him back out of a playful wager. He would never doubt her knowledge of trivia again. From a reference book on her shelf, she showed him that two different actors *had*, in fact, played Darrin on *Bewitched*.

After cashing his check from BigWay, he called her and said she could pick anywhere she wanted to go. Money was no object. He suggested several nice restaurants—an Italian one with candles propped up in old wine bottles, a steak place where you could choose your own piece of meat, and even the Chinese place in Juárez where Pancho had taken his girlfriends.

When Elena passed on any of these fancy places, he was surprised and a bit relieved. A formal dinner date wasn't something he'd done before. He worried that he wouldn't have anything nice to wear. Not to mention what to order. Since he could purchase beer for him and wine coolers for her from the laid-back BigWay cashiers, he'd never worried about being carded.

They could go over the bridge to Juárez, as they'd talked about before, but that wasn't something he'd done since Chewie left for the Air Force. Rauluis was glad Elena had never asked about his trips to J-town. While they happened before she got to El Paso, he knew he didn't want to tell her about all the bars they cruised or how stupid they got, much less the women in the back rooms.

A walking tour of the Lower Valley was set for the first day off they both had in common. Elena had decided that she wanted to see all the sites and landmarks in Lomaland that he'd mentioned over the summer. He thought about gathering all his Map Books and handing her the collages of lists, stubs, sketches, postcards, but that wouldn't be the same, he figured.

When he tried to change her mind, she said, "Por favor, amor." The trinity of "or's" hanging in the air like if they came from a poem.

Poooooorrrrrrrrr

Faaaaaaaaavooorrrr

Amoooooooooorrrrrrrrr

The morning that he was to guide his girlfriend through his childhood neighborhood he woke up feeling real anxious. Like suiting up for a big game. Like getting written up at work. Like learning a few days ago that Laura was coming back to this side. While he still wasn't sure what to think about his cousin's impending return, his emotions stirred deep in his stomach.

He knew that eating his favorite breakfast of huevos con chorizo probably wasn't the best idea, so he settled for a tall glass of juice and one of the pan dulces he'd scored from the woman in the BigWay Bakery Department. She continued to flirt with him, although he'd mentioned Elena's name after "girl-friend" more than once. Free pan dulce was free pan dulce, one of the other sackers told him.

He decided to meet Elena at Peoples' Park, since they hadn't been there in a few weeks. Each had a distinct connection to the gathering place in the Lower Valley. No matter where he went in El Paso with Elena, the spot where they first met would be a gold star (School Supplies—Aisle #12) in his mental Map Book.

His Cali girlfriend was already at Peoples' Park talking to a group when he arrived. For a weekday morning, things were pretty quiet. He eavesdropped on the group's conversation as he strolled up. When he heard a somber tone in their voices, he loosened his hold on his good mood.

"What's up?" he said, taking care not to sound too upbeat.

"Hey, cariño," Elena answered and gave him a quick kiss. "We're just catching up."

More new faces than old ones were gathered. They continued to stand around as if they were waiting for instructions of what to do next. In the few moments of silence, some of them walked off to see to other things, rummage through bags of clothes that Elena had brought, and maybe find out where their kids were if they had any. Rauluis now wished that he'd cruised BigWay to check for any discarded fruit before coming to the park.

"Seems slow around here today." He was the one to break the heavy silence. "Thought there'd at least be a game going on." The basketball court was empty and the ball he'd left wasn't in sight.

When he noticed that not even Elena was saying anything specific about the weird vibe in the air, he decided to stay quiet and look forward to their day together. He slipped his hand in hers and squeezed it as a signal. They exchanged glances and excused themselves from the group that remained.

As they walked past other circles of people (few regulars, plenty of drifters), he thought he heard whispers of something but nothing that made sense.

"Ready for your tour?" He pushed ahead with their plan to explore the surrounding landscape. "A bet's a bet."

"Yeah, totally," she said in an upbeat tone. "Listo, Ca-pi-tan Cruz."

Her salute made him laugh and temporarily forget the awkwardness at Peoples' Park.

The night before, he'd thought about drawing a map. But having lived on his own and worked in the Lower Valley for almost a year now, he was impressed that his memory was like a whole library of maps. He unfolded and refolded several mental diagrams as they walked.

Streets/Roads
Avenues/Drives
Intersections/Dead Ends/Detours
Barriers-Borders-Basura
Landmarks (Lots of them)
Omniscience::Cielo Voice

In the hours before falling asleep, he'd traveled every inch of a remembered life in Lomaland and the surrounding desert. While he never confused his practice journeys with dreams, there was a cloudy texture to his visions of this desert community. He constantly felt like he had to blink away a dusty film. Maybe that's why his eyes always felt so dry with lagañas when he woke up. (Eyedrops—Aisle #3.)

A few minutes into their private tour, it felt as if sand had begun to seep from the pores of his imagination. It clung to the sweat on his face and neck. He stopped wiping them with his shirt when he noticed that Elena wasn't bothering with her perspiration. The drinks they'd bought at Lucero's Market were half gone, so he knew they'd have to make another stop in the coming hour. By midmorning, the sun preyed on them. A quick flip through the main mental map for this journey revealed another tiendita not too far off that sold aguas.

The first tour he'd given of where he was born and raised was as much a physical one as a symbolic one. His past was present in the places he pointed out to Elena. Landmarks each told a story in Raul Luis "Ruly" Cruz's past.

North Loop Clinic
Cristo Rey Church
Pokey Roney Ranch

Whenever they reached another stop, where a large dot might appear on a globe, he'd share another part of his history.

El Gran Arroyo
Lomaland Park
El Arbol Viejo

He didn't describe the structure or space that stood before them but the memories it contained. With each detail he shared with his West Coast girlfriend, more maps were created, more detailed ones, young adult versions. Each step of their tour charted years of emotions.

As he continued to narrate their journey of the Lower Valley going east on North Loop Drive, he was surprised that he had stories and stories about every block. The words and sentences kept coming, in no real order, as if someone were ripping random pages from a book and he was the omniscient narrator.

"What's with those jugs?" Elena asked.

"Where? Those in the yard?" he asked in reply.

"Yeah. That's the third house, at least, I've seen. The yards are fenced by them." She pointed to a beige brick house on the corner of Courtland Drive and Lomita Drive. "At first I thought it was only someone being weird, but now I wonder."

"Well, like a lot of things here, it depends who you believe."

"What do you mean?"

"Just that there's at least two reasons for the jugs of water."

While they took sips from their second round of cold drinks, they moved at a casual pace. The sun that had been with them since the morning did a good job of avoiding the few clouds in the sky.

"Well, I'll give you my cousin Laura's story first. It's more interesting." He let his hand touch Elena's, both damp from sweat, as if to signal that he was going to share a personal footnote.

"If it's as good as the ones you've told me about playing around Lomaland, I can't wait."

"Well, you see, there's all kinds of talk of mysterious things happening. Lomaland is said to be filled with ghosts and witches."

"Wait a minute. Are you gonna tell me this desert is haunted?"

"Not exactly. These aren't scary ghosts or witches. Then again, they're not as cute as Tabitha." (He was glad that he didn't have to explain all his TV references.) "Well, Laura told me that our tío, I forget which one, told her that people started filling empty plastic gallons with water when neighbors started having things stolen.

"Nothing expensive, just sprinklers, rakes and shovels, small toys, things people left outside. You know how we are."

At this point of sharing in his story, they stared at a bright blue house surrounded by plastic milk jugs, each filled to the top with water. Their different-colored caps made them look like decorations.

"That no matter what they did, the stealing kept happening. Nothing the cops or even the gangs did stopped the strange robberies. Everyone was all freaked out.

"After months of more stuff, more-private things like laundry and statues of saints going missing, that's when most people in Lomaland, especially the viejitos, decided it must be a fantasma. Since no one had seen anything or anyone actually take anything, they just called it a ghost."

"Okay, I see . . . but what does that have to do with the bottles of water? What's the point?" Elena bent down to hold one of the jugs and studied its contents. Dirt and dried milk particles floated inside the water, like a Christmas globe or something.

"Well, someone told someone and someone told someone else, you know how it is, that if you filled jugs with water and placed them around the edges of your lawn you'd be protected. Ghosts and witches can't cross over water, it turns out."

"Really? Naw, you're making it up. Right?"

"No, I swear." He raised his left hand, then switched to his right hand. "If I'm—When Laura ever comes back, I'll have her tell you."

"All right, I believe you, but I want to check your sources, señor." She gently bumped into him and gave him a kiss on his cheek. Their sweaty faces slipped against each other.

They walked a little longer past a stretch of empty lots. They sat down on a fallen cottonwood tree next to a dry ditch. While he was used to the vacant sections of the Lower Valley, he had begun to notice something different about this part of El Paso on his walks to work. Real estate signs, sheets of wide plywood nailed on tall wooden posts, stood out against the landscape of sand/weeds/rocks.

The company names and logos brightly painted on the signs contrasted with the desert's flat beiges and muted greens. He considered if any of the Lower Valley residents paid much attention. Why would they? Most of them had lived here for more than one generation, like his great-grandparents, his grandparents, even his parents till they moved.

He sensed that the Realtors, with last names like Salazar, Rodriguez, and Guzman, were selling more than property. If you were to call the listed phone numbers, as his parents must have done when they moved, you would probably hear them use words like "change," "value," and "progress." The same words his mother used to sell them on leaving Lomaland for good.

No longer at an age where he would let himself be uprooted, he was beginning to figure out that definitions of words as simple as *change value progress* weren't the same for everyone. The promise of those words mattered only to those who benefited.

"So, c'mon, I'm waiting," Elena said as she got up from their little break.

"Huh?" he asked, brought back from the lessons inside his head.

"You know, what's the other story about the water bottles?"

"Oh, yeah, it's not as cool as the first one, but it's funny."

"Don't tell me that. Now I'm going to feel all bad if I don't laugh."

"You better." He tickled the sides of her stomach, and she wiggled away. He chased her for a bit until they got tangled in each other's arms. They hugged and kissed under the partial shade of a cottonwood. Neither of them seemed to mind that the white-yellow sun had left them sunburned in addition to sweaty and sticky. He didn't, for sure, and tried to sneak his hands under her shirt.

"No, tell me. No more stalling."

"Okay, I can't remember who told me this. Or where I heard it. Maybe I made it up.

"Some neighbors border their yards with the bottles to keep dogs from shitting on their grass.

"I know, I know it sounds dumb, but all my aunts used to do it, maybe still do, and they swore that it worked. My mother always thought it looked too tacky, so she didn't try it. Instead, Pancho got stuck having to pick up the crap from the stray dogs in the neighborhood."

"Are you serious?"

"Yeah, he did. I faked my allergies good."

"No, not about your brother. People around here believe that there's some magic or power in the water that keeps poor dogs from doing their business in their yards?"

"No, I don't think it's like the ghosts or witches. It's more of a game, I think. Something to keep the dogs guessing. Like did you see the bags of water at the tienditas we went to this morning?"

"Oh, yeah, what about them? Do they keep ghost dogs from entering the place?"

"No, smarty. The hanging bags of water keep the flies away."

"What? You're making up more stuff. More Map Book stories."

"No, really. The first time I saw the bags of water I asked the lady, and she told me in Spanish that the flies get scared when they see their reflections in the water and don't stick around."

"Are you sure you didn't misunderstand her? Your Spanish is almost as bad as mine."

"No sé de que tú hablas," he said in a purposely bad Spanish accent.

"Flies, witches, dogs—too much, Rauluis. I can't wait to tell my mom this, she loves to hear about crazy stories. I always make fun of her for reading the *National Enquirer*."

"Hey, at least it's reading."

"I know, but it's not like real reading. You know, books, or even magazines."

"Okay, College Girl."

"Hey, it's just that . . . well, I guess I am a book snob."

"And that's why I love y—." He only managed to cut off the last two vowels from the phrase that slipped out of his mouth.

"Ah, that's sweet. You're the best guide ever. This is way better than when my dad took us to Alcatraz."

He didn't know if it was good or bad that she hadn't made a big deal of him saying, "I love y—." And when she took his hand and held it real tight as they walked farther east on North Loop Drive, he figured that she understood how he'd meant it. Serious and fun.

It didn't matter. The warm emotions of their afternoon together pumped through his body and made him think he could walk more miles through the vast desert. If he hadn't had to be back for a work meeting later that day, he would've suggested that they take a shortcut he knew.

From North Loop Drive, it was through some bushes, past the rusty shell of a pickup, and then you hit a long caliche road. It cut through the desert and was a clear path toward Lomaland. While it had been a long time since he'd made the trek, he remembered the times he and Laura had taken the road home. Whether they were coming back from Lomaland Park or maybe the Lafayette Tiendita, the road was something he always looked forward to.

Like this afternoon's journey with Elena, those walks as a boy always left him feeling tired and full of energy. As if no matter how thirsty he got, it was worth it.

The dry heat of the desert lived inside of him as much as his memory of almost drowning.

Hours into the one and only Lower Valley tour he'd ever been asked to give, he sat across Elena at the Bus Stop Diner scarfing down his third mini hamburger. With his mouth full, he allowed his girlfriend's voice to lead him as easily as she'd followed him through the sandhills and canal roads.

"Don't freak out or anything, but I need to tell you something." She pushed the basket of fries to the middle of the table. He took one and dipped it in ketchup as a way to let her know he was ready. "You know back at the park this morning. Well . . . the reason we were acting kinda weird . . . is because of Marito. . . . No one's seen him for a few days, almost a week. Like if he just left. . . . Without saying anything."

The pauses and hesitations in her voice set off several alarms in his mind.

"Damn, I knew something was going on." He rewound the events of this morning and stopped at the point where he met Elena at Peoples' Park. She was right. Marito wasn't in any of the frames that he scrolled through. *How could I miss that? What was I thinking?* He answered his own questions by remembering that today wasn't about looking out for Marito or any of the park's residents. Today was about spending one more day with his girlfriend before she left El Paso for good.

"It might be nothing, but everyone's worried." Elena tried to sound hopeful and put her hand on his across the table. "I told them that Marito would turn up, but I didn't do a very good job of reassuring them."

"Yeah, he's probably just off on a walkabout, like we were today. Nothing major."

"Yeah, we don't really know what Marito does when we're not around. He could have a family somewhere. Maybe he's shacked up with a secret lover."

Her hopeful attitude, like many of her other beautiful qualities, had a powerful effect on him. He trusted her good intentions.

They finished their lunch saying very little. Fatigue gathered in his achy shoulders and sore thighs.

He tried to mentally go through the remaining stages of his Lower Valley tour, but no matter how much he tried to look ahead, what rested behind them felt more present, like if he was looking through a plastic bag of water at a magnified past.

"Hey, Luis, Raul Luis . . . Cariño, you ready?"

Before any memory-episodes of Marito could swallow him, Elena's voice made him realize that he hadn't noticed her go to and return from the bathroom.

Before they exited the Bus Stop Diner, he also went to the men's room. Stomachs full and legs rested, they walked out into a bright afternoon.

Standing on North Loop Drive, he called up one of his mental maps: His old address to their right and Peoples' Park to their left. One direction would keep them on the tour he'd planned. The other would cut their journey short.

Without saying anything, they both walked back toward their starting point. Nothing they'd shared over lunch had seemed to convince either of them that things were all right. That Marito would be back at the park, his bike and cart safely parked under the trees.

As Rauluis completed this journey through the Lower Valley, Elena by his side, an itch crawled up his legs. No matter how much he scratched and scratched, it persisted.

He kept an eye out for an aloe plant. "The desert heals more than hurts," he remembered his mother promising her son.

 The final week of Elena's summer in El Paso was brutal. Her leaving him after less than two months hurt so bad. During this period, he stayed over at her place as much as he could. Although neither of them talked about it much, he couldn't stop thinking of their inevitable separation.

"You knew she'd be going back to California," he told himself. "But, shit, why so soon?"

It was all he could think about. When he got written up for calling in sick and missing too many days of work, he didn't care too much. It was a jale, as Alberto always said it was. And these days he was being pulled in only one direction: west = California = Elena. Nothing about collecting carts, doing go-backs, not even chasing down shoplifters mattered.

He was in love. If not for the first time, never in this way. When she tried to get him to talk, like right before they fell asleep, lying next to each other, not touching, he tried to play off his sadness and confusion.

"It's no big deal. I know we'll stay in touch," he offered with his back to her.

"Yeah, but it doesn't have to totally suck, you know," she said and held him.

"Yeah, I know, but it does. Nothing I can do about it, right?"

"Well, you can come with me."

"I don't know. What would I do?"

"There's all kinds of things to do in Berkeley."

"I mean for money and stuff."

"There's a grocery store not too far from the apartment I'll be renting."

"Yeah. Maybe . . . but you already have two roommates."

"They'll understand. Maybe we can find our own place."

"Lots of maybes. Anyways, I'd be messing up your plans."

She got him to face her and held him tighter. Her torso molded perfectly next to his, her thighs wedged their way into his hip. When he felt himself getting hard, he forced himself to focus on what she was saying.

"What do you want, Raul Luis?" Her tone was sincere, emphasized by his two names said apart.

"I don't know." His tone was pure sadness.

"Do you want to stay? Do you want to go?"

"I'm stuck . . ."

"Here?"

"No, somewhere between staying and going. I don't know . . . I don't know anything else than living here."

"But do you like being here? Do you still think you're drowning?"

"Yeah, some days it feels that way. But it also feels safe, you know. Like I have a place here."

"Well, how are you supposed to grow if you don't leave?"

"What do you mean?"

"Roots are supposed to help us branch out, right?"

"That sounds cool."

"Well, come with me then. Do it. Don't be afraid."

"It's not that I'm afraid . . . more like I'm still trying to figure things out . . . understand what got left behind . . . stuff that's buried."

"I'm not sure what to say. You need to decide for yourself. No one but you should make your choice."

Even after he felt her roll over and fall asleep, he stayed awake for a few hours thinking. Everything she said or asked made sense. She seemed to know exactly what was going through his head and his heart. And this made it even harder for him to decide what to do. Time was running out.

One thing he was able to decide was that he didn't want to see her off. He'd watched enough scenes on TV and in the movies to know that good-byes were either real tearjerkers or half-ass hopeful. He didn't want to experience either of these when she left for good.

On one of their last dates, they went to a concert across the state line in New Mexico. He'd bought the tickets when she told him one of her favorite bands was coming to the area. While he'd been to concerts before with Pancho and a few with Alberto, this was the first one he'd taken a date to. He never thought of the rock shows at the El Paso County Coliseum as a place to go with a girl, much less a girlfriend. The women there never seemed his type—too tough and pretty gross. Alberto did prefer the tattoo-and-leather type. Elena was definitely not a rocker chick.

Tonight's concert was more of a performance than a spectacle. He couldn't even tell it was in a basketball arena by the way they'd set up the stage. With the spotlights mostly on the lead singer, it felt as if he, the guitar player, keyboardist, and drummer were the only ones that mattered. As if the thousands of people in the audience were incidental.

During previous hard rock concerts that he'd been to, there were so many moments when he'd forget where he was and think the music was playing live inside his head. The coliseum, a venue better suited for circuses and rodeos, had terrible acoustics. The distorted sounds of blaring guitars and thumping bass attacked him from all sides. Tonight's New Wave band, one Elena had turned him on to, played spacey keyboard music that crept through his skin, all his senses bathing in the lingering melodies.

On his feet for almost the whole concert, he even caught himself dancing a few times. He didn't worry about what any of his limbs might be doing. And Elena didn't seem to mind either as she moved easily in the space next to him.

Their shared rhythms were among the many reasons he felt he loved her. He would miss having her next to him, and he felt unsure of what might happen once he was alone again.

On the drive back home from their concert date, his thoughts alive and kicking, he kept his foot steady on the gas pedal. He was the only one awake, so he had the stereo controls all to himself. The cassette deck played one of Elena's mix tapes: "Fave Songs::El Paso Summer."

His girlfriend's body was turned away from him, her legs pulled up on the passenger seat and her head buried against the window. Even if he hadn't been driving her car, he wouldn't have been able to sleep. Too much to think about. The unlit road ahead seemed like an extension of the darkness back inside the basketball arena. With the headlights lighting up only a few yards ahead, he felt like they were drifting through a river, a straight one, not the curvy Río Grande. Outside every window, there was only black. Nothing to recognize or identify in the desert landscape.

As he ejected the tape to flip it over, he heard Elena's steady breathing in the silence of the car. All those lonely times in his bedroom, mostly in the new house, he couldn't have imagined this feeling. He was tempted to let go of the steering wheel to see if (as silly as it seemed) the force of his love for Elena would carry them back across the state line. He'd thought of suggesting that they stay in a hotel after the concert, but he knew she had a community project in the morning. If it wasn't the final one, he would've tried to change her mind.

A few miles before the next exit, he did his best to keep from feeling miserable on such a great night. He wanted to hold on to the excitement of the concert and think about how it would find its way into his Big Chief Map Book. For sure, he would keep the ticket stub and the wristband they gave them for their seating section. Maybe Elena could help him write down the names of the songs the band had played. While he wasn't good with titles and always messed up the lyrics, he was developing an emotional connection to the music that Elena had brought into his life.

Her tastes were becoming his own, from music to food, waking up earlier, sleeping on his side, even stuff like reading. On the long drive to the concert, she'd read him a few pages from the book she was currently reading. Some story about a man who travels in a boat down a jungle river, lost and paranoid about what awaits him. The descriptions sounded more like they were inside the character's head than anything about the setting. Strange, but cool, especially the way Elena read it.

He had plenty of vivid moments from their time together to push aside the thought of her departure. But no matter what memory he queued up, there it was: She was leaving. He'd done everything he could to keep it from coming up tonight before the concert. She must've sensed that he didn't want to go into it, so they avoided talking about it. They also made up games to play on the drive up and listened to songs from every cassette in her case. The trip to the concert passed too quickly.

And when a road sign emerged on the highway, he thought he might be able to make it last longer. The next exit would take him in the direction of California. Of all the times that he had imagined driving that far west, he never considered that it could be for a girl. The idea first came to him watching TV when Richie and the Fonz had gone to Hollywood to become movie stars. Ruly and Laura figured if the gang from *Happy Days* made it out there then why couldn't they do it? He remembered that they'd asked his mother if they had any family in California, figuring that that would be another reason to go. When she mentioned cousins that he'd never met, even one who was his exact same age, he thought about it for a long time.

Now that Elena would be returning to the Golden State (a nickname he'd learned from *Big Blue Marble*), a familiar sadness surfaced inside him. A yearning that wouldn't drown. The dark space of the highway he drove on made the depressing emotions heavier. He turned the brights on to see more of the road ahead. He tried to count the hash marks as he drove over them to occupy his bleary thoughts. With each yawn, the energy of the concert wore off, and he started to feel stiffness in his back and calves. A long sip of a watered-down soda did little to fuel his energy or lubricate his irritated eyes.

This road trip was helping him learn an important lesson: He was good at distances from a distance. It was everything in between, the miles, the choices, the relationships, the here and the there, that gave him trouble.

Point A <————————————————> Point B.

One of the few things he never forgot a teacher saying was, "The shortest distance between two points is a straight line." While he usually accepted everything said in class as true, it now seemed that there were too many variables to consider—side roads, damn detours, rest stops.

When he was little, before they left Lomaland for good, Dad would get them all in the car and take them on what he proudly called "Vacations." Ruly grew to dislike these family trips that didn't go anywhere near Disneyland, which his classmates wrote about on the first day of school after summer vacation, or the Grand Canyon, where the Brady family went on one of his favorite episodes.

The worst part of these so-called vacations was that Dad couldn't resist pulling over while driving through towns with boring names like Lordsburg, Raton, Van Horn. Not glamorous like San Bernardino, Orange County, Beverly Hills. Although he, as well as Pancho and Laura, welcomed any opportunity to stretch their legs, they never stopped at the one place they always wanted to see.

Mile after mile, the billboards appeared outside their car's windows along with endless desert. Each set of bright red letters on an even brighter yellow background revealed just how close they were.

THE THING?

Pointing.

MYSTERY OF THE DESERT

Urging.

5 MILES TIL THE THING?

Heart beating fast.

4 MILES TIL THE THING?

Bodies shifting & shifting.

3 MILES TIL THE THING?

Mouths salivating.

2 MILES TIL THE THING?

Hands gripping door handle.

1 MILE TIL THE THING?

Pulling up door lock.

½ MILE TIL THE THING?

Rolling down window.

¼ MILE TIL THE THING?

Leaning back in seat.

THE THING? NEXT EXIT.

Swallowing disappointment.

Ruly, Pancho, and Laura slumped back in their seat and watched the yellow trailer with THE THING? written on it in bloodred letters out the back window as Dad steered straight ahead. While Ruly did think Dad was a good driver, one that could handle flat tires, nearly empty gas tanks, and old windshield wipers, he didn't understand why Dad chose to stop at those stupid historical markers along state roads. The bland wood and faded black print announced how boring they were and kept Ruly from ever reading them, like many of the assigned pages in his social studies books. He figured if The Thing? had had something to do with Cabeza de Vaca or Pancho Villa or Geronimo (a trinity of names Dad reported when he got back in the car after reading the marker more than once) then Dad might have found it worth stopping for.

A decade and more past Dad's vacations, driving back from the concert in Las Cruces, New Mexico, each time he crossed over into the other lane, he jerked the steering wheel back to his side. He went ahead and cracked his window to allow some cold air in, closing his mouth and inhaling through his nose. His lungs filled up and seemed to awaken.

He glanced at the gas needle and saw that he would have to make a pit stop. Although he wanted this night to go on forever, the last thing he wanted, as the guide of his first journey across state lines, was to get stuck out in the middle of nowhere. Dad would never let him live that down.

As if on cue, he spotted the lights of the next gas station. The voice inside his head told him that they'd make it okay. He took one hand off the wheel, lowered the stereo's volume, and peeked over at Elena. "Why do you have to leave?" he asked before he placed his hand on her shoulder, letting her know that they were pulling off the interstate. She shifted and placed her hand on his as she slowly began to wake up.

On their last day together, he tried to act as if it was just another morning. He went out and picked up some breakfast taquitos and orange juices at the Whataburger drive-thru. At an intersection, he bought the newspaper. Without even looking at the day's headlines, he knew that today's date would always be an important one. The songs coming from Elena's "Bitchin' Mix Tape" left him feeling a little upbeat. Driving back to her place didn't seem so dramatic after he completed this familiar routine.

After eating and reading through the paper together, which he promised to continue doing on his own, they decided to take a short walk before she had to hit the road. From her place, they followed a walking trail to the mountains surrounding the university campus. Other evenings, they'd come out here to be alone, find an isolated spot, and make out like crazy.

Today, they didn't even hold hands. A distance had presented itself that he didn't know how to negotiate. His emotions were unmapped. With a lump in his throat, he was relieved when she finally said something.

"So, this is it, huh?"

"Yep."

"I'm gonna write, so you better."

"Can they be postcards? I'm good at those."

"Sure, but a letter, even a short one, now and then, would be cool."

"Okay, no problemo. I better start now, since I'm a slow writer."

"Good deal."

A period of silence accompanied them while they walked up a trail on the mountain.

From their high vantage point, he watched a parade of cars and trucks moving steadily along I-10, traveling east and west. Beyond the traffic, some kids were playing in the shallow Río in front of cardboard and scrap wood shacks that dotted the Juárez hillside.

In the foreground, off to the right, on this side, the ever-present ASARCO smokestack stood like a misplaced beacon that welcomed everyone driving in on I-10 from the west. Faded white letters ran vertically down the side. AS__CO. The four out of six letters that were most visible spelled a Spanish word that summed up the awful taste in his mouth.

Looming above these boundaries, Cristo Rey watched from his cross on the mountain. *Cielo Voice.* His arms pointed in opposite directions. It was hard not to think of sides from this spot on the mountain.

Should I stay? Should I go? Or is there a third option?

"What are you thinking?" he asked Elena, who was also looking out at the border between there and here for probably the last time.

"Why?" she asked.

"You have that look on your face."

"I love— I love that you know me so well. I know it's not fair, but I want to know why you won't come."

"To California?"

"Yes, why can't you leave El Paso?"

While he'd managed to keep his emotions in check in this final hour, saving snotty tears for later, he hesitated for a long while before he answered her question.

Even on such a big occasion, so much on the line, one word would have to do: "Cuz."

Her expression showed that she accepted his curt answer even if her body language said she didn't completely understand.

She hugged him tighter than he held her. He kissed her from her lips to her neck to her shoulders.

Before he let go,

need to breathe

reach for surface

wait on rescue

he embraced the moment as another lesson in drowning.

C

cuz

z

1 Most nights, their bodies formed a lowercase *t*. He, the vertical line, she the horizontal. Tonight, they were lined up more like a crucifix. Her stomach bulged where they crossed each other's torsos. Even if he'd wanted to get up, drowsy after another night of binging on TV reruns and chicharones, he wouldn't have been able to lift her.

He didn't know how much she'd weighed at her last doctor's visit, but he knew from carrying around as big a panza most of his life that she was really heavy. In their fleshy cross, he dozed off as his breathing matched hers. Their stomachs rose and fell in sync.

The dreams had been getting vaguer every night they shared a bed. While at first they always involved people he knew or situations from TV movies of the week, the most recent dreams had become ordinary situations filled with the faces of strangers.

In their latest incarnations, the cousins are in line at BigWay Foods. They're standing next to each other, not saying much, stepping forward with the rest of the line. And while there isn't much else going on, he isn't totally bored.

Laura is always reading in his dreams. Never books. Fashion magazines, *TV Guide,* even those horoscope booklets found in the checkout aisles.

"Why aren't we getting closer to the front of the line?" he says and nudges his cousin in his dream. Everything about her is the same as the girl who slept in the next room the summer he left Lomaland for good. "Where are all the people coming from?"

"Wait, I'm reading. Can't you see?"

"I'm standing here, of course, I can see. But I have to go . . ."

"Always in a hurry. There's a line, Cuz, hold your horses."

"You know I'm allergic."

"Real funny. It'll pick up, give it a sec."

In the dream, while his cousin's words do little to comfort him, her tone, the casual manner of her voice, leaves him with a strong sense of being in the right place. Whether or not he knows where he is, being with Laura always feels like sharing the same oxygen.

He remained still for a long period in between being asleep and being awake. Trusting that together they'd take care of each other, he didn't worry about who was the "mamá," "father," "mijo/mija." Those labels common in Mexican-American families like theirs seemed dated, not good enough for who Cuz and Cuz had grown up to be. Who they were now. We don't need our family, they agreed in not so many words. We're making a new one.

On this night, after he finally rolled out from under Laura, he found his way to the toilet and sat for a good while. He felt he needed to pee for at least two people as he fought to stay awake, not shut his eyes.

The last few weeks seemed to be as hazy as this moment.

Although he was beginning to recognize the stay-go pattern in his relationships, especially with women, he still hadn't developed the emotions to understand the connections between presence and absence. So, in a strange way, it made sense for Laura to reappear not long after Elena left El Paso for good. Like if, maybe, they were the same woman but in different skins. He pushed this out of his head as soon as he thought it. They were nothing alike, really. Only his profound love for both of them came close to comparison.

In the rush of welcoming Laura back to this side of the border and helping her move into an apartment, he hadn't had a chance to share too many details about his summer love. (He liked the sound of that, like a song title from the sixties or something. "Summer Love.")

Laura's pregnancy overshadowed any emotions he was dealing with. Cuz needed him, nothing else ever mattered. As their special bond allowed, they easily navigated the distance caused by her migrations south/north of the border.

And while she hadn't shared too much of what had happened since she'd crossed over, he knew she'd tell him when she needed to. So, in the interim, he tried to map her journey from pieces of conversation. Their interactions with family members at this time were few, so that didn't offer much. On the phone with old friends, she mostly joked and didn't reveal anything he hadn't already suspected.

Maybe that's why he started staying over at her apartment when she returned. To gather information. From all his work on his different Map Books, he'd become good at pasting together collages of facts and memories and gossip.

Unlike the summer when he learned how to drown, all these years later he was the one playing the role of houseguest (like they sometimes did on sitcoms when they wanted to introduce a new character. Chachi came to mind.) One thing was for certain in his TV-like life: if Laura was going to reveal anything—especially who the father of her baby was—he was the person she trusted most.

Back in the apartment's only bed, he took the accustomed position—on the left side, face to the wall, back to Laura. They'd fallen into this arrangement as quickly as they'd accepted it when she'd stayed over at the new house that summer. On those nights, his cousin had snuck into Ruly's room and crawled into his bed while he slept. Since she would sneak out before he woke up, he was always unsure whether she had been part of a dream.

From the first nights as adults sharing a bed, he got better at separating reality from dreams. And if there was any chance for confusion, the size of her body made sure that he knew it was there.

Right arm came first. Over his chest, tucked into his neck. Left thigh next. Under his waist, pushed up to his back. Her belly completed her sleep-hold on him. Roundness left its impression down the middle of his body. Her breasts cushioned themselves against his shoulder blades. All of it felt like he was being fitted for an extra skin, a sweet-smelling one that had been tailored. They seemed locked in this position for the remainder of her pregnancy. Although he wanted to know if it was a boy or a girl, she wanted to be surprised. "It's like opening presents before Christmas morning. You know how I am."

Even on the hottest of nights, Cuz crawled in behind Cuz. The double bed was barely big enough for his belly, and hers only made the one-bedroom apartment that much more intimate. He knew that if anyone, especially some-one in the family, saw them this way that they wouldn't understand. ¿Qué van a decir?/What will people think? In English/Spanish, they both expressed embarrassment.

But he knew there was nothing sexual about their relationship. No longer a virgin but now an experienced sexual partner, he knew their intimacy was totally different than what he'd experienced with Elena.

Even when Laura's nipples poked him, he didn't get excited. In fact, the first time he felt the moist bumps on his back, he thought of Dr. Goldfarb's instruments, not of some centerfold's breasts. Taking an unplanned break from sex seemed natural after the passionate summer with Elena. In fact, what he most enjoyed about sharing a bed with Cuz was that she would always pull him back into the innocent spaces of their child selves.

One night, she got them talking about Chicken Sundays. He hadn't thought about that family tradition in years. While his memories of Sundays were mostly about church and eating menudo or gorditas after Mass, he was struck by how much he remembered about Chicken Sundays.

Shortly after they moved from Lomaland to the new house, his family began going to the Caravan Bar and Grill on Sundays. (It also helped that they stopped going to Cristo Rey Church then, too.) He remembered Dad driving up Lee Treviño, getting on I-10 and rather than turning up toward Montana, like they did when they went to the Cinema Park Drive-in, Dad took the Zaragoza Exit.

As Ruly and Laura remembered the drives from the Lower Valley to the Caravan, they both agreed that much was changing in their side of El Paso. Widened roads, renamed streets, so many stores in a new shopping center. Everything was now closer in terms of miles, it seemed, but many memories were being pushed beyond the boundaries of their experiences. *If the desert completely disappears, where will our pasts be buried?* he wondered more than once.

He knew that any story that involved fried food would keep Laura quiet enough for her to fall asleep. He relied on the virtual pages of his Map Book to reconstruct those Sunday afternoons when he'd dress up like a cowboy. Boot-cut jeans. Pearl-button shirt. Bolo tie. Tony Lama boots.

The Caravan's dining area was all paneled walls and the bar was all mirrors. "Do you remember the fuzzy red carpet?" he asked Laura. She did.

While his cousin and brother rushed the buffet line, he preferred to stay behind with Dad and watch him flirt with the waitresses. He didn't even consider if his mother minded. She seemed happy to enjoy her one day off. Her new position as warehouse supervisor had made it possible for the family to afford Chicken Sundays, he figured. All those beers and piña coladas his parents ordered weren't cheap. The tips Dad gave were also generous.

"Remember how me and Pancho used to chug the free Coke refills?" Her voice began to slip into sleep. "We must've had six or seven."

Once they had a contest of who could drink the most glasses of soda between plates of fried chicken, corn on the cob, pork and beans, and potato salad. Pancho drank at least ten. Ruly and Laura tied at seven and a half. He remembered his stomach got so big that he had to undo his cowboy belt buckle, polished silver with a copper horse in its center. The buckle was one Dad had given him for his birthday with a western belt, RULY etched on the back.

"Hey, Cuz, do you remember when everyone started calling me that?" He nudged her and watched drool forming around the corner of her mouth. "You asleep?"

She grumbled some answer, but all he could make out was her slurring "Ruuuulllyyyyy."

In all the times they went to the Caravan, he never danced. "Do you still like to country dance?" he asked, not expecting her to answer. Her heavy breathing would border on snoring in a few minutes.

Lying awake in the dark, he remembered that she and Pancho used to go out for the bunny hop and sometimes the two-step.

"What was that song you guys liked? Amarillo something. . . . Amarillo Dawn . . . Amarillo Afternoon . . . by Morning. Yeah, you had the singer's poster up before you replaced it with Michael Jackson's."

She shifted her body as if to let him know she was still listening. His Celtics XL T-shirt that she'd made her own rode up her back and revealed stretch marks. They reminded him of the patterns he had studied in Lomaland's desert. Waves rolling across the sand.

"Remember how my folks used to act all silly and everything on the dance floor?" he continued. "Moving in and out of the other couples."

Once he knew by her breathing that she was asleep, the last thing he thought of was how his parents must have really loved each other back then. And he figured that holding a woman so close means you love her more than if you are a good dancer or not.

Before he could begin thinking about the few dances he'd shared with any of his girlfriends, he felt Cuz turn over, pushing him against the night table. The ashtray full of change and keys spilled on the floor. He hoped the noise would wake her up, so he could move, but he was the only one still consciously thinking of Chicken Sundays.

Minutes later, he slipped out of bed and headed to the kitchen with slim hopes that there were any leftovers. Laura usually devoured them before going to bed. He found some hardened corn tortillas and cheese. Instinctively, he reached for his comal, but it sat unused at Chewie's Casita. If he stayed at Laura's any longer, he'd have to go get it.

While he waited for a regular pan to heat up, he felt the thickest memory of all on his tongue. Maraschino cherries. Juicy, cough-drop-size cherries that the Caravan waitress would put in his soda. He wondered if the cute waitress had done this for Dad or his brother but preferred to think that he was the only one who got this treat. He remembered he'd wait till he was done with his soda before he poked the straw into the super-sweet cherry and pulled it out. Like putting his tongue out for the Eucharist at Mass, he would lay the fleshy fruit on his tongue and suck out all its juice before he chewed.

Tearing through a decent quesadilla, he knew that tomorrow he and Laura would go get some fried chicken. She liked Church's while he preferred Kentucky Fried Chicken. Whichever they decided on would be okay. The side dishes would also be agreed upon, gravy mandatory for both of their large appetites. What he wasn't sure about was how he would explain stopping by BigWay to buy maraschino cherries (Aisle #10? Aisle #11?).

2

Even after having attended two times a week for more than a month, he still couldn't believe what he was doing.

Each time that he walked back into Ysleta High's gym he knew that this wasn't what he'd had in mind back in high school. And even if he laced up some high-tops and had a basketball to shoot, there wouldn't be any points added to the home team score. The main lights and colorful scoreboard weren't even turned on, one of his former duties as Team Manager.

He was able to take pride in the simple fact that he was standing courtside on the polished-wood floor. Mighty under headdress of feathers, the profile of the Indian at midcourt still gave him goose bumps. If he closed his eyes and concentrated, he might be able to hear the all-girl drum corps playing the fight song. "All Hail, All Hail to Ysleta." And, of course, the arousal of cheerleaders— pom-poms, perky breasts, maroon bloomers.

Instead, in the dimly lit area behind the bleachers, all he heard was the echo of a group of pregnant women breathing over and over again. Their inhaling and exhaling as familiar as bouncing balls.

"C'mon, Cuz, breathe—breathe . . . ," he said as one of the "coaches" urging his partner on. "You can do it."

"Go Indians, go," he added to see if his cousin was actually listening.

When he felt her elbow jab him in the stomach, he knew that she was indeed focused on his voice. He muffled a laugh and continued repeating the lines he'd practiced over and over: "Breathe . . . Relax . . . Breathe . . . Rest . . ."

He let his mind wander high into the rafters, and if he tried real hard, he could almost hear applause trapped in the gym. It didn't seem that long since he'd handed water and towels to the varsity B-ballers. And when he gave Cuz her water bottle covered in Minnie Mouse stickers, he realized that not much had changed since his graduation. Still Team Manager. Except now he was solely responsible to a mother and her baby. A team of three.

Over the period of attending birthing classes, he'd given up trying to make the other couples understand that he wasn't the father, much less that he and Laura weren't husband and wife. And while he still didn't miss attending school, Laura had become the dedicated pupil. He smiled every time her hand went up to answer the instructor's questions, mostly rhetorical. The female instructor welcomed the exchanges and always gave a positive response.

"Yes, you're right, Laura, it's important that you get plenty of rest."

"Of course, you need a dedicated coach."

"A baby is definitely a blessing."

Laura held her head up higher every time she came closer to being the teacher's pet. He would've bet against anyone if they'd said Laura would be good at anything that required studying. Like him, she'd always seemed to learn more from TV than from a school subject.

He guessed that was part of what brought them back together at this point in their lives. Laura was pregnant. And he was the closest thing she had to a husband-father. If someone were to ask him why he was doing this, he'd say, "Cuz." They would either understand or not. Their problem, the cousins agreed without saying it.

At their last class, he'd heard from someone in the expecting parents group that men developed cravings when their wives were pregnant, but he thought it was all bullshit. While Cuz pigged out on pork rinds, cranberry juice, chile-coated pecans, and Chico's Tacos, he practically ran out of the room when she went on one of her binges. He'd resigned himself to cleaning up after her, but what he wasn't doing was cleaning *her* up. No way. He didn't go near her slobbering self. The crumbs and who knows what else that clung to her oversized T-shirts and sweatshirts were super gross. It wasn't until he armed himself with a Dustbuster and a variety of sponges that he felt okay about mothering Laura.

Cousin or no cousin, he still had to get used to spending so much time with a woman, a pregnant one no less. He'd never officially lived with Elena at her summer place, but they might as well have. The last few weeks that they were together, he'd pretty much crashed there more often than not.

Now that he was without a girlfriend again, he didn't want to think about the past too much or worry about meeting someone new, so he focused on his cousin's needs.

Week 1—Tomato Seed

Week 2—Prune

Week 3—Lime

Week 4—Peach

As the weeks of Laura's pregnancy added up like the different fruits the birthing class instructor referenced for the baby's size, it seemed that she couldn't get enough schooling. The instructor suggested that Laura register for some other parenting classes. Only after she bribed Cuz with fried burritos and root beer floats did he agree to go with her to the local community college.

Since he hadn't followed through with his idea to begin taking college classes, he didn't want to revisit his decision. Or lack of. Some thought he should definitely go to school: Elena, Dad, even Laura. While others felt that he should continue working full-time: his mother, the guys at BigWay, probably Alberto.

Truth was that he was stuck in the middle. Again. The too-familiar feeling of being between expectation and resignation. Really, he'd told Elena in their last phone conversation, he did miss school—the routine, the learning, the snack bar—but he didn't miss homework or boring teachers talking all the time.

"You want to grow, don't you?" Elena had asked him.

"Naw, I've never liked being the gordito of the family." He hoped she still thought of him as funny.

"I'm serious. No kidding about your future."

He wanted to tell her that she sometimes sounded *too much* like a parent or a supervisor.

"Yeah, I guess," he said instead. "How hard can it be?"

In that conversation a few weeks back, she'd listed her university classes and the kind of assignments she had due. All sounded hard to him. But the kind of classes you take at a community college can't be as hard, right? He said this to himself as he wandered the Student Services Building at Valle Verde, the college's main campus in Lower Valley El Paso.

While Laura waited to talk to a woman behind a desk, he peeked into different windows of the administrative offices. He was leafing through a schedule of classes for next semester when an older man asked if he needed help. Surprised that he was the one being asked, he remembered sending in some paperwork but he didn't know what came of it. For all he knew, some more forms waited at his parents' house. Since becoming Laura's surrogate partner, he hadn't gone over too much.

The older man directed him upstairs to check at Window #5. A helpful lady took his Social Security number and said he was enrolled as a probationary student. He pretty much understood what that meant before the woman's long explanation of what he had to do to be fully registered.

After updating his address—Chewie's Casita would do for now—he met with an admissions counselor. She explained the differences of part-time versus full-time, what possible majors he could choose, and the basics that were required. He politely nodded when she asked if he understood.

In no time at all, like when he was first catching on as Ysleta's Team Manager or as a BigWay employee, he was almost an officially registered student for the upcoming semester. When he looked over the printout she gave him, he saw that the price for taking five classes was about two weeks' pay. When the counselor also mentioned budgeting for books, maybe lab supplies, parking fees, he almost changed his mind. But she suggested he go talk to the financial aid office.

He was about to put it off and go find Laura, who was probably looking for him, when he saw a familiar female face from the High. He might've pretended not to see her, but the toy truck at his feet cornered him.

"Sorry, he's— Hey, Ruly, long time. How are you?" Before he could answer, he allowed himself to be hugged.

Looking down at a small boy, she said, "C'mon, get up. Sorry—he's bored."

"No, no problem." In a few quick moments, he took the image of a varsity cheerleader and spliced it with this young mother. Debra Bejarano, Ysleta Indian varsity squad co-captain.

"Is he your son?"

"Yeah, one of them. Mijo, say hi." The boy held on to his troquita and crowded next to his mom.

"He's cute. Likes trucks, huh?"

"Yeah, he can be a travieso but not as bad as his older brother."

As he and Debra waited in the financial aid line, he learned that she was in her fifth semester at EPCC. She was studying to be a Sign Language teacher. He was surprisingly honest and told her he wasn't sure about coming to school. And he didn't mind working more than forty hours at BigWay.

Unlike Elena, Debra seemed to understand his indecisiveness about taking college classes. She had also spent most of her time working since graduating from the High, up to three jobs at a time. After her first baby, she quit working, she told him, got married, and depended on her husband (some older guy from Phoenix) to support her.

And while Debra didn't give too many details about what had happened from that point to the present, he figured a second baby and a divorce brought her back to school.

Although Debra was older, he felt she talked to him as someone on her level. And it didn't hurt that she was still attractive. Even with a few more pounds than he remembered from watching her cheer at Ysleta's Hutchins Stadium. When she bent over to pick up some papers she dropped, he got a good look at her butt. More high school cheerleader than single mother of two.

He sensed a rare opportunity to ask her out, but was interrupted by a familiar voice.

"Dee? Hey, girl. Check you out."

Laura went right past him and hugged her old high school friend.

"Laura. I didn't have a chance to ask Ruly. We were—"

His cousin turned to him and slapped his arm. "Hey, I've been waiting downstairs forever."

"Sorry. We were just catching up. My fault." Debra said and smiled in his direction as she bailed him out.

At this same time, he saw that Debra's son was making his way over to another section of the administrative building. When he sensed that Laura and Debra were too caught up to notice more than each other—especially after Laura's big belly took center stage—he raced over to the curious child.

By the time he reached the boy, he had to act quickly. Like Spider-Man, the boy had crawled up a short wall and was sneaking into an office. As the only adult paying attention, he felt compelled to jump into action. With one arm, he reached out for the boy. His other free arm, hand stretched, palm out, caught the boy's desired object, a desk globe, not too different from the one Ruly's tía gave him (which must still be in his old bedroom). Rather than try to talk the travieso into returning the globe to the desk, he carried the boy and his trophy back to his mother. The boy was heavier than he looked and his hair smelled like potato chips.

In the steps it took to get back to where Debra and Laura were last talking, he imagined that his daring rescue would do well to maybe get him a date or at least a phone number.

"I saved your niño" was a good pickup line if he'd ever heard one. Better than "You still have great legs. Wanna go to the movies?"

"Oh, my God, ay, what did you do?" Debra rushed over to them.

He was about to answer her question when the globe fell out of the boy's hold and rolled across the floor. Like a bowling ball, it picked up speed and headed for the stairs. He handed the boy to his mother and chased the globe. This moment seemed like something out of a movie. More *Meatballs* than *Raiders of the Lost Ark*. None of the people sitting behind desks seemed to notice his starring role in this matinee.

By the time he returned the globe back to the office where it belonged, he was bummed to learn that Debra had left. Laura said they were late for a doctor's appointment or something.

As he and his cousin finished up at the financial aid office, they didn't say much about seeing someone from their high school years. At least this time they were glad it wasn't someone they'd rather avoid. You couldn't go too many places in the Lower Valley without a spontaneous YHS reunion. *Once an Indian, Always an Indian.*

On the drive back to Laura's, they picked up fried-food baskets at the Dairy Queen drive-thru. They remembered when Laura used to work at the one on Zaragoza Road, how her supervisor hit on her all the time. She started to share that she had gone on a date with the older guy, but she abruptly ended the story by stuffing onion rings in her mouth. She swallowed them down with a large gulp of a chocolate milk shake.

He was going to bring up the kind of men she used to date, maybe get closer to learning something about the baby's father, but he let her change the subject back to something that mattered more at the moment.

"Dee said you looked good."

"What? . . . No, you're lying."

"Naw, Cuz, she asked me about you."

"Like what?"

"I don't know, stuff we ask about guys when we want to know."

He was having a hard time paying attention to the road and was tempted to pull over. By taking the side roads, little traffic, few stops, he was able to stay involved in this important question-answer.

"What? Does . . . you know, does she like me?"

"Ahhhhhhh, how cute. 'Does she like me?' You've always been so cariñoso. Remember—"

"Just tell me what she said."

Laura put more onion rings in her mouth, reached in her pocket, and handed him a note from Debra. With one eye on the road and the other on the scratch paper, he got a feeling in his stomach, near the bottom, between his belly button and crotch. While he knew he would stress out about what to say, when to call, how to act, he held on to the excitement of a former cheerleader practically asking him out.

3

Eyes closed. Bedspread tossed off.
Head on fluffy pillow, thin pillow between legs.
Fidgeting.
Twisting.
Squirming.

When he had trouble sleeping, he tired himself out by going over the blueprint of his first home. The rough mental sketches began appearing after his family left Lomaland for good and continued for months in the new house.

The images behind his eyelids would've seemed drawn by his hand except that he couldn't draw for nothing. And his blueprint of the two-bedrooms-one-bath house was almost all straight lines. With each step he traced in his head, he appreciated how the house in Lomaland grew out of a desert canvas, exposing itself room by room, brick by brick.

Taking about sixteen steps from the street to the side door, pausing, pulling on the screen—that was the one constant in each mental journey. There was a front door and a back door and many windows, but it only made sense for him to use the side door. He was always tempted to knock, although he was certain the house was empty.

In the moments when he was awake and asleep, the Lomaland house held shapes and memories if not furniture. When his subconscious allowed entrance to his first home, he took his time in the living room, where more memories with family existed than in all the home movies he'd ever watched. The main room of the house's interior was the biggest and gave him the most to survey. Often, he'd be asleep before he even finished looking over this one room and before he stepped into any other space in the house. Especially if he was inexplicably drawn to any of the objects in the room, like the electric heater. The white metal appliance in one corner of la sala hummed its presence. No one else ever seemed to notice the noise it made. He also remembered a TV and stereo in this room, but it didn't surprise him that the heater's distinct rhythms played only in his ears. Many times, like when his parents argued, he squeezed his body between the couch and the heater. Cuddled by the heater's own heartbeat, he would often doze off. Pancho would come wake him and take him back to their bedroom.

He remembered that the hallway nearest the heater led to the bedrooms and the doorway on the opposite side led to the kitchen. Whichever direction he chose to follow in his first house was like passing through a curtain of memories, more undeveloped images than tangible ones.

Exclusive viewings of his mental maps revealed fuzzy events that played more like music than home movies. Mariachi songs from scratchy records. Ancient sounds coming from instruments as old as relatives in faded sepia photos. Watery syllables of their native language that had brought them over to this side from Mexican pueblitos (names he always meant to write down).

"Where are we from?" he asked often, especially during the holidays when more than one distant relative showed up at a get-together. He thought it was somewhat odd that he never really heard his parents' generation talk about where their parents' generation came from. All he was sure of was that he, Pancho, Laura, and the rest of their cousins weren't the first ones to learn and recite the Pledge of Allegiance.

On a rare night off from working at BigWay, his self-guided tour of his home in Lomaland didn't bring sleep. He crawled out from under Cuz and went into the apartment's front room (more of a TV room than a living room). Pushing the buttons on the cable box, he found mostly static filling the screen. When he did get a channel, it was some dumb news show or a long commercial. At the end of the second row of buttons, his luck changed.

Familiar characters in western clothes and cowboy hats and sounding like vaqueros took their place on the TV screen. He pulled up a beanbag and lowered the volume to where he could still hear it. Cuz was always a light sleeper, and in her last three months of pregnancy, she seemed to be even more sensitive to sounds, from crunching to farting.

Through two segments with commercial breaks, he followed the drama of *The High Chaparral*. As in other episodes, Blue Boy was in some kind of serious trouble. And of course, Manolito and Buck had to come to his rescue. He wondered if he had seen this one before as the beanbag took shape around his body. The muted light of the TV sometimes induced sleep. Just as his eyelids were beginning to remain closed, he felt Cuz come into the room before she planted herself in front of the TV. He leaned forward and rubbed his eyes. Light from the bedroom brightened up the space around Cuz, as if her pregnancy gave off light.

"Your dad a glassmaker?" he asked out of habit.

"No, you know he's a car salesman, menso," she answered as usual.

"C'mon, I'm watching this."

Manolito was about to lose his temper in a bar and let the local cowhands know that he meant business. From years of TV watching, he could have guessed what was about to happen, but he was still excited about the consequences of Manolito's temper laced with his charm.

He listened to the dialogue of the TV western while Cuz stood her fat ground and started some litany about being "Hungry, oh, Cuz, so hungry." Annoyed that her body was taking up more and more space in the apartment, he tried to concentrate on the smashing of chairs, bashing of beer bottles, and of course, the crashing of a chandelier. Leaning to one side, he witnessed Manolito give one of his victorious gritos and run upstairs with a señorita from the cantina.

"All right, goddamn it, but you gotta go with me." He climbed out of the beanbag and went to put on some sneakers and his pitchfork cap.

He knew the Chico's on McRae was still an all-night high school hangout, although he hadn't been there in some time. Especially not during the weekends. He liked to think that he had too much going to mix in cruising the local hangouts like he used to in Chewie's Cheby with the guys. No time for partying.

With all the vehicles lined up around Chico's, he predicted that all the booths inside were full as well. He suggested that they should go somewhere else. Cuz said she wanted Chico's. Hinting that they could go to another Chico's Tacos location, Montana Avenue or Washington Park, even the Northeast one, he was surprised that she said it wasn't the same. "How can it not be the same?" he asked. "They are the same. Chico's is Chico's." When she started rubbing her belly and giving him her latest "I'm going to be a mommy" face, he made his way around to the back of the building and parked BEBBA half on/half off the curb. The new 4x4-sized tires he'd bought for it were good in tricky situations. He'd use some money from next month's check for new upholstery.

A crowd of teenagers from Lower Valley high schools, as revealed by their letterman jackets, filled the booths in the back. A few families, barefoot niños and everything, huddled in the tables up front. And on each white Formica table, he spotted the usual parade of paper boats full of red-orange chile sauce. A few of the soggy containers did a poor job of keeping the rolled tacos from bloating over the edge.

He guessed that when you were pregnant the foods that you craved and were repulsed by were often the same. Some dude at the birthing classes had said he was having his wife's cravings of chile rellenos, but he'd thought the fat ass was just saying it as an excuse to stuff his face. He still went ahead and ordered a double order of tacos with extra cheese, half of Cuz's request, for himself. Three large fries completed his order.

While Cuz waited in BEBBA and he waited for his number to be called, he thought he recognized someone in back, one of the guys from the varsity Indians but not a starter. He didn't let himself be noticed. Since he'd moved in with Cuz, he didn't go out much. Of course it was hard to go anywhere and not see someone from the High. You practically couldn't go to any grocery store or the bank without seeing someone from the past. It was as if all 600+ of his fellow graduating classmates had stationed themselves for good in this town. For better or worse, most of the city's high school graduates (and certainly, dropouts) stuck around. And if, by chance, you got out, you inevitably came back.

Recently, he'd run into a classmate while pumping gas. He'd considered Melissa Ramirez one of the prettiest girls ever since freshman orientation. He remembered she wore her light brown hair feathered, like most of the girls sitting in the High's auditorium, but Melissa seemed to be the only one he noticed. Her hair reached past the middle of her back, and when she turned to the girl sitting next to her, he could tell how fine it was. The strands were like Christmas icicles, clinging to her fingertips and falling loose with a flick of her hand.

Standing in Chico's Tacos, waiting impatiently for his order, he remembered Melissa's initiation into Moccasins, a popular club for Ysleta High School girls. From the morning embarrassment of having to beg at the Free Bridge to crawling around Bassett Center, the pledges were made to earn their place in Mocs. Of course, not just any girl got a chance to make a fool out of herself. She had to be popular, liked, or if nothing else, part of the all-girl drum corps.

He tried to picture Melissa's hair as he'd first seen it when a truckload of girls pulled up to this Chico's. Because of what hell they'd been through all day, the pledges were unrecognizable. She and the other girls being initiated were all one clump of gray-brown crap. The sweat suits he'd seen them in earlier that day were now a crusty shell, like those beetles he used to flip over on their backs. "Cucarachas" was what Alberto and the other guys called the pledges.

When the Moc pledges stumbled out of the pickup in Chico's parking lot, leaning against each other for support, they must've regretted their desire to ever be popular. And thinking back on that night years later, he couldn't fully understand why you had to be crushed before you were put up on a pedestal. High school definitely didn't make any more sense now than it had then.

He had thought of Melissa over the years, and that night of the initiation had left a certain taste in his mouth. And now, by chance, he got a whiff of a batch of tacos and fries that a customer carried past him. The steaming smell of grease and salsa lingered in the blueprints of his memory-episode.

Back then, when the president of the Mocs dumped Chico's leftovers on the pledges' heads and then told them to pick a guy to hug, the large crowd in the parking lot gasped. While every dude watching took an instinctive step back, Raul "Team Manager" Cruz leaned forward. It could've been the MD 20/20 he'd been drinking that night, but he wanted to think it was his high-school-self being brave, for once.

Whatever it was, it worked. Melissa stepped toward him, lifted her arms and threw them around his torso. Her hair could have been covered in dog shit and he could've still imagined its silky softness. She must've been surprised that he didn't cringe. That's the only way he could explain why she hugged him for so long. He didn't remember if he hugged her back or if he just allowed himself to stick to her Chico's-sauce-covered body.

Of course none of this came up when he saw her at the gas station. They shared a short conversation where he learned that she'd married a guy in the military. That they'd moved back to El Paso when he was transferred to Fort Bliss. She was happy to be back home and that her kids would be close to their cousins. The draw of staying or returning to El Paso was stronger when you have kids, he figured.

As if Chico's Tacos were a vault where high school memories were stored, he started to think that he didn't have anything holding him back or anyone holding him here. Yeah, he'd miss his family, especially Cuz, and most certainly Mexican food, but what flavors were out there that he hadn't tried? Elena had said something like that one time when she asked why he couldn't come visit her in California. She always talked about exotic foods from other cultures that weren't only Mexican. He didn't remember any of their names, but he could still hear the excited tone she used when she talked about her favorite dishes from places in the Bay Area.

He was snapped out of his wandering state when the number for his Chico's order was called. Being sure to ask for extra salsa and napkins, he snaked through the long line of people, carrying the box of tacos and French fries. Grease already stained the wax paper, and the spicy steam rising from the Styrofoam cups of sauce sparked a deep-rooted appetite.

Walking with his head down, careful not to spill the taquitos, he didn't notice them in time. When he finally did see them huddled around BEBBA's passenger's side, he wanted to turn around, tuck the tacos under his arm, and sprint down McRae, past I-10, all the way to the Lower Valley and not look back. Of course he knew that if he didn't get Cuz her nightly craving, he'd never hear the end of it. And her whining was nothing compared to her yelling. Although she was sharing her organs with a growing baby, she was still able to hold more than enough air to communicate her frustrations.

"What's up, Ruly-Ruly? Long time no see, ése." The cups of soupy salsa splattered over when Carlos shoved him in the arm. While he hadn't used Alberto's weights since he started staying with Cuz, it seemed that that was all Carlos had been doing since he graduated. Two other guys, Paul and Fermin, standing nearby, also looked the same as they did at the High. For a second, Raul Cruz had to remind himself that he wasn't Team Manager anymore.

And if he had any doubts, seeing Cuz in the passenger seat all pregnant certainly helped him understand that indeed times had changed. Instead of being the poor dope trying to be near the Mocs and the Letterman Club—part of the High's inner circle of popularity—he was the substitute father of an unwed mother-to-be. He placed the box of Chico's on Cuz's lap and wedged himself into the driver's side. With a quick move to push the key into the ignition, he signaled that he wanted to get the hell outta here.

"Hey, we hear you've gone from Manager to Coach." Carlos smiled as he reached into the passenger side window and picked a fry out of the box. Cuz had already torn through the wax paper and was stuffing a handful into her mouth.

"Did you tell—" He stopped himself and turned the key. He wished more than anything that there was a working stereo. A hollow dash smirked back at him.

"Yeah, you know," he mumbled as he gave BEBBA some gas. She sputtered any grumblings that he choked back. "I had to, she's my cousin."

Carlos turned to his buddies, a fat smile on his face: "Are you just cousins, or are you cousin-cousins?"

He wouldn't have heard anything weird in Carlos's statement if Cuz hadn't reacted the way she did. "You're sick, stupid cabrón." She pushed Carlos's head with greasy fingers. The dude stood back, swiped his head, and stared back with a shitty look.

For a second, Raul was back on the sidelines. Sweaty towels. Slobbery mouthpieces. Old cleats. No CRUZ on the back of his uniform. He hated the feeling that settled in his gut, a weight as heavy as the baby fat he carried from eighth grade to high school graduation. And when something finally came out of his mouth, he was surprised it wasn't vomit.

"Shit, vato, I wouldn't go near her, cousin or no cousin. Who knows who's put it to her?"

Whether intentionally or not, his foot pressed all the way down on the gas pedal when Cuz spoke. And although he didn't hear what she yelled, he knew from the shapes of her mouth and how quick the guys took off that she was pissed.

In a deafening silence, he drove back to her apartment with his shirt and crotch soaked in cheese sauce. She squashed stray taquitos on the floorboard when she stormed out of BEBBA and slammed her apartment door without looking back.

His ass settled in a puddle of warm sauce as he tried to figure out what the hell had just happened. It was too confusing. Nothing that they'd covered in the birthing classes. After a few minutes, he couldn't think of anything to say that would help.

One thing he knew for certain: he wasn't getting into the apartment tonight.

As he put BEBBA in Drive, he only hoped that his shit wouldn't be on the street tomorrow morning. Or worse, that he'd find his clothes soaked in motor oil like he remembered Laura had done to a former boyfriend's stuff.

4   A WOMAN *WITHOUT* A MAN IS LIKE A FISH *WITHOUT* A BICYCLE

        MAKE BREAD NOT BOMBS

        GO CAL BEARS

The stickers on the sealed boxes made Elena's absence more present. As hard as it still was these months later, he tried to take his old friend Alberto's advice: "Don't think about her. Better not call anymore. Ruly-Ruly, forget her."

If he stayed busy, he pulled off the first one. He knew that long-distance phone calls were expensive. And now that he was back at Chewie's Casita, giving Laura time to cool off, it was time to work on the last one or risk having his amigo give him a hard time.

In the time since Elena had left El Paso, he'd moved aside his memories of his first love like he did the boxes she left behind. First, they stayed under the kitchen table, where he'd placed them the day after she drove off to California. Then, when he forced himself to clean up the place, he moved them to the front room, next to the bookcase with the mini set of encyclopedias (C–Ch, M–Mi, R–Ro, E). Stacked three boxes high, they served as a makeshift end table. Since he didn't have any lamps but the one in the bedroom, he dropped his work shirts, dirty socks, and anything else he didn't want to leave on the floor on the end table boxes.

When he finally resigned himself to doing laundry more often, he moved the boxes again. One fit under the bed, the other two were too tall. Another one didn't take too much room in the bedroom closet where he threw his shoes and boots. The last one, a banana box he'd brought Elena from BigWay, taunted him with its size. Who knew what was in it, or any of the three, for that matter. If she hadn't left it on the dresser, in the closet, or in some drawer, he figured that she didn't think to leave him anything worth unpacking. Probably just school papers and stupid books that she'd stopped asking about.

He tried to use the last box as a footstool as he watched TV. It also did okay as a temporary stepladder while he rehung a cross that had fallen. If he flipped the banana box on its side, a slight shift of its contents, it fit snugly between the radiator and the trash can. He did consider that whatever was inside might be affected by the heat in a few months, but it probably wouldn't be there that long. Based on past experiences, there was a better chance of the contents of boxes being thrown out, given away, or sold at a garage sale than damaged.

When his family left Lomaland for good, remembering the details too well, his life became burdened by unfamiliar people and places. The new neighborhood was easily found off North Loop Drive, past Zaragoza Road A large sign, VALLE VISTA—BEST VIEW IN EAST EL PASO, advertised the modern homes being built in this growing area, which had spread out from the Lower Valley. A popular migration from some of the oldest neighborhoods to the far, open landscape of the desert swept up his family.

"Look at all the stores," his mother boasted as they drove toward their new address those years ago. "I bet that you can find some toys and games here."

He did like the idea of getting new things to play with that summer. While he'd made it a point to pack as much of his stuff as he could from his old house, Dad had told him he'd have to get rid of some things. A box labeled GOOD-WILL was placed in his room. He didn't know who that was and didn't like that strangers would be getting his things. The box of donations ended up containing mostly broken pieces of toys from past birthdays and Christmases. So the possibility of shopping for new toys did help him store away the awful feelings of having to move.

Because of the memories he rediscovered as he got older, there was a vague sensation of stepping away from his childhood home toward some unknown place that would shelter his teenage years. This emotional journey was made up of many details: Dad's calculated trips from one address to the next. The putting/placing of old furniture in new rooms. The buying of a second TV. The meeting of other boys and girls his age. The new songs he couldn't dance to. The pool where he never learned how to swim. The teachers who congratulated him on speaking clear English. Dark brown schoolmates that challenged his pink tongue. The canals that ran water to alfalfa and cotton fields. The paths where cholos lurked.

He felt his family's move to a bigger house-yard-neighborhood-community did include his birth-map instincts but not his emotions. Like the comal that he made sure they brought from Lomaland, he learned, he had to feed the fire in his chest, one way or another. The sacred rituals of prayers in English and Spanish, eating too many flour tortillas, and even working on his Map Books were never packed away in boxes left taped and put in the storeroom out back of the new house.

The cuartitos alive in his body, which grew to fill the spaces of the larger house, came to be where he stored his memories. When the mental images became too much, he used bags, boxes, bottles, drawers, and when there was someone—Laura, Alberto, Elena—to listen, his stories revealed his migrant sensibilities.

Ultimately, when considering what got packed away and forgotten versus unpacked and remembered, he realized that if they had asked Ruly if he wanted to be part of that first move, he would've said, "No, it seems too hard."

It would take several years for him to begin learning the meaning of "quest." He'd recently watched a movie with that word in the title and liked how it related to his life so far. And although the teen wrestler ended up with the older woman in the end, he decided that part of his quest from here on out was letting Elena (and her stuff) go.

While his exile from Laura's apartment prompted his return to Chewie's Casita, he probably wouldn't have bothered with the scattered boxes if his Air Force amigo wasn't coming home on leave in a few days. Although he'd kept his best friend updated on his breakup with Elena, he hadn't shared too many details about what he'd been doing since then. He couldn't remember, but he thought he'd hinted in his last postcard that Laura had reappeared on this side, but he didn't offer any other details.

Anyway, he didn't know how to explain moving in with an unwed pregnant woman who happened to be his cousin. It seemed like too much of a hassle. He figured if he made Alberto's former living space look close to what it used to then maybe they could pretend that nothing had changed since they graduated from the High.

When Alberto landed back in El Paso, they picked up where they'd left off. With a crew cut that the airman's head seemed suited for and muscles on top of those he'd already had, Alberto showed up when Raul really needed a distraction.

And despite his attempts at camouflage, the boxes of stuff Elena had left behind were evidence that he'd had a girlfriend for 79 days. Of course when Alberto looked over his casita, he didn't tell his buddy that he'd kept count in his Big Chief Map Book.

"Fuck, if I was you, I'd have already gone through her shit and thrown away what wasn't worth a shit." Alberto dug through Elena's cassette cases and tossed them aside until he found something he recognized. "This is good. We should take this."

Raul didn't want to make a big deal out of his old friend's intrusion, so he decided to go along with their plans for the night. It seemed they both needed some R&R.

With the single from the year's popular sound track blaring, Alberto drove toward the Border Highway. They cruised their old stomping grounds around the Lower Valley, although they both kept saying at every intersection how much the neighborhoods had changed. In a little bit over a year, there were more stores and fast-food joints than during their high school years.

"I didn't think I'd miss Hell Paso," Alberto said over the music, "but I did."

"Your letters made it sound like you were having a blast."

"Shit, being overseas was big-time fun, but there are those things you grow up with, you know, that you don't even know are important." He pulled into a Whataburger drive-thru as if to give one example. They ordered their usual #3 combos (no onions but with onion rings instead of fries, extra-large Dr Pepper) and scarfed them down in the comfort of his new car. The cherry red Firebird blew more than the doors off Chewie's Cheby. Raul hadn't told Alberto, but he was impressed with his friend's new wheels and appearance, sharp clothes and more cologne than he remembered him wearing before he enlisted.

"This burger's good, but tomorrow I'm telling my nina to make some tortillas de harina. Those are what I would have killed for while I was away. I went without the taste of comida for too long."

Raul nodded while finishing his onion rings and let Alberto go on about being thousands of miles from home. Their talking kept his mind off him feeling a different kind of homesickness, the one where you know you're missing something although you've never really left.

"One time this Puerto Rican dude invited me over and his chick made tortillas. They were all right, but they were nothing like the . . . man, maybe we should have hit up a burrito place . . . yeah, I'm gonna eat about two dozens of those bad boys tomorrow. With huevos con chorizo, mole and beans, chile verde, even enchiladas."

"You better take it easy or you'll gain back all that weight you lost. And to eat tortillas with enchiladas is so dumb. Tortillas with tortillas, I don't get it."

"C'mon, Ruly-Ruly—an enchilada burrito is almost as good as a tamale taco."

Both friends laughed, as much about Alberto's appetite as his use of the nickname he'd given him those first days as Team Manager. He handed Alberto some napkins out of reflex and told him that they should get on their way if they were going over to J-town. He knew they'd be out late no matter what time he and his amigo got started. Still, he had to at least pretend to care that he had to work tomorrow. He'd begged his supervisor for the night off, telling him that he had a family obligation. It wasn't that much of a lie, since he considered Alberto more like his brother than Pancho.

Without him having to spell out the details, he knew Alberto sensed that he was still bummed about Elena leaving. Alberto had been cool enough to insist that they go to J-town for a blowout, like they had done back when they were at the High. Only now, Alberto wasn't leading him by the nose, clearing the way with his years of experience. This time they were partners. Like Butch Cassidy and the Sundance Kid, Starsky and Hutch, Ponch and Jon, Ruly-Ruly and Chewie Baca.

The last few hours were as blurry as the mirrored tile on the walls of this place. Who knew how the hell they ended up here? The spinning lights made everything even more distorted. He kept blinking his eyes, hoping that would help clear up his cloudy vision, but he slowly realized that smoke was being pumped in from somewhere around the stage.

The dancer onstage looked as familiar as any girl in the High's yearbook: dark hair, long and straight, a flat nose above full lips. He wanted to call her Irene or Lucy, even María Something. When she turned her back in his direction and bent over, he tilted his head to see her upside-down face. "Naw, don't know you," he said. He saw Chewie clapping his ass off. The dancer took his friend's dollar bill and slipped it in the waistband of her G-string.

He sipped the drink in front of him and was happy the melted ice had watered it down. The countless reflections staring back at him agreed that he was totally pedo. He needed a glass of water bad. Maybe coffee.

Chewie had bills in between each of his ten fingers and fisted his hands when he got real excited. Raul couldn't tell if his friend was psyched about the next dancer coming onstage or something else altogether. And as much as he wanted to get home and go to bed, as he decided when he threw up in the alley outside, he'd known from the time Chewie picked him up that they would eventually end up here. Wherever this was.

The Royale Cabaret was one of several topless bars off the main strip in Juárez. Its fancy neon sign and tuxedoed bouncer out front were a more respectable face than the type of entertainment inside. While he was no expert in titty bars, this one tried to look classy. Though you couldn't tell by how dead the place was. Other than him and Chewie near the stage, he spotted three other hombres (puros mexicanos, western hats and all, not pinche pochos, T-shirts and tennies) reclining in the shadows of the club.

Raul shut his eyes every now and then, welcoming the soothing effect of the cavernous bar. Behind closed eyelids, he felt the bass of the music crawl around his body. It did its own lap dance from his torso to his groin and back up in the opposite direction. His body was tired enough to surrender itself to the seductive beats of Top 40 hits from el otro lado. As with many bars and clubs in Juárez, the songs the dancers moved to were in English.

When a New Wave song he remembered from Elena's favorite mix came on, he snapped out of his sleepy state and sat up. Chewie must've seen him come to life and patted him on the shoulder, motioning for him to get closer to the stage. He grabbed the bills Chewie waved around and slid his chair closer to the lit stage. While the two old high school buddies still couldn't hear each other over the music, they exchanged glances and lots of head nodding.

About an hour or who knows how long later, as they drove over the bridge back to the Lower Valley, he realized that it was probably one of the last times he'd have an excuse to go partying in Juárez. Whether it was the crappy taste in his mouth or the concert-of-a-hangover he was sure to have, no bout of nostalgia would be strong enough to push him over the border again anytime soon.

At Alberto's side all night long, he came to realize that the past could deport you to a place in your memory. And no matter how much you declared yourself to the present, you were hopelessly uprooted.

And he knew that this wasn't the quest he'd been on since throwing his cap in the air with hundreds of other high school graduates.

While he didn't yet have the exact words to match his changing emotions, he'd learned that he couldn't be Ruly-Ruly any more than Chewie Baca was still the average student who preferred the snack bar to the classroom.

You move on. Right? You have to.

And he did.

5 Raúl Luis Cruz
English 1301
Dr. Sánchez
EPCC

My Sacred Space: A Desert Tail

When I was little, I spent my summer days and nights running around Lomaland. This is a neighborhood in the lower valley full of sand hills (that's why it gets its Spanish name).

What made Lomaland so special was that, in my years as Ruly (my name as a boy), I was happy there. I know that the desert can seem boring or ugly to a lot of people, but when your little it can be full of imagination.

In the mornings, after I had eaten breakfast (huevo con chorizo, mashed beans, and tortillas de arena, my favorites) I would leave our warm kitchen and go see what all the other kids in the neighborhood we're doing. We would gather near our house in an empty lot, were someone said a church stood years before, and see if there was enough of us to play a baseball game. If not enough kids showed up we would see what other fun we could have before the sun went down. And it was always sunny in Lomaland.

Unlike my brother Francisco (we called him Pancho) who was one of the older kids, I never got to decide anything. I was the one who was sent to get the snacks and drinks and fetch the bats, balls and gloves. I followed each order Pancho gave like a brave does for a chief. I did complain only a little.

Since I wasn't always needed, I had time to do other things, like exploring. And of course lizard hunting, which became my obsession when I made my first sling-shot from a Y-shaped tree branch and a strip of inner tube. Pancho showed me how. While my parents' thought my brother was watching me, sometimes I was really out wondering in the desert, a maze of mezquite trees, yucca plants, cactuses and a lot of wild weeds.

From my first hikes in Lomaland's dessert, I felt exposed and safe at the same time. I wandered what it would be like to get lost and live among the lizards and rabbits and other creaturas. I always managed to find my way back before anyone missed me or became worried.

There were parts outside of Lomaland where I wasn't supposed to go. My parents gave strict orders not to go farther than the end of our block, past the house of Don Rayo (a blind man with a huge Saint Bernard) or near Hillcrest Junior High (once a school for "Jesus-priests" my grandparents told me).

The skeletons of priests buried underneath the school's football field kept me away from that side of the road, but every summer I got more and more curios. In the last full summer I spent in Lomaland, I needed to know what was past La Loma, the biggest hill around. Really big, it was like a mountain that I needed to climb.

Almost two years ago I went by myself back to Lomaland. I stood in the desert lot behind my old house, hoping the new family wouldn't see me peeking. When a boy walked into the backyard, I got down. Hiding, a lizard ran under me. When my eyes followed it, I felt myself return to my life as "Ruly."

Not knowing exactly what I was doing, I picked up a rock and moved closer, trying not to scare off the lizard. It was in front of me with its head up as if waiting for something to fall from the sky. I don't know why, but I took careful aim, I through the rock, and it hit the living target. The lizard's body escaped. The tale stayed behind, making a cool pattern in the sand.

I walked into the sand hills, my hand around a rock, sweat on my forehead, hoping to see more lizards. If not for the sun setting, I am not sure if I would have realized how late it was. And thirsty and tired. I rested in the desert for a long time before going home.

Waiting to speak with Dr. Sánchez about errors in his essay, Raul sat in his desk, not doing anything but counting the minutes left in the class period. He had his textbook open to an assigned chapter, but he still wasn't too interested in reading. In a few weeks, it would be spring break, so that was good. While he didn't have any plans, he craved having more time to himself, like he used to. Working part-time at BigWay while taking three classes was harder than he'd imagined. He didn't know how someone like Debra, who was attending school and working full-time while raising two boys, could do it.

It was good that she was so busy. In the time since they'd started dating, he had gone from just finding her attractive to really liking her. It wasn't the other L-word, he told Cuz, at least not yet. And of course the great sex they had didn't hurt. So, if Debra was free more, he knew what he would want to be doing. All the time. He sensed from the sounds she made, especially when he was exploring with his mouth, that she too enjoyed sex with him.

Thinking of their last time in bed, he felt himself getting hard, so he changed his thoughts back to school. In his first college semester, he was doing okay. Of his three classes, History was the easiest. The teacher was this big-haired lady who gave quizzes every week. Open-book ones. So he got the hang of it pretty quick and got good grades. He didn't see how anyone *couldn't* get an A in the class. Maybe just those who sat in the back and never brought their books. When they asked dumb questions, he wondered if they even bought their texts.

He hated math. The same as high school. Unless they were somehow related to sports, numbers never did hold his attention very much. And when numbers were combined with letters, he was really confused. If he didn't want to fail Algebra I, he knew he should take the instructor's advice and get some tutoring. Just in case, he would check on the drop date.

As for this English class, he never knew anyone could make him write so much. So far this semester, he'd written more than he probably did in all his years of school, from K–12. Unlike reading, especially when it competed with his TV watching, writing was beginning to come easy to him. One of the best things about it was that you could do it anywhere. As long as you had a pen or pencil, some paper, Dr. Sánchez always said, you have the rest you need inside of you.

In the first days of class, Dr. Sánchez, who resembled a Mexican Santa Claus more than a college professor, told the class that he had written several books and passed them around as if to prove it. Sitting next to the other first-year students, Raul wondered what the books were about. Not wanting to look too curious himself, he flipped through them and was happy to see that some were illustrated with cool charcoal sketches. Since the images were signed "M. Acosta," Raul figured someone else had drawn them. And some were short poems, in English, Spanish, and a mix of the two.

But what he most liked about Dr. Sánchez was that he was honest with them. So honest that before he said anything about grammar/mechanics he talked about being a Chicano and a Pinto. While Raul felt confident about his understanding of "Chicano," he learned that "Pinto" was not just the name of a bean. As an ex-convict, the burly professor said, he knew the value of Time-Space. "Don't waste either one," he said. "You'll regret it. ¡Orale!"

When he went home that day with Dr. Sánchez's syllabus and reviewed some of the readings, he was reminded of a conversation he'd had with Elena last summer.

"So, what do you call yourself?" she'd asked him as they walked around Peoples' Park.

"What do you mean?" he asked, caught off guard, although he sort of knew what she meant.

"You know, who are you? Your identity." He didn't know if the last two words were also part of the question.

"Well, you should know who I am. You're kissing me, aren't you?"

"Don't be silly, you know what I mean." They sat in their favorite spot, the wooden frame of an abandoned sofa near the trees around the park.

"Like what they called me at school?"

"Well, sort of. What did you check to apply for college?"

At that time he didn't want to admit that he hadn't filled out any forms. That he had no immediate plans to take college courses.

"Well, I know I'm not white. And I'm not as dark as my cousin Laura," he said trying to sound funny.

"Duh!" She took a firm hold on his hand as if to say that she wasn't playing.

"If you're gonna be rude ...," he said in a playful tone.

"Sorry, and I don't think you're Chinese or anything."

"Although Dad says we have some Chinese blood from a long time ago."

"Really? Like on my mom's side. We could be related."

"Don't say that. I don't want to think about kissing my long-lost cousin or anything." He took a chance and tried to begin kissing her. And he was successful in interrupting her questioning, at least for a short while.

She kept after him, though. "Then you checked a box, probably the 'Hispanic' one?"

"Doesn't everyone?" he said while moving away from her to give himself some room. "Don't we have to?"

"Well, there's the 'Other' box. On most forms, that's another option."

"Yeah, but what does that mean? 'Other'? That you're an alien, a freak, some kind of Thing?"

"No, it means that none of the other boxes fit you. That you identify as an 'Other.' Some even have a blank line you can fill in."

He remembered her taking a stick and drawing a line in the ground at Peoples' Park.

_____.

The deep hole at the end seemed more like an exclamation point than a simple period.

"Yeah, I guess that makes sense," he told her while he looked at the blank space at his feet. "You can't expect four boxes to cover everyone. I guess that's what I am."

"Who?...What?"

"The blank line. To be filled in. Undecided."

"Cool. I get that."

He was glad she accepted this response even if it was somewhat of a bullshit answer. He'd felt that Elena's questions had been a kind of test. A multiple-choice exam. He hated those in school. Although the right answer was there in front of you, it was still hard. The answer seemed to be staring back at you, taunting you, like some game. All tests sucked, as far as he was concerned.

Remembering that talk from when he still wasn't a registered student, he finally had a good response for Elena's college-type questions: *Who are you? What do you call yourself?*

While he'd checked the "Other" box on EPCC's forms and written "Mexican-American" on the blank line next to it, he sensed now that he was different from any of the printed choices. Not a "Pinto" like Dr. Sánchez or a "Chicano" like Chewie. Not even the vague line after "Other" that most left blank.

Like the multiple-choice tests he was improving on, the best answer to his ex-girlfriend's question had always been inside of him. And only now was it surfacing.

While he'd realized it during one of Dr. Sánchez's classes, he felt proud that it was through his own thinking, not some boring book or some girl he was trying to have sex with, that he'd realized he was most like a hyphen. The small dash between "Mexican" and "American." The typewriter key between the zero and the equal sign. Top right-hand corner, closest to the letter *p*.

For his next essay, he told Dr. Sánchez during a conference that he'd started writing about himself as an in-between space. HYPHEN = BRIDGE, he'd written on a napkin during lunch at Chico's. Like that point when he crossed back from

Juárez and he had to answer another test-like question: "What's your citizenship?" Not ever thinking about it, seriously buzzed most of the time, he used to answer, "American, sir." The "sir" helps distract the border guards, Chewie coached him, so that they won't notice you're drunk off your ass.

Why didn't I ever answer "Mexican-American"? he wondered. Probably too confusing. But what was wrong with that? It was confusing. Even when he wasn't fucked up, crossing back from J-town always felt like one of those *Twilight Zone* episodes. The ones that Laura liked to watch after the late news. The black-and-white stories always had some person facing a crisis—alien abduction, time-space warp, virus or disease—that left the person stuck between reality and the unknown.

More aware, that's what he most identified with now. In the middle, where the hyphen always rests.

Like most other ideas he was having as a college student, he had to think about them again and again before he wrote them down. Wanting to do better than the B+ he received on his essay about growing up in Lomaland, he wrote several drafts and proofread more, as Dr. Sánchez instructed.

During spring break, Debra complimented his dedication to school when they were over at Laura's. The old friends had reconnected since seeing each other at EPCC. He was relieved when Debra took over his baby-watch duties, and Laura seemed to welcome an experienced mother's advice. He still pitched in, like picking up and delivering some baby stuff Debra had stored away. Knowing that Laura's due date was approaching, he was happy to help her make room for the baby. While he missed hanging out with his cousin, he'd also missed the space he'd made for himself at Chewie's Casita. And it was a much better place to be alone with Debra than her apartment littered with dirty clothes and broken toys.

As for his essay, which he'd titled "Somewhere in the Middle," he felt proud of the feelings that emerged. He wasn't freaked out that he still had more questions than answers. "Is it possible for a hyphen to grow, or even disappear, during a lifetime?" He used the question in the last paragraph of his essay. Something Dr. Sánchez said could work as final arrival to a paper rather than a predictable conclusion. He received his highest grade on this essay.

In the weeks after spring break, he started showing up early to campus. It helped that he no longer had to worry about getting tutored in math. The sucky feeling that he would have to re-take math faded every time he visited with

Dr. Sánchez, who was always outside on the patio before class, a cigarette in one hand and a coffee cup in the other. Raul didn't smoke and preferred hot chocolate, but he considered trying caffeine if it would make him as wise as his profe.

In the classroom, Dr. Sánchez looked real serious, all business. But outside he was more laid-back, even when they talked about his writing, how it was improving and starting to feel more honest.

"You're on a journey," Dr. Sánchez told him one day, "to discovering your voice."

"Really? So, I'm maybe going to get an A?"

"No, I'm not talking about grades, hombre. I'm talking about your mind, your soul. Tu mentealma."

He wasn't sure what that meant, although he knew the two joined Spanish words. From class lectures, he'd learned that more would follow.

"You come from a people that live stories as much as tell them. Los antepasados are always guiding us. A sacred path. A pilgrimage. We've been following it for generations.

"Our role as writers is to have the vision to know what direction we should go in. What signs to look for. What songs to hear. What poems to write. What foods to gather."

Raul resisted the urge to take out his notebook and write down every word from the Chicano sage (a word he'd learned from reading a handout in class).

"¿Intiendes mendes?" Dr. Sánchez grinned and patted him on the back, like a firm shove in the right direction.

"So I *am* getting an A?" He asked this as more of a joke than a worry.

"Chale. Only if you go to this."

Raul took the flyer his favorite teacher handed him and followed him to class.

CENTRO DE SALUD
FAMILIAR LA FE
Presenta
Una Noche de
Literatura & Cultura

Thurs., April 26, 7 PM

Canned Goods accepted
at door for
Segundo Barrio Food Bank

6   "Mandona" (*not Madonna*) was a rarely used Spanish word collected over his nearly twenty-one-year-old life. And to call his cousin bossy was just the beginning. She always got her way, as far back as he remembered. (Sort of like the 1980s icon.)

Even as children. While Ruly looked up to the older Laura, he knew from watching home movies in the closet that she was also known as "La Niñita" in the family. This term of endearment was as familiar to the cousins as "Gordito" and "Morenita."

"Have you ever noticed how you can add '-ito/-ita' to any word and make it cute?" he'd asked Laura when they were younger.

"Yeah, I know, Tía does it all the time. Tortill*ita*. Bes*ito*. Pans*ita*. Lom*ita*. A bunch of random things, like what she keeps in her junk drawers. Bunch of nad*ita*."

Laughter: her distinctive gurgling and his deep grunts.

"I wonder why three letters can change regular words, especially since Spanish isn't that easy," Laura offered her curious prim*ito*.

"Yeah, some days my tongue will do those weird sounds, but other days, like when I'm playing with Los de Abajo, I can't get the words out. They won't form in my mouth." He opened his mouth wide and wiggled his tongue for full effect.

"Like when you meant to say 'lots of dogs' but said 'lots of farts.'"

"Shut up, that wasn't funny . . . it's not my fault that I can't roll my *r*'s . . . who needs stupid Spanish anyways?"

Growing up, he was glad that he wasn't alone in being stuck between languages. If someone was going to make fun of his verbal farts at least it was Cuz.

Before she was a willful teen or a pregnant young woman, as La Niñita, Laura's every step was watched over.

Christmas home movie: A curly-haired infant totters from the sofa, past a floor of discarded wrapping paper to a tiger-striped cushion. Atop the orange-black animal, she smiles away from the movie camera. Everyone is watching: grandparents, aunts, uncles, cousins, all the family, except a mother or a father. With all eyes on La Niñita, she smiles and giggles at her audience.

From viewing these warm images over and over again in his closet-theater, he knew that Laura as La Niñita was loved. Con mucho cariño.

Since the home movies didn't capture the rest of their lives past childhood (none filmed outside of Lomaland), he was glad that his and Laura's memories were more accurate than any family portraits.

Thomason Hospital was a perfect setting for his thoughts to journey over the past. Like all the nurses, doctors, and patients who busied the hallways, his mind was crowded with activity. Thoughts coming and going since he'd arrived an hour or so earlier. He'd been detoured on his drive from work to school. As with most big surprises he experienced, today's involved his cousin Laura. It began with a short note: "Headed to hospital." He'd been as anxious about the words as he was about the source of the handwriting. Not Laura's. Maybe Debra's.

Is she going into labor? Isn't it too early? Is she okay? These questions kept looping in his mind like film on a projector wheel as he raced to the county hospital.

"Breathe," he told himself behind the wheel. "One. Two. Breathe, Menso!" When he called himself "Menso," he knew Cuz's spirit was riding shotgun. Her voice steadily helped him pay better attention to the signs ahead.

Arriving at the hospital without remembering too much of the drive over, he was sort of freaked when he saw his mother there. Of course—she was the one responsible for the familiar penmanship.

Before he could ask about Laura, his mother said, "False labor pains, I think. . . . She's asking for you."

He held on to these words as he hustled down the hospital hallway.

Cuz was asleep when he walked into the hospital room. He sat next to the bed and thought about waking her but didn't. The TV was on without any sound. Some soap opera with nurses that weren't as cute as the one he'd glimpsed at the reception desk. He changed the channel and came across an episode of *Welcome Back, Kotter* that he hadn't seen in a while. Surprised that he remembered the characters and catchphrases, he laughed at all the funny parts although he didn't raise the volume. A few minutes in, he heard another laugh. *Gurgle-gurgle. Gurgle-gurgle.* As distinct as Horshack's.

Cuz was real groggy. From sleep. Probably meds.

Under the bedsheet, in a hospital gown, hair pulled back, she looked wasted. He couldn't think of a time that she'd appeared this out of it. Not even when she had real bad days in the first months of her pregnancy. Her helpless expression made her appear as much like a little girl in a home movie as a mom-to-be in a hospital.

"Why are you smiling like that?" she asked as she tried to sit up.

"You, Cuz. You make me smile."

She groaned. Somewhat touched, somewhat in pain.

He helped her sit up, put her legs over the side, and got her some ice water from the bedside table. She drank three glasses in a hurry. Whatever she had experienced earlier today had left her dehydrated.

Without asking for help, she motioned that she wanted to go to the bathroom. Supporting her extra weight didn't seem a chore. Almost second nature. They held on to each other tight the whole way.

She did give him a funny look when he didn't immediately walk out as she sat on the toilet. He waited on the other side of the door. And he resisted the temptation to ask her any of the questions spiraling through his head.

What happened? Is the baby okay? Was Epstein Mexican? What names are you thinking of? How about Barbarino? Or Beccarino if it's a girl?

She did better walking back from the bathroom on her own. When he saw she wanted to adjust the incline of the hospital bed, he searched for the remote. It was buried in the sheets, so he had to untangle them. Holding her belly, she glanced at the TV. Still no volume. She served as the laugh track as she made her way into the adjusted bed.

"Cuz, I need you to do something for me."

"Sure, what do you need?" He clapped his hands, ready for any request. *Once a team manager, Always a team manager.* "Another pillow. More water. Chico's maybe. You name it."

"No, nothing like that. At least not for now."

"Yeah, sure. What?"

"Don't say you'll do it if you won't."

"I will. Promise. Cross my heart."

"Promise-promise. Or just-saying-you'll-do-it promise?"

"What? . . . Just tell me."

His cousin's request was a simple favor, it seemed, but when he summarized her words to a list, they ranked from the concrete to the abstract.

La Loma
King of the Mountain
Climb
Sacred
Manda

In the hospital, he kept telling himself that he could promise to complete her sacred petition. That is, if she meant what he thought she did. But why did she want him to, was the question he was going to ask before she interrupted his lingering thoughts.

"You owe me, Cuz."

"What?" He sat on the edge of the bed, blocking her view of the TV rerun.

"I saved you."

"When?" He scooted closer to her.

"Just promise me. Just—"

She was about to offer more before she started groaning. He backed away, not sure if he was causing her pain. Her groans grew louder, almost to the point of screaming. Before he could act, she pushed a button on her bed's remote. In seconds, a team of nurses and a doctor rushed in. They hurried him out of the room.

Not sure what to do next, if he should wait or go look for his mother, he moved toward a window at the end of the hallway. While he'd lost track of how much time had passed since he read the note, he guessed from the fading sunlight that it was early evening. The silhouette of the mountain landscape, watercolor hues running across the horizon, appeared much more vivid from this west side of town than from his desert home in the Lower Valley. It was beautiful and disorienting.

Stuck at the hospital, doctors and nurses coming in and out of rooms, he studied more of the view outside the window. When he saw other medical buildings, he remembered his visits to Dr. Goldfarb's office years ago. Instinctively, he knew that he would never outgrow his allergies of the desert despite what Dr. Goldfarb had promised. Any thoughts of being separated from the landscape of his birth seemed unrealistic.

"We are where we're born," his mother told him as a boy.

His interpretation: We breathe the polluted air. We inhale the particles. We swallow the dust. No matter what.

Allergies grow up with you, he realized. They mature, they age, they become other allergies. Dancing to disco. Waking up early. Fixing grammar errors.

If he was going to carry out Laura's Manda, he learned that he'd have to make peace with the desert.

After a long period and no doctor, nurses, not even his mother coming to let him know what was going on with Laura, he reluctantly made his way down to the parking lot.

As he steered BEBBA in the opposite direction from an explosive sunset, he caught a fleeting glimpse of the cross on the mountain. At the highest peak of the sierra, Christ the King stretched his arms out to the sides, palms up, as if about to dive, like a clavadista in Acapulco (another episode-story from *Big Blue Marble*). The blessed symbol for thousands in the borderlands was the image he recorded when he left Laura in the care of the hospital staff.

You Owe Me

I Saved You

Promise-Promise

Laura's words were titles of mix tapes, personal and distinct.

Later that night, her voice playing in his head as he tried to fall asleep, he remembered one of their favorite outdoor games growing up in Lomaland. King of the Mountain. Along with the kids from the Trailers (Junior, Tere, Lisa) and Los del Abajo (Lorenzo, Victor, Samuel), Laura and Ruly gathered at the steepest side of La Loma, the highest hill in their desert neighborhood.

The objective of King of the Mountain was simple, as decided by the older kids in Lomaland. You started at the bottom of La Loma, waited for a signal, usually someone whistling, and you rushed your way to the top of the hill. First one to the top was the winner.

Speed wasn't the most important skill. Balance and persistence were needed. And that was if the other players decided to leave you alone. Which never happened. Since you were allowed to interfere with anyone around you, you could do pretty much anything to get past your opponents. It didn't take much. Sometimes a slight push or kick would send your competition tumbling back to the bottom. You could always count on getting bruised and cut up and definitely scratched.

You had to have good footing at all times. While Ruly always wore his Kmart work boots and Laura her trusty tennies, a few of the older guys went barefoot. Most of the bottles left from the weekend drinking circles of men were avoided, but occasionally someone would run home hopping, blood trailing them to their doorstep.

As one of the youngest, Ruly decided that it wasn't important for him to reach the highest point of La Loma. He really liked helping Laura keep her crown as Queen of the Mountain, as she'd named herself. One afternoon, in one of the last games they would play in Lomaland, he learned how Laura was more than just a cousin.

Victor, the middle child of Los de Abajo, had shown up mad about something that had happened at home. (Ruly and Laura knew the house at the bottom of the hill was crowded with people and problems.) For each turn of this particular game of King of the Mountain, Victor kept getting to the top and doing anything to stay there. Slapping. Punching. Biting. Spitting. Cussing. If there had been any rules to their game, he would've broken them all.

"Stop being a cabrón."

"Let go of my shirt, dork."

"Damn, ése, that hurts."

"Why are you being . . . ?"

"All right, I give, you win."

No matter what protests any of them shouted at Victor, the angry boy was going to be the first to reach the top of the high mound—*sand weeds rocks.*

Knowing that they'd be called in any minute to wash up before dinner, Laura gave Ruly a look that said, "Get ready."

As soon as his cousin heard the whistle, she rushed up La Loma and quickly did away with the smaller, clumsier players. Then she set her sights on Victor, whose heavy boots, black like his hair, dug deep into the dirt. His mistake came when he took his eyes off the top and looked back down. That was when Laura made her move. Before anyone could warn Victor, she rushed toward him, reached for his belt loops, and pulled his pants down.

The sight of Victor's bare butt still made Ruly&Raul laugh all these years later. The anger in Victor's face that had given him an edge all afternoon disappeared when he turned, fell, and rolled over. With all eyes on him and laughter coming from every direction, he seemed to have two choices: Go after Laura or sit there and join the fun.

It might've been the day's heat or the warm dirt all over Victor's butt that made him burst out laughing. Brushing his messy hair out of his face, his teeth stood out on his dark face. His smile-laughter gave Laura permission to do the same.

Hush-hush, gurgle-gurgle. Hush-hush, gurgle-gurgle.

Soon, each of their Lomaland friends was cracking up, the sounds of a good time filling the desert around them like a playful sandstorm. Meanwhile, Ruly had taken advantage of his cousin's strategy and now he stood atop La Loma. He raised his arms in the air like if signaling a touchdown and danced around for his big score. Although this moment lasted for only a short while before Victor's little brother came and pushed him down, Ruly was happy to have a chance to be King of the Mountain, standing tall over Lomaland, as close to *CieloSky* as he'd ever been.

As he drifted off to sleep, his cousin still in the hospital for observation, not by his side, he took comfort that he'd learned to queue up his childhood memories at the exact moments when he needed them most.

7   Thoughts of what lay ahead blustered through his mind. More than coarse sand, plenty of rocks, countless weeds, and patches of cacti. Hopefully not stickers, those pesky ones that jumped at your ankles. He hated those small thorns (Espinas? *Not pineapples.*)

No matter how careful he was while playing in Lomaland's desert, he brought back home a family of stickers. Impossible to remove. The bigger ones clawed their way through his tube socks and pricked his skin.

Given his allergies, he always itched. Since he was too lazy to remove the stickers, they'd stay on the dirty socks he threw in the hamper, and even after his mother did the wash, the stickers would be there next time he wore the socks. The desert never let go, one of the very first lessons he had to learn.

WEST = California: Beaches. Ocean. Elena on Telegraph Avenue.

NORTH = Cold: Igloos. Glaciers. Santa Claus.

EAST = Sights he'd never see: Statue of Liberty. Eiffel Tower. Great Wall of China.

SOUTH = The Past/México: Cruz Clan. Santos Familia.

Of course, the personal details he associated with the four directions were from his mind's compass: instincts rooted in the Chihuahuan Desert that included three cities and two countries. He'd come to understand deeply over the years how distance meant more than miles or kilometers (he'd never learned the difference since he missed that episode of *Big Blue Marble*).

Taking the long way to Lomaland, he drove on North Loop Drive past Lower Valley landmarks. First, he resisted the temptation to stop for pan dulce at Aztec Bakery. He didn't want a heavy stomach, so no Little Debbie cakes from Mini Market either. When he drove past where Peoples' Park used to be (a sign soliciting new owners and a chain-link fence), he didn't search for last summer's hideaway. No bad memories today, especially about Marito's mysterious disappearance.

For being so early, this morning was already very warm. A rock mix tape he'd made played on the boom box in BEBBA's passenger seat. Pitchfork baseball cap. Backpack: *The Metamorphosis* (Elena's paperback), blank spiral notebook, pen/cils, tissues, milk jug of water.

As he steered BEBBA through a favorite shortcut down a canal road, a chorus of dogs barked from backyards. When he came out on Yarbrough Drive, he noticed that there were more houses in this neighborhood than before. Even the homes he remembered appeared different, extra rooms added on, converted garages.

His cousin would soon become part of this tradition of multiple generations gathered under one roof. Even if it was temporary, Laura had agreed to live at his parents' house after she had her baby. His mother had called to give him an update on his cousin and mentioned this latest arrangement. The news that Cuz would be a more permanent part of his immediate family comforted him. Maybe he would even move back in to help out. Or better yet, he thought, he could go between Chewie's Casita and his second home. He seemed better prepared to negotiate that kind of physical distance. For Cuz, he was willing to navigate the emotional journey.

Lomaland Park in the old neighborhood was empty except for a few viejitos walking around the perimeter. They wore sweaters although the morning air was still. Some dogs rummaged through Dumpsters. The lucky ones tore through fast-food leftovers. No kids. The park seemed like a whole other place with vacant basketball courts and motionless swings. Not one of the sacred spaces where he and Laura had spent so much of their childhood. As the only evidence that this was the same park, the grass was pretty green for this time of year.

Although it would add to the distance he'd have to cover today, he decided to leave BEBBA at Lomaland Park. From there, he walked until the paved roads and sidewalks became desert. For now, the landscape was flat and easygoing, as he'd mapped in his head. Spotting traces of footsteps in the sand made him think that kids coming home from Lomaland Elementary still used this path as a shortcut, just like he and Laura had done.

Not having eaten breakfast today, he felt dust devils turning in his empty stomach. His pits and crotch already moist with sweat. No matter how much he blinked, dryness filmed his eyes. The rising sun assured him that it was a good idea to wear a T-shirt (Front: BIGWAY FOODS; Back: T.R.I.E.S.) and corduroy cutoffs in addition to his ragged Diablos baseball cap. High-tops were laced tight, tube socks at mid-calf. The backpack he carried didn't slow him down. He chugged what was left of his water.

Ruly felt the climb would leave him breathless.

Raúl Cruz knew the key would be to keep his legs moving.

Rauluis thought this could be a cool thing to write about.

Cuz: "Saved you. Remember? You would've drowned."

Laura had said other things between her cries of pain at the hospital, but these were the phrases that guaranteed his carrying out her Manda of climbing La Loma in their old neighborhood. He didn't know if anything waited for him at the top or what Laura wanted him to do when he got there.

At the onset of this journey, he didn't think of what other past events might have brought him here today. Not leaving Lomaland for good. Not becoming part of the High's football team. Not falling in love for the first time. Not Cuz crossing over and crossing back carrying a child.

A promise-promise between Cuz+Cuz was the sole act that prompted his first step. Second even firmer. A third stamped his presence on the loose caliche trail.

And as tempted as he was to keep looking down (no lizard sightings yet), he lifted his eyes. The climb seemed steeper than any former self remembered. Twice as old as the last time he walked this path, he felt the flesh-colored sand shift under his steps. The rising landscape embraced his adult size.

Brown.

Everything in his sight, behind and ahead, was one color. The arthritic limbs of the mesquites he instinctively avoided. Even partially buried rocks took on a darker complexion. Tumbleweeds (green once) in different sizes, their pale color heightened when huddled up like football players.

And lots of random junk: Paper grocery bags. Rusted bicycle rim. A recliner in decent shape. Of all things, a wig.

Brown. Brown. Brown. Brown (maybe dirty black).

Although brown was one of his favorite colors, along with shades of blue (globe blue, La Virgen blue, veins-under-his-palms blue), at this moment brown overwhelmed him. Closing his eyes was his only idea to clear his mind. No good. Grainy specks dried his vision of Lomaland's desert even more. Like adjusting the knobs on his old TV set, he made himself focus on anything else. Keeping his mind busy would allow his body to carry on, so he ransacked his mind's Map Books.

TV: Favorite episodes of *Big Blue Marble* & Cal Worthington commercials.

SPORTS: A football stadium cheering: "*Goooooooooo Indians. Fight fight win!*"

JALE: Stocking boxes at work was hard, but at least it was indoors and he got paid for it.

A sandstorm of experiences browned his mind.

SCHOOL: He'd already pre-registered for two summer classes (Algebra I and Chicano Literature with Dr. Sánchez).

SEX: Pleasuring himself as much as his girlfriend.

(LOVE: "Debra" did have the right number of letters and ended with an *a*.)

As more minutes passed, each personal time-space that he imagined helped him avoid suffocating on brown.

CUZ: Warm bed, watching TV or a video (no ghosts on the wall).

BABY: Womb = Water. Birth = First Breath.

FAMILY: More than a House.

CASITA: Home.

At the midpoint of climbing La Loma for Laura, he was out of breath. To keep his promise-promise, he tried another mind game.

Listing always worked to make tiring tasks go by faster. Whether it was cleaning up the dog shit at his first house, running stadiums with the varsity Indians, or getting through twelve-hour shifts at BigWay, he learned to use the alphabet to create random lists.

A—apples (caramel) B—bologna (fried, edges burned) C—cupcakes (chocolate, white frosting) D—deviled weenies (way better than Spam)

He covered a letter with every 3–5 steps on the unsteady desert trail that snaked upward. Almost like he used to do walking home along the canals. Not watching where he stepped. His socks were covered in thorns. He pulled them up each time he reached down to scratch his calves.

K—ketchup (on hash browns next to scrambled eggs) L—leftover pizza (more Laura's favorite) M—Mom's meat loaf (jalapeño stuffed inside)

He now felt that he should've made time for breakfast. Hungry, he began to fantasize about what would be his first meal as soon as he made the climb back down.

Q—(Dairy) Queen (sometimes he cheated on his lists) R—rolled tacos (Chico's, of course)

Either distracted by his hunger or surrendering to the pain from the rocks in his shoes, he tripped and dropped hard to the ground.

Covering his face with his cap, he soaked in his sweaty fatigue. Ache cloaked his body. The sun preyed on him. His skin remembered.

Disoriented, forgetting his place in the alphabet, a mestizo meal mentally appeared.

tortillas (de harina, always) freshly made

green chile con carne with arroz

frijoles, asadero cheese, aguacates, some limón (lime not lemon)

Through squinted eyes, he made out the shape and color of the sun directly over him. More white than yellow. *How many flour tortillas can I eat right now? I bet a dozen easy.* When he placed tortillas on his comal, he left his hand on it for as long as he could hold the heat. Seconds. Flip. Do it again. Longer. The hotter the comal got, the better the tortilla tasted, he told Laura when she called him "mensito" for burning himself. He liked to get one side browner than the other. Not too brown, only some spots like freckles on the tortilla's face. Brown blemishes on white skin.

Flat on his back, sand caked on sweaty shirt, he inhaled and exhaled deep breaths. Turning away from the sun, he was drawn to the cloudless sky.

So much blue. Thirst. California ocean. *HeavenCieloSky.* Neighborhood pool. *You owe me, Cuz . . . I saved you . . . You would've drowned . . .*

He didn't have a response for Laura when she shared her secret at the hospital. It was less a confession than a way to ask her Manda, he'd decided the night before.

Whatever his cousin's motivation was, his almost-perfect memory of that day he learned how to drown after leaving Lomaland for good was forever changed. Those moments right after surfacing, leaving a world underwater, dropped on cold tile, swallows of air, now revealed Laura, wet from head to toe, worried expression, moving aside for the lifeguard.

Like a home movie that had come off its spool, he rethreaded the episode-memory and played it slow to be sure that it had been his cousin who had reached down for him. And like watching reruns of his own past, from one moment of drowning to the next moment of drowning, she was the one who had always been there to help pull him up.

Cuz: "Breathe, Menso."

Cuz: "You promised."

Lungs replenished one more time, he pushed himself off the desert floor.

Step. STEP.

Kick. KICK.

Dig. DIG.

He ran as best he could the rest of the way to the top of La Loma. And only stopped pumping his arms to bite a sticker out of his palm. The more he got in stride, the less he stumbled and had to put his hands down for balance.

More rocks jumped into his high-tops. He compensated by digging into the sand with his toes. Like a running back, he stayed low through the shorter mesquite bushes and drove his legs past cactuses. His backpack kept slipping to his side, so he tucked it under his arm like a handoff.

Rather than tire the higher he climbed *making a new path from older ones* he gained momentum.

Arriving at the top, he fought the urge to bend over.

To refill his lungs, he strained his arms above his head.

King of La Loma one last time.

Promise-Promise.

As if he'd been planning it long before today's Manda, he searched and found a yucca plant, broke off a dried branch, and carved five letters into the earth.

One *U* rested between two *C*'s and two *Z*'s.

It wasn't permanent like the limestone cross that flagged the mountain peak on the horizon, so he made sure to write it down. After he made the sign of the cross, a deep hunger pulled his weight to the bottom of La Loma.

Acknowledgments

Love to my family: Polo and Chuy, who made La Loma a Sacred Place; my Mom for her support although she may have imagined a different career for me; my Jefe for feeding my appetite for stories and hungrily reading the books I shared; my Brother, Robert, Jr., and his family (Marty, Diego, and Alex) for always keeping an open door; and Estela Monsiváis for caring in two languages.

My deepest gratitude to the University of Nevada Press, especially Margaret Fisher Dalrymple, who responded to multiple drafts and promptly answered each phone call/e-mail; Joanne O'Hare, who asked about my novel each time we talked; and the wonderful staff, who showed care for my first book of stories.

From the beginning, I've been blessed with the friendship of Kevin McIlvoy, who assigned writing a first chapter to a novel, received the seeds of this book, and made sure that they took root, and Todd McKinney, my brother in words, rhythm, and corazón.

So proud to be part of El Paso's River of Voices: Arturo Islas, Ricardo Sánchez, Dagoberto Gilb, John Rechy, Ray Gonzalez, Abelardo "Lalo" Delgado, José Antonio Burciaga, Alicia Gaspar de Alba, Carolina Monsiváis, Benjamin Alire Sáenz, Pat Mora, Rubén Salazar, Estela Portillo Trambley, Christine Granados, Sergio Troncoso, Sheryl Luna, Claudia Guadalupe Martínez, and those to follow . . .

I couldn't have grown as a community and literary advocate without these organizations and academic institutions: Con Tinta Advisory Circle; The Border Book Festival; New Mexico State University; Colorado College; Saint Mary's College; and Arizona State University.

A big abrazo to my writer/poet friends who kept me working with their words of encouragement, as well as their own publications: Francisco Aragón, Manuel Muñoz, Michelle Otero, Maria Melendez, Alberto Ríos, Demetria Martínez, Luis Urrea, Lucrecia Guerrero, Denise Chávez, Rene Saldaña, Stella Pope Duarte, Lorraine López, Kathleen Alcalá, Cyd Apellido, Lilly Morales (who opened my eyes to more of the border), and Helena María Viramontes for simply suggesting I try a change of point of view.

My sincere regards to old school friends who said they liked reading my stories although I may have changed the facts. "Once an Indian, Always an Indian."

Gracias to the publications (*PALABRA*, *BorderSenses*, *Chrysalis*) and editors (John McNally, Marcia Hatfield Daudistel) that published me between books.

I appreciate those who make teaching at El Paso Community College more than just a job, especially Jeanne Foskett, Ysella Fulton Slavin, and Caroline Woolf-Gurley (RIPPLES Rocks!); Claude Mathis and Dr. Richard Rhodes, administrators who truly support the arts; and those students who believe (almost) every word I share.

Countless Chuco Town diners provided tables for my journals, notebooks, and pens—their hardworking staffs refilled many cups of coffee and baskets of tortillas.

Rigo, my carnal, don't ever stop reminding me what is at stake and showing us why our work requires more labor.

Cuz, may you always enjoy a happy life and share it with your wonderful daughters and lucky students.

Caro, I love you for recognizing the survivor in me and allowing me to witness your own creative activism. And for our greatest collaboration, Pablo Ricardo Monsiváis-Yañez.